The MISTMANTLE CHRONICLES

D0060534

THE MISTMANTLE CHRONICLES

BOOK ONE

Urchin of the Riding Stars

by

M. I. McAllister

Illustrated by

Omar Rayyan

miramax books

HYPERION PAPERBACKS FOR CHILDREN
New York

Text copyright © 2005 by M. I. McAllister

Illustrations copyright © 2005 by Omar Rayyan

First Hyperion Paperbacks edition, 2006

1 3 5 7 9 10 8 6 4 2

Printed in the United States of America

ISBN 0-7868-5487-1 (pbk.)

Library of Congress Cataloging-in-Publication data on file.

Visit www.hyperionbooksforchildren.com

For Caroline Sheldon,
with thanks to Jo Boardman
for the squirrel

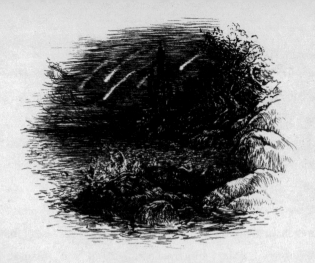

PROLOGUE

ON THE ISLAND OF MISTMANTLE, before dawn on an autumn morning, a squirrel lay on her side and watched the shooting stars dash across the sky. It took her mind from the pain.

It was a rare night when the stars left their orbits and swirled so low across the sky that it seemed you could reach up and touch them. These nights did not happen often, and when they did, they always meant that a great event would happen. For good, or for bad? Nobody could know which. Even old Brother Fir, watching from the highest turret in Mistmantle Tower, didn't know.

The mother squirrel didn't know, and didn't care. She lay panting, longing for help with the long, hard birth. But she was a stranger here, and knew nobody.

Her own island was far away, and she hadn't dared to stay there. A prophecy had been made about this baby: *He will bring down a powerful ruler*. If the king had heard that, he would surely have had the baby killed, being ruthless enough to do it. She had hidden on the first trading ship she could find, and escaped.

She had hoped that the ship would go to Mistmantle. She had heard great things about the secret island, where a kind king ruled from a high tower on the rocks, and red squirrels, hedgehogs, moles, and otters lived and worked together. It was a good, safe place, protected by the enchanted mists folded around it like a cloak. Because of that protection, very few ships ever reached the island—but, at last, this one had. Already in birth pain, she had slipped from ship to shore and crawled to the shelter of the rocks.

No creature was near. Those who were awake were high on the hilltops, watching the stars. A sudden spear of pain made her lurch and gasp, but it took her breath away so completely that she could not even scream.

Birth should not be like this. Something was terribly wrong, and she was alone. Raising her head, she could see lights shining high in Mistmantle Tower; but it was far away, soaring toward the night sky.

As stars swirled over the island, the squirrel's baby slithered into the world, a pale scrap of a thing with thin, downy fur, which glimmered under the starlight. With the greatest effort she had ever made in her life, the mother sat up, nuzzled him, and bit through the cord.

"Heart keep you," she whispered, and laid the warmth of her face against him. "Be happy. May someone find you and love you." Before she could give him a name, she was dead.

The baby lay on the shore, pale as moonlight, showing up clearly against the dark rocks. A gull flying overhead caught sight of something like a scrap of fish, swooped, snatched him up, and rose into the sky. Mistmantle Tower was near. That would be the place to perch and gobble down the meal.

In a dash of silver, a star rushed past; and another. The gull swerved and soared. A falling star dazzled it, and another made it veer from its course. Scared and angered, it opened its beak to screech.

The newborn squirrel fell, spinning, gaining speed. If he had hit the rocks, he would never have breathed again; but he fell into shallow water, and the waves washed him onto cold, wet sand.

In Mistmantle Tower, animals had crowded around the windows all night to watch the stars. The best was over now, and they were smothering their yawns with paws and settling into their nests for a brief sleep. But in the highest turret of all, Brother Fir remained watching, leaning his paws on the sill to ease his lame leg. The squirrel priest was old, but his eyes were still sharp, and he missed nothing. When he saw something white tumble from the sky, he leaned out to see better. Sometimes fragments of rock would fall to earth as the stars passed, and it could be one of those.

Below, from another window, Crispin stretched forward and turned his face to the sky. He was a young squirrel living in the tower, an attendant to the hedgehog King Brushen. Though he was young, he had just been made a member of the Circle, the small group of animals closest to the king. He craned his neck from the window.

When he, too, saw something white spin down through the air, he leaped from the window and ran swiftly down the wall to the shore.

In the dim, early light, Crispin knelt by the thing at the water's edge. He had expected something hard and bright, like a precious stone, but what he'd found was a curled-up scrap that could be anything. A starfish?

It moved. As Crispin watched, it gave a thin cry, uncurled, and waved a tiny paw in the air. Crispin heard the shuffling step of Brother Fir behind him but was too fascinated to look around.

"It's a baby!" he said.

"Well, Heart bless it, so it is!" said Fir. "Pick it up, young Crispin, don't leave it there!"

Crispin wasn't used to babies. He scooped it up awkwardly in two paws, afraid of hurting it, but it stretched and wriggled; and without thinking, he cradled it against the warmth of his shoulder. Brother Fir took off the old gray cloak he wore.

"You young squirrels don't feel the cold," he said. "You're always going out without your cloaks. Wrap him in that before he freezes."

"How did he get here?" Crispin wondered aloud, watching the baby's face as he wrapped the cloak around it. "He must be very new."

"A few hours old, I think," said Fir. "And most unusual. Look at that fur!"

Crispin didn't know what newborn babies were supposed to look like, but he knew there was something strange about this one. It was paler than the sand.

"We need to find his mother," he said. "She must be worried."

"She must be dead," said Fir bluntly. "Or dying, or she's rejected it. A mother separated from her baby would be screaming to split the rocks. She'd have the whole island out looking for him."

Crispin handed the baby to Fir, ran around the shore to find a group of otters, and sent them to search for the baby's mother. He returned to find a chubby female squirrel bounding rather heavily down the beach, and even from a distance he could hear her calling to Fir.

"What you found?" she bellowed. "A one of them stars?"

Crispin flinched. Apple was a warmhearted squirrel, but not very bright and extremely talkative.

"Morning, Brother Fir, sir— Oh! Morning, Crispin, I've come looking for stars—I mean, bits of stars—I been up a tree all night to watch them stars. Don't know what bits of stars look like when they're on the beach, but I come looking, all the same. You found one?"

"Better than a star," said Fir. He lifted back a corner of the cloak, and the baby blinked sleepily.

"A baby!" Apple's deep brown eyes widened. "Ooh! Can I have a little hold?"

Crispin thought this might not be a good idea, but Fir handed her the baby. She made little comforting noises to it as it nestled into her fur.

"Whose is he?" she asked.

"He's lost," said Fir. "He was washed up by the sea. We're looking for his mother."

"If you can't find her, I'll have him," she said promptly. "I don't mind. I'll take care of him. I love babies, me."

"Thank you, Apple," said Fir as he took the baby back. "We'll take him to my turret, to warm him by the fire. Will you find a nursing mother who can feed him, in case his own can't be found?"

"I'll look after him," called Apple over her shoulder as she hopped away.

"Don't let her near him!" said Crispin. "She doesn't know her teeth from her tail tip. She'd forget where she'd left him."

"She's a motherly soul," said Fir. "And she wouldn't bring him up alone—there's a whole colony of squirrels in Anemone Wood, all bringing each other up. They're capable of raising one extra youngling between them. They cope well enough with their own. You seem to have survived."

They began the long climb back to the tower. Crispin would rather have skimmed up the walls, but he slowed down to keep pace with Fir.

"You told her he was washed up by the sea," he said.

"Hm. I certainly did," said Fir. "He must be an orphan, and not from here. We've never had a squirrel that color before. That makes him different enough from the other squirrels, without them thinking he came tumbling down out of the sky on a night of riding stars. And if I know Apple, she'll soon forget that we had anything to do with him. Let her think she found him herself. We'll tell him all he needs to know when the time is right."

They stopped by a window so that Fir could ease his lame leg and get his breath back, and Crispin looked down at the tideline. It was scattered with all sizes of shells, colored pebbles, driftwood, shining clusters of seaweed, tattered feathers, and the spiny shells of sea urchins.

"Urchin," he said. "Can we call him Urchin? He was found on the shore."

Fir raised a paw. "May the Heart bless you and keep you, Urchin of Mistmantle," he said.

And far away on the other side of the island, a wave of the sea lifted Urchin's mother, cradled her, and carried her gently away.

CHAPTER ONE

FROM THE HIGHEST POINT OF WATCHTOP HILL, Urchin could see the whole island.

For days, squirrels and hedgehogs had dragged rough branches up this hill. The wood for their bonfire was ready to light now, stacked up so high that Urchin knew he had to climb it. He was old enough to manage it, and young enough to want to. Springing swiftly from one branch to the next, twirling his tail to balance himself, he reached the very top, gripped with his hind claws, and dusted moss from his fur. He was still as pale as honey, with the red squirrel color only at the tips of his ears and tail. When he straightened up, shook his ears, and looked out over Mistmantle, he felt he was lord of the island.

Tonight would be a night of riding stars. The animals would gather here as the air turned cool, light the bonfire, watch the stars swirl and dance through the darkening sky, and guess at what great things would happen next.

Anemone Wood spread out below him to the south, with a first touch of autumn turning the leaves to crisp gold. Farther away, on the shore, otters chased each other in play. A line of small rowboats bobbed on the water. Urchin could never understand why otters were so fond of boats, when they all swam so powerfully. Maybe they just liked anything to do with water.

A tall ship was moored by the jetty, with its sails furled and its painted figurehead gleaming with color in the sunshine. A work party of squirrels and otters had been lined up to unload it, passing crate after crate along the line. Urchin guessed at what might be in those crates. Wool for cloaks, maybe; paint for the workshops—or rare wine for King Brushen's cellars? Tomorrow he would be down there, doing real, grown-up work, helping to load the ship with timber.

He didn't really want to think about tomorrow. Balancing and curling his hind claws, he turned a little farther to gaze far over the treetops to Mistmantle Tower, and his heart stretched out to it.

The tower was the place he longed for. On a high outcrop of rock, gleaming in shell pink, white, and pale, sandstone yellow that was almost gold, Mistmantle Tower rose like a statue to the sky. From a turret, a pennant fluttered in the breeze. A young female squirrel was hopping up the steps carrying something in a basket, and the moles on guard stood back to let her in. She might be one of the queen's attendants. Urchin envied her. He even envied the kitchen mole who appeared at a low window and threw dirty water into a drain. From the king in the Throne Room to the kitchen mole in the scullery, life in the tower must be wonderful.

He had been there, of course. All the Mistmantle creatures were invited to the tower for great occasions, like the Spring Festival. Apple said that when she was little, there had been all sorts of wonderful feasts and festivals with banquets, music, and garlands. There wasn't so much of that now, but at least Urchin knew what it was like to stand in the vast Gathering Chamber of the tower.

He had been there for the naming ceremony of Prince Tumble, the only child of King Brushen and Queen Spindle. It seemed that all the island's creatures had crammed into the tower that day. Wonderful Threadings hung from the walls, stitched and woven pictures showing stories of the island; but there was neither room nor time to take a good look at them. Even following the crowd up the stairs had been confusing. Urchin had wondered how anyone ever found their way out.

The procession had been magnificent. The animals of the Circle had entered first; then there had been a gasp of admiration as the three Captains of Mistmantle stepped proudly down the hall with gold and silver glittering on their robes and circlets of gold on their heads. First Husk the squirrel, then Crispin the squirrel and Padra the otter. Brother Fir had followed them, limping, in his plain white tunic. Then, at last, tall, strong, and splendid, came King Brushen, with Queen Spindle at his side and all the colors of a jewel house gleaming from their mantles, and the queen's friend, Lady Aspen the squirrel, with

11

the bright-eyed, wriggling baby hedgehog Prince Tumble in her arms. Finally, with every animal stretching up on its clawtips, Brother Fir had lifted up Prince Tumble and blessed him.

Urchin had not been back to the tower since. He looked past it, into the enchanted mists that surrounded and protected the island so well that few ships ever reached it. Islanders who belonged here, if they left by water, could never return by water. The mists would prevent it. The otters took care never to row their boats beyond the mists.

He was trying to work out how long it would be until nightfall when a fir cone hit him on the shoulder.

"He's showing off," said a squirrel voice.

"Ignore him," said another.

Two other squirrels had reached the hilltop, Gleaner and Crackle. They were never apart, and always looked at Urchin as if they'd just been planning something very nasty for him. Crackle seemed to go out of her way to make trouble, but Gleaner did it without even trying.

Urchin looked past them and saw other animals working their way up the hill, the squirrels taking shortcuts as they leaped from one tree to the next. Gleaner and Crackle were followed by Urchin's great friend, Needle, a hedgehog with unusually sharp prickles, and around her—not too close—was a scampering, clambering bunch of very young squirrels, barely old enough to get up to Watchtop at all without being carried. Beyond them Urchin's foster mother, Apple, lumbered up the hill, keeping mostly to the path. When she did jump on a branch, it bent alarmingly.

"Urchin!" squeaked a small squirrel in excitement.

"It's Urchin!" cried another, bounding forward.

"Wait there!" called Urchin. If they climbed up to meet him, they'd probably bring the whole heap down on themselves, so he sprang down to them. He was popular with the young squirrels, and in no time they were swarming over him, wanting rides on his back and holding out their paws to be swung around. Needle came and stood beside him.

"There's Captain Crispin on the beach," she said. "And Captain Padra."

Urchin looked down to the shore and saw Padra the Otter lolloping from the water and rolling in the sand to dry his wet fur. Captain Crispin stood by, holding his cloak.

All three captains had been friends since they were small. In time they had been chosen to be pages at the tower, then promoted to the Circle, and now they were captains, the highest rank on the island. Captain Husk was the king's most trusted friend and adviser, and mostly stayed in the tower. Captain Padra had always taken special care of the shores and the creatures who lived by water. But Crispin took a particular care for the woodlands and the Anemone Wood creatures—he even appeared to take an interest in Urchin.

He was Urchin's hero. If anyone had asked Urchin what he'd like to be, he could have truthfully said, "I want to be like Captain Crispin." But he wouldn't have told anyone that. It was a treasured dream, not to be spoken. And they'd only laugh.

Besides, nobody *had* asked him. He'd be loading timber onto ships for the rest of his life.

The youngest of the little squirrels had fallen over and was whimpering. Urchin picked her up and sat on a log with the squirrel on his lap and Needle beside him.

"Isn't it wonderful up here?" Needle said. "Look at that ship!" Then she looked down at her paws. "Sorry."

"It's all right," said Urchin. "I don't mind." He knew she hadn't meant to remind him of his future loading and unloading ships.

Crackle popped up behind them.

"Oh, so Needle's still speaking to us," she said. "You don't want to talk to him, Needle, he's just joining a common work party, and you're a tower hedgehog. You'll be off to the workrooms tomorrow, won't you? Painting, weaving, sewing, making the Threadings, goodness knows what else. Very talented, aren't we? Very privileged. Much too good to speak to the rest of us."

Needle turned quickly.

"Ouch!" said Crackle.

"Oh, did you get caught in my spines?" asked Needle politely. "You shouldn't get so close to me. Ignore her, Urchin."

"You must be looking forward to tomorrow," said Urchin.

"I haven't liked to talk about it," Needle said awkwardly.

"What, because you've been chosen for training at the tower and I haven't?" said Urchin. "Talk all you like. I'm very glad for you. It's just that . . ."

He looked at the shore again. Captain Crispin was no longer there. A few squirrels and otters sat on the jetty, dabbling their paws in the water.

"I had dreams," he said quietly. "Sometimes I think I'm meant to do something special." He wriggled his paws. "Maybe it's because of not knowing who I am. I don't even know how I got here, or where from. I don't know who my parents are—or were—and I don't even look like the rest of you. Apple always told me I was special. I used to think, perhaps, I'd been chosen for something. I . . . you won't laugh, will you?"

"Of course not!" said Needle.

He wouldn't have said this to anyone but Needle. Even with her, it wasn't easy.

"I was born on a night of riding stars," he said. "Wonderful things are supposed to happen after those nights, but I don't think anything very exciting followed that one. It was as if . . . well, as if *I* was what happened. As if I was sent here that night, and I have something vital to do. And I've tried really hard at everything I've ever done. I knew I wasn't really a Mistmantle squirrel and I'd have to make an effort to become one. And I *have* made the effort, but I've got nothing to show for it. Nothing except loading ships for the rest of my life."

"What makes you think it's for the rest of your life?" asked Needle. "You might go on to . . ."

She stopped, as Apple had finally appeared at the top of the hill. She was looking down at the moored ship while she got her breath back.

"Unloading boats!" she grumbled, and flopped down heavily beside Needle and Urchin. The log rocked, and the little squirrel squeaked. "It's all wrong, this. They never used to do it this way. They never had no work parties, and that and all the work that needed doing got done, all the same, and we had a lot more fun in them days."

Urchin and Needle grinned swiftly at each other. There was no point in arguing, or in speaking at all, once Apple had something to say.

"The boats all got unloaded and loaded up, too, and all the nuts and berries and that all got gathered up and stored, and all the making of cloaks and cordials and the fishing and the work on the boats, and looking after the tower and making medicines, and keeping our nests nice, all that, it all got done. And these days it's all work parties, isn't it?" She looked around for support. "Isn't it, though?"

"Yes, Apple," said Needle.

"It's work parties all the time now, and before you're up in the mornings it's 'all the West Shore otters report for beachcombing' and 'all the Anemone Wood squirrels to report to the cone stores' and I don't know what else. Here's Urchin looking after them little ones—hello, little one—climbing trees, all the things he should be doing at his age and tomorrow he's got to go and . . ."

"Load timber!" squeaked Gleaner, and giggled.

Needle's spines bristled. "And what work will you be doing, Gleaner?" she asked sweetly.

"They haven't told me yet," said Gleaner with a wriggle and a shrug. "They're still thinking about me. They may be considering me for work in the tower." She wriggled again. "Of course, I don't suppose I'll get in, but it's very nice to be considered."

"Who said you were being considered?" asked Needle.

"Mind your own business," snapped Gleaner, and added in a whisper, "you should have been culled at birth."

"*Culled?*" said Urchin. "That's not funny!"

"And that's another thing that never used to happen in the old days," said Apple crossly. "There wasn't no culling."

The small squirrel twisted to look up at Urchin. "What's culling?" she asked.

"Never you mind, bless your little ears," said Apple.

"There was a mole baby taken to be culled last week," said Crackle loudly.

"That's enough out of you!" said Apple.

"But it's kind, isn't it, to kill the weak ones," said Gleaner as Needle took the little squirrel by the paw and dragged her away to play. "It's cruel to let them live if they're weak or they're not right. Far more sensible to kill them off. They do them in very quickly."

"They dope them first, don't they?" said Crackle.

"You just be quiet," snapped Apple over her shoulder. "It's a terrible thing, and we never used to do it in the old days."

Gleaner sat up very straight. "It's the king's law!" she said indignantly. "You can't say the king's wrong!"

All Mistmantle animals were fiercely loyal to the king, and always had been. Turning against the king was unthinkable. Hedgehogs especially were famous for their loyalty and hard work, just as otters were known for their courage and good humor, and squirrels for their bright spirits. Moles were so much underground it could be difficult to get to know them at all, but they were determined and reliable.

"He's a real good king, a good king," agreed Apple firmly. "He's just got some funny laws, that's all. Like that . . ."—she glanced at the little squirrel, who had escaped from Needle and was climbing up Urchin's leg—". . . that law we were just talking about, and them work parties. And them's not good laws, in fact, that thing we're talking about, that's a bad law, there's no good in that, can't be, but he's a good king, a right good king, but them laws just isn't good laws, that's all, he's got some bad laws."

"Pardon?" said Urchin.

"Oh, don't make her say it all again," sighed Gleaner.

"I wish they wouldn't, though," said Needle quietly. "My mum's having another baby, and I just hope and hope and pray that it's all right. I couldn't bear it if . . ."

Urchin looked down at the small squirrel, but she was staring at something a little way off.

"The baby should be all right," he said.

"But even babies that are just a bit weak and small get culled," she said. "Or a teeny bit lame or short-sighted."

"What's the little one staring at?" demanded Apple loudly. "Oh, my goodness, it's him!"

"It's Captain Crispin!" exclaimed Urchin. He jumped to his hind paws and nearly dropped the little squirrel as Captain Crispin leaped from a tree and landed on the hilltop.

"Good morning!" he called. "What a splendid woodpile!"

As a captain, he wore a gold circlet on his head and a belted sword at his hip. Thrilled and flustered at the same time, Urchin bowed awkwardly and wondered if his fur was dirty or sticking up. That was the trouble with being pale. The dirt showed. And he wished he'd been found doing something more impressive than looking after a toddler. He stammered a good morning.

Apple curtsied and wobbled a bit. "Good morning, Captain Crispin, lovely morning, Captain Crispin, sir, we've built our bonfire, sir, we're all ready for the stars tonight, we'll be having a grand supper up here, I've brought some of my apple-and-mint cordial, would you like some cordial, sir?"

Urchin's claws curled in embarrassment. Apple's cordial was famous for repelling insects, but it tasted terrible.

"Thank you, Mistress Apple, but I'll do without that pleasure today," said Crispin. "But I'd like to speak to young Urchin, if I may. Urchin, will you come with me?"

Urchin, astonished, tried to stammer a reply. He glanced at Apple for help, didn't get any, and only just remembered to hand the young squirrel to Needle. He dusted down his fur as he ran to Captain Crispin's side, and they walked down the hill path.

Crispin asked Urchin how Apple was, and what work had been

19

chosen for him, and how the autumn harvest gathering was doing, while Urchin tried to guess at what the best answers would be and to say something intelligent without showing off. But Captain Crispin was so friendly and natural, that in time, he forgot to be shy. Finally, Crispin turned to him and asked, "Will you be on Watchtop Hill tonight, to watch the stars?"

"Oh, yes, sir!" said Urchin.

"Only, if you'd like to, you could come to the tower," said Crispin. "Captain Padra and I are going to Brother Fir's turret room to watch from there. Probably the best view of the island. You're invited, if you'd like to join us."

Urchin felt a shiver of joy through his fur even though he was sure he must have misheard. He opened his mouth, but nothing came out. Finally, he managed to say, "Me, sir? The tower?"

"Certainly you, Urchin, if they can manage here without you," said Crispin, "and if you don't mind missing the bonfire. Make your own way to the tower, around twilight, and I'll tell the guards to expect you. They'll direct you to Fir's turret."

"Thank you, sir!" gasped Urchin.

"Thank *you*, Urchin!" said Crispin, and with a leap he was bounding down the hill. Urchin watched him until he was out of sight, then ran full tilt to the nearest tree, shinned up it, and turned somersaults for pure joy. A night of riding stars, the tower, and Crispin!

CHAPTER TWO

U RCHIN'S FUR HAD BEEN WASHED AND BRUSHED until it shone softly in the lamplight inside Mistmantle Tower. He wore a cloak, a new dark red one, partly because the nights could get cold, but also to honor the occasion. He couldn't go to the tower without a decent cloak. The guard pointed him toward a staircase, and he was springing up three steps at a time before he reminded himself that this was Mistmantle Tower, and he was here to meet two captains and a priest. After that he ran up lightly, imagining a sword at his hip.

He passed the workrooms where Needle would start work tomorrow. They were locked now, but he could picture them full of parchment, canvas, silk, needles, shuttles, and every shade of every color he could dream of. Rolls of canvas and stone jars of paint were stacked outside the doors, with skeins of soft wool.

Mounting the next staircase, he was startled by color. The walls here were hung with Threadings and paintings showing ancient stories of the island's past and its heroes. Some of the pictures were old and needed dusting, but Urchin still gazed. The animals looked as clear and vivid as if they lived. The colors and patterns enchanted him. Then he pulled himself together and pattered up the wide stairs, because he mustn't keep Captain Crispin waiting. There was a narrow, twisting flight next, and another, and another, before he found the small oak door at the top.

With his paw shaking, he took a deep breath, knocked, not too hard, at the door, and waited for a guard to answer it. But to his great surprise it was opened by a tall, pleasant-faced otter wearing a circlet and sword.

"Captain Padra!" he gasped, and managed to bow, though he was so startled he had to balance with his tail to keep from falling straight back down the stairs. There was something larger than life about Padra the Otter. But he had a kind expression and bright, intelligent eyes, and looked as if he would always be ready to laugh.

"Urchin! Come in! Welcome!" he said, and held out a paw to shake. "I'm Padra! Crispin, stop staring out of windows and come and meet your guest."

The small, round room had a sweet, fresh scent of smoke and apple from the logs crackling gently in the grate. The room was spotlessly clean and simply furnished, with a jug and wooden goblets on a low table. A bench had been drawn up near the fire. And all around the tower were windows, high, arched windows, some of them a little open to the autumn night. In the twilight, they looked into a sky of violet and apricot. Crispin came to meet Urchin with a goblet of spiced wine.

"Now you see why Fir's turret is the best star-watching place on the island," said Crispin. "The only problem is choosing your window."

"Thank you for letting me come, Brother Fir," said Urchin, and the old priest's eyes twinkled.

"You must see my gardens," he said. "Hm! Did you know there were gardens, right up here, up in the sky?"

Urchin leaned from a window and realized for the first time how far up he was. Far, far below him the sea hushed and swished, and the stars seemed close enough to touch.

"You live in Anemone Wood, don't you?" said Fir. "Come over here. You can see it from the northwest window."

He steered Urchin from one window to the next. It was growing dark, but Urchin could see his favorite pine tree and Watchtop Hill, where little lights bobbed and moved as animals gathered to watch the stars. Fir proudly showed him the window boxes.

"Parsley, marjoram, basil, peppermint, thyme," he said of one, and then, "sea thrift, periwinkle, and . . ." He stopped and turned up his face to the sky. "Hm. There goes a star. D'you see?"

Padra and Crispin darted to the windows. Something silver flew across the sky, twirling and sparkling, then another and another. There was a pause; then from the eastern sky the stars twirled into

23

sight, twisting like otters at play, dancing, swirling farther away and out of sight. Then there was only one, then one more, and the sky was dark again.

"Wonderful!" said Crispin.

"Worth staying up for," said Padra. But Brother Fir said nothing, and Urchin knew that the priest felt as he did himself. It was too breathtaking for speech. The beauty and terror of it had reached into Urchin's heart, and he could not speak for fear of breaking the spell. He stayed at the window where the chill night air still seemed sparkling with starlight. Then he spun around when he realized Crispin was saying his name.

"I'm sorry! Sorry, sir; did you want me?"

He wondered if it was time for him to go. The two captains had seated themselves on low stools by the hearth with goblets in their paws, and Padra grinned.

"Urchin's still up in the sky," he said. "Quite right, too. But it'll be a little while before the next lot, so you may as well sit down and get warm. Over here," he added, as Urchin hesitated. "Come by the fire."

"Wonderful stars," said Crispin. Urchin took off his cloak. "But not as good as the night I found you."

Urchin thought he must have misheard. "*You* found me, sir?"

Padra chuckled quietly. Crispin smiled down.

"Apple forgot," he said. "She only remembers what she wants to remember, so she thinks she found you all by herself. We let her go on thinking it."

"But Crispin found you first," said Fir. "Then I came hobbling behind him. He took you from the wet sand."

"You saved me, sir!" cried Urchin, and added, "Excuse my asking, but do you know how I got there?"

A glance passed between Crispin and Fir. "We tried to find your mother," said Crispin. "There was no trace of her. We saw you drop out of the sky, and that was that."

"I beg your pardon, sir," said Urchin, "but you might be mixing me up with somebody else. I don't think I dropped out of the sky."

"Oh, you did," said Fir. "Yes. Hm. I saw you, too, floating down. Hadn't a clue what you were, but you didn't look much like a star. We kept quiet about it. The other animals might have formed some extremely strange ideas about you if they knew you came tumbling down like that, especially on such a night. And I'd go on keeping it quiet, if I were you."

"Yes, sir, but how . . ." began Urchin, and stopped, because it seemed like a silly question.

"How did you get up there in the first place?" asked Fir. "Hm. It's something I should very much like to know."

"Maybe a gull tried to carry you off and dropped you," said Padra. "But if so, it's amazing that you survived."

"And I've kept an eye on you since then." Crispin smiled. "You've turned out all right."

"Which is just as well," said Padra. "Crispin's finally worked out that he can't look after himself. I could have told him that years ago. Come to the point, Crispin."

Crispin put down his goblet and turned to Urchin. "I need a page to help me, Urchin," he said. "Somebody who can do some fetching and carrying, be my messenger, help me at court, and so on. There would be some guard duties, but you know what it's like here—nobody needs much guarding. And a page learns to handle a sword, but it's so peaceful here, nobody needs to fight. I only use mine for fencing contests, calming down rowdy sailors from the trading ships, cutting ivy in the woods, that sort of thing. The point is, I need somebody to be my right-paw squirrel. What do you think, Urchin?"

Urchin felt his heartbeat quicken. He doesn't mean me, he thought. He's asking if I can think of anyone.

"He does mean you, Urchin," said Padra gently, as if he had read Urchin's thoughts.

"Take time to think about it, if you like," offered Crispin.

"I don't need to," said Urchin, and found he was almost breathless. "It would be wonderful. But are you sure, sir?"

"I wouldn't be asking you otherwise," said Crispin. "I've watched you grow up. I keep an eye on all the island's squirrels, and I know you'll do very well at court. I would have asked you sooner, but I had to wait for the king's permission."

Urchin thought of that morning, when he had stood on top of Watchtop Hill and envied the kitchen mole. Now he was to be a page, and spend every day in the company of Captain Crispin. He'd serve in the Gathering Chamber, and maybe even in the Throne Room and the royal chambers.

"It's all my dreams, sir," he said, and found he was whispering in awe. "I'll work hard, I promise. I won't let you down."

"I know that," said Crispin. "Shake paws on it, then." And as they shook paws, he looked past Urchin at the window. "There's a stray star out there. They'll start again soon. Urchin, when you go home tonight, get your belongings together. Tell Apple where you're going, and I'll let your work party know they can't have you. Come to the tower first thing. You'll have the room next to mine."

"Yes, sir!" said Urchin, and bowed awkwardly because he wasn't sure what to do—bow, fall to his knees and kiss Captain Crispin's paw, or jump in the air and turn somersaults.

Padra stood up. "The stars are starting again," he said. "You'll get the best view looking southeast."

Before dawn, Urchin left the tower. Starlight and his excellent night vision were good enough to take him home to Anemone Wood. His head and heart sang with the knowledge that he was going to the court. He would work, learn, and fight if he had to, at Captain Crispin's right paw. Captain Crispin would depend on him to polish his sword and circlet, hold his cloak, and run his messages. He would listen to the captain's troubles, wait on him at table, and make sure everything he needed was ready before he even asked for it.

The morning was not far off, but he thought it would never come.

Urchin was not the only squirrel hurrying home from the tower that night.

Gleaner had not had a good day. She had quarreled with Crackle. *(Stupid name! Crackle!)* So wherever she watched the stars, she didn't want to be where Crackle was, which was a pity, because Crackle was going to Watchtop Hill. Then, as if that weren't enough, *Urchin* had been invited to the tower! *Urchin! Only* to the tower, and *only* by Captain Crispin! Gleaner squirmed with jealousy. Urchin wasn't even a Mistmantle squirrel. Probably wasn't a proper squirrel at all.

So why shouldn't she go to the tower anyway, by herself? Pleased with her own boldness, she had run to the tower and scurried nimbly up the walls. The roughness of the stone and her excellent balance kept her from falling.

She peeped through a window she thought might be Captain Crispin's. No sign of Urchin there, or anybody else. She ran a little farther and tried a window on the next floor. This was fun, this spying.

She was lucky. Not Urchin, not Crispin, but somebody well worth looking at! She found she was spying on the most beautiful squirrel on the island.

Lady Aspen! Gleaner gazed at Lady Aspen and adored her. She almost forgot to breathe. She was near enough to see the silver bracelet on the left forepaw and the elegantly polished claws. The bracelet flashed in the candlelight as Lady Aspen groomed her tail with a small ebony brush. She was the loveliest and most refined squirrel on the island, Queen Spindle's dearest friend—and everyone knew that she was to marry Captain Husk.

Gleaner was losing her grip on the window ledge. She scrabbled, turned her tail to catch her balance, and ran on up the tower. She would have liked to see the queen and the little prince, but that was too much to hope for. At the window of an empty room she stopped to watch the ride of the stars, then ran on upward until she heard voices. An otter laughed. Scrambling on, she found herself among the trailing leaves and overhanging herbs of Fir's window boxes.

Good. Plenty of room to hide. With her ears twitching, she picked up and recognized voices—Urchin's, then Fir's and Captain Crispin's, so the otter must be Padra. She clung on. It was impossible to hear everything while hanging upside down from the bottom of a window box with thyme tickling her nose and lavender in her ear, but she heard all that Crispin said to Urchin. By the time she ran down again she knew that Urchin had fallen from the sky. It could be useful, that. You never could tell.

As dawn filtered across the sky, Urchin lay on his back in a fir tree, watching the last flourishes of starlight as he imagined his future. There was no point in trying to sleep. He ran down and filled a canvas bag with his few possessions— a spare cloak, a ball, some counters for games, and a few cones and nuts to nibble on—said good-bye to Apple, and bounded through the wood to Mistmantle Tower. It was a long way, and he didn't want to be late.

Something was wrong. Terribly wrong.

When he thought about it afterward, he couldn't tell how he knew it, but long before he reached the tower and saw the guards, he was feeling uneasy. He had never seen so many guards before, all grim-faced as they rushed in and out of gateways. From somewhere inside the tower he heard terrible sobbing and wailing, with one high and desperate voice rising above the rest. Animals were scurrying toward the rocks and whispering to each other, looking up at the tower but hanging back as if they were suddenly afraid of it.

Something clenched at Urchin's heart. His paw tightened as if he could hold on to his dreams, but he had a sickening feeling that they were slipping away.

CHAPTER THREE

HE STILL HAD TO REPORT TO THE TOWER. He smoothed his fur nervously and climbed the stairs to the great wooden doorway where two armed moles stood on guard.

"Nobody gets in," said one.

"None in, none out," said the other.

"But I was sent for," said Urchin. He couldn't let Crispin down, so he stood his ground. "I have to report to Captain Crispin."

"None in, none out," repeated the mole.

"I'm under captain's orders," said Urchin.

"So's everyone," said both the moles, but they glanced at each other. They clearly didn't want to risk disobeying a captain.

"Please, can you get a message . . ." began Urchin, but the guards looked past him, stamped to attention, and saluted. There was a rush of paws on the stairs, and to Urchin's great relief Crispin appeared, breathless and keen-eyed. He put one paw across Urchin's shoulders.

"He's with me," said Crispin sharply, and the door was opened at once. In the wide, high-ceilinged entrance hall, the sound of crying was suddenly louder. Animals whispered to each other. Urchin was trying to take it all in when Padra bounded toward them, and his face was grave.

"Padra!" said Crispin. "Everyone's rushing for the tower. What's happening? Is that the queen crying?"

Padra put a paw on Crispin's shoulder. "It's little Prince Tumble," he said, and his voice was low with trouble. "Crispin, he's dead."

The words hit Urchin so hard that he couldn't understand them. It couldn't be. The prince was young and full of life.

"No!" said Crispin. "How?"

"That's the worst," said Padra. "He was murdered."

Urchin gasped. "You must be mistaken," said Crispin.

"No mistake," said Padra. "I couldn't believe it myself, until I saw him. The queen found him just outside their chamber, stabbed to the heart."

"But . . ." began Crispin.

"I know," said Padra. "Nothing like that happens here. Nobody on the island would do anything like that. Only, somebody did."

Crispin was already leaping up the stairs, and Urchin wondered what to do. He supposed he'd been forgotten and wouldn't be wanted now, but he hadn't been dismissed.

32

"Crispin," called Padra, and nodded toward Urchin.

"Wait here, Urchin," ordered Crispin. Then he appeared to think again. "Do you still want to start work today, in the middle of all this? It won't be easy."

"You might need me, sir," said Urchin. He wanted to be useful, and he couldn't bear to go straight back to the wood.

"Come on, then," said Crispin. "Stay well back and do exactly as you're told."

Urchin ran after Crispin up the wide stone stairs. There were brackets on the walls for torches and lamps, with soot stains above them. Turning sharply to the right, the two hurried along a corridor hung with Threadings, and reached a ring of animals who shuffled quietly aside to let the captain through.

The silence was solemn and fearful. Urchin stood with the others, leaning sideways a little to see past Crispin. Another squirrel was bending over the still body of a small hedgehog. A very small hedgehog. Prince Tumble, hardly more than a baby. Until then, Urchin had not quite believed it.

Terrible grief was on the squirrel's face as he bent over the body, but he had a lordly air about him and had taken command. Urchin hadn't often seen Captain Husk. He would have recognized him from his captain's sword but, more than that, he had an air of real authority that proved him to be a captain. He'd know what to do. It was reassuring to know Captain Husk was in charge.

Crispin pulled the circlet from his head as a mark of respect.

Kneeling beside the body, he moved it gently, and Urchin saw the dark red stain on the little hedgehog's chest. Through the half-open door of the chamber he glimpsed the king and queen huddled together, but the queen was silent now, as if tears were not enough.

Urchin looked away quickly. It didn't seem right to see them grieving in their own chamber and without their robes and crowns. The other animals stood with lowered heads and drooping ears.

"It's a clean stab wound," Captain Husk was saying, "and there are no bloodstains in any direction, so we can't tell which way the murderer went. At least it was quick, and the prince couldn't have known much about it. He must have died without crying out, because nobody heard a thing. The king and queen didn't know he'd left the chamber until the queen found him."

"So the murderer must have lured him out," said Crispin. "Must have stood here and called him, but he'd take care not to wake Their Majesties." He shook his head and twitched his ears. "Somebody the prince trusted, I should think. I watched the stars from Fir's turret, then looked in here on my way to patrol the shores at dawn. They were all asleep then."

Husk stood up. "I've summoned all the animals to the Gathering Chamber," he said, "all the adults and the young ones old enough to work. And I've sent otters to find out where everyone was last night and first thing this morning. We don't know when it happened, but he—oh, Heart bless him, Crispin, he was still warm when the queen

34

found him. We all have to give an account of where we were, even captains. We'll speak to the creatures when they're all here."

Crispin nodded. "We should robe," he said. The captains all had robes to wear for important occasions. "Come with me, Urchin. You can help me robe. I'm sorry, it's a wretched start for you."

"Is that a good idea?" asked Husk. "A new page starting work at a time like this?"

"He has to learn," said Crispin; so Urchin, relieved to be given something to do at last, pattered after them through the Gathering Chamber. Padra, coming from the other direction, joined them.

Urchin had never seen the Gathering Chamber empty before, and couldn't help staring about him. Long arched windows on three sides of a curving bay let in the light. Benches had been placed along the walls, and at the south end was a raised platform, the dais, with carved chairs and a plain table. He had only been there for feasts and cere- monies, when there might be long trestles overflowing with good things to eat and the hall would be hung with Threadings, decorated with garlands, and warm with candles. Today it was bare and plain. Empty, it seemed even more enormous than ever, and their paws sounded too loud on the floor.

Padra, Husk, and Crispin strode grim-faced down the hall, paws resting on their sword hilts. Without speaking, they marched to the anteroom adjoining the hall.

"Robes are in the carved chest, Urchin," said Crispin gruffly. Urchin heaved open the chest—it smelled of spice and sandalwood, and the lid was heavy—and with great care, lifted out the first mantle, holding it across both forepaws to keep it from trailing. It was sea-turquoise with silver embroidery, and Urchin had never touched anything so beautiful in all his life.

"That's Captain Padra's," said Crispin. "Attend to him first. Captain Husk and I wear the green-and-gold ones."

"I'll robe myself; don't trouble your new page," said Captain Husk quietly. He lifted his robe from the chest and drew away from the others to put it on, while Urchin helped Padra and Crispin into theirs, though it was really Padra who helped, saying things like "the cuffs have to fold back," and "fasten that on the second hook, not the first." The collars and cuffs were deep and richly decorated, and the hems touched the floor.

"The moles have explored every tunnel," said Husk, folding back his cuffs. "They've found no signs of intruders. They'd know from the vibrations if anybody had dug a new one."

"Nobody's arrived by sea, and nobody left the ship," said Padra. "There were otters guarding it all night. Thank you, Urchin."

"So it does have to be an insider," said Crispin heavily. "Nobody's going to own up, and nobody saw anything. I can't believe such treachery could happen here."

"None of us believed that," said Husk, "or we would have been more careful. But now that it's happened, and we have no idea who did it, we must solve this murder the old way. The ceremonial way. We must cast lots."

"Cast lots?" said Crispin with a frown. "I'm not happy about that."

"I've never understood how it could work," said Padra.

Urchin was hoping somebody might tell him what "casting lots" meant. Crispin turned to him.

"You need to understand this," he said. "Casting lots is an old way of solving a mystery—very old; we rarely do it now. A token for each type of animal is put into a bag—one each for squirrels, moles, otters, and hedgehogs. One is drawn out, and that shows that the murderer is from that group. Then the clawmarks of each of that kind of animal are put into the bag, and the animal drawn out is the murderer."

"So how *does* it work?" asked Padra.

"We will be drawn to the right name," said Husk. "It has its own power. The power of the murderer's guilt, maybe. Or even Prince Tumble's spirit."

"We should ask Fir about this," said Crispin.

"He's looking after the king and queen," said Husk. "They need him. Urchin, take the red velvet bag from the bottom of the chest and place it on the table, please. We'll need it. Then come with me—if I may borrow your page, Crispin. Bring the purple velvet cushion from the windowsill. We need something suitable to lay him on."

Red velvet bag. Purple cushion. Urchin padded behind Husk to the royal chamber as animals began to gather silently in the Gathering Chamber. It should have been wonderful—all three captains of Mistmantle were seeking his help now—but it was all happening in a

37

nightmare. At Husk's order, he stood at the open door with the cush-ion balanced on both forepaws. Fir was kneeling on the floor, holding the queen's paw.

"Your Majesties," said Husk gently, with a bow, "it's time to take the prince to the Gathering Chamber. He must be there for the cast-ing of lots."

Fir's ears twitched. "I do not like the casting of lots," he said. "It may not be fair."

"Peace, Brother Fir," said Husk. "All will be done wisely, with honor. If the lots name somebody who is clearly innocent, we will disregard them. If there is evidence, of course we'll consider it. But the lots may at least point us in the right direction. Unless, of course, the king objects . . ." He bowed again. "Will you allow the casting of lots, Your Majesty?"

"Do anything, Husk," said the king gruffly, and to Urchin he looked suddenly old and wretched. Husk solemnly laid the prince's tiny body on the cushion, took it from Urchin, and cradled it back to the Gathering Chamber, where the animals were now crowded together. At the sight of the small, still body, they gasped.

Husk mounted the step to the platform, where Crispin and Padra waited silently, their paws folded and their heads down, while Urchin hoped someone would tell him what to do. It would be terrible to stand in the wrong place or get in the way, and he tried to catch Crispin's eye.

"Stand at the door of the anteroom, Urchin," said Crispin, and

Urchin took his place. He was near enough to see and hear all that was happening. Husk laid the cushion on the table.

"I'll see to it," he said quietly to Crispin and Padra. "I have to, I'm responsible for this. I was on duty last night, and if I'd patrolled earlier, if I'd posted more guards, if I'd just been a bit sharper, this couldn't have happened. It was on my watch."

"Don't blame yourself, Husk," said Crispin.

"But I do," muttered Husk bitterly. Then he turned and raised his voice to the crowd.

"Creatures of Mistmantle," he declared, "squirrels, hedgehogs, moles, and otters, we will draw lots to find the murderer of our dearly loved Prince Tumble. The tokens will be placed here."

Crispin lifted the red velvet bag from the table. One by one, Padra took four leaves, holding them up for all the gathering to see before he placed them in the bag. On each leaf was a mark—red for squirrels, black for moles, green for hedgehogs, blue for otters. Husk turned his back as Padra and Crispin mixed and rearranged the tokens in the bag.

"Now, Captain Husk," said Padra.

The silence was tense and fearful. Urchin's hind claws curled. He saw the wide eyes and clenched paws of the watching animals. Teeth were gritted. Nerves were stretched.

Husk drew his paw from the bag. From his post by the door, Urchin could see what he held, and a shudder ran from his ears to his tail tip.

"The squirrel token," announced Husk. "The murderer is a squirrel."

Every mole, every otter, and every hedgehog quietly released the breath it had been holding. Squirrels stood still with set faces. Urchin bit his lip.

Urchin curled his paws and longed for this to be over. Crispin and Padra must have felt the same, because they were briskly lining up the squirrels, trying to get it over as quickly as possible. Crispin beckoned Urchin into the queue. Every squirrel claw was different, and the animals all knew each other's clawmarks as they knew each other's faces. Each squirrel made a clawmark on a leaf and dropped it into the outstretched bag. Urchin, pressing his mark into a beech leaf, tried not to shake; and finally, Crispin and Husk slipped in their own leaves. Their faces were calm and set, but Urchin's heart twisted in pain for them.

"Husk, shall I do it?" offered Crispin.

"It's better if it's not done by a squirrel," said Padra. "Shall I?"

Husk shook his head. "It's my fault and my responsibility," he said. "I have to see it through."

He turned his back, folded his paws, and appeared to be praying. Padra tossed the leaves in the bag. Squirrels clutched each other's paws. Feeling sick with anxiety, Urchin swallowed hard.

Husk turned, thrust a paw deep into the bag, and drew out a leaf. Then he took a long, shuddering breath. The pause was terrible.

"No," he said hoarsely. "It has to be wrong."

Urchin found he was trembling. He couldn't help it. Padra and Crispin stepped up to Husk to examine the leaf.

"No!" said Padra quietly. "It's a mistake."

"No," said Crispin, shaking his head, his eyes widening. "No."

Husk's paw shook. He held up the leaf, and a gasp of horror shuddered through the hall as he spun around to meet Crispin's eyes. *"Crispin! YOU!"*

CHAPTER FOUR

IT COULDN'T BE. Urchin tried not to stare at Crispin, but he didn't have to look at him to know it wasn't true. It was as if he could feel something in the air, something not quite right, like a note of music out of tune; or going into a room and knowing that somebody is hiding. Something false. With all his heart, he knew Crispin was innocent.

Crispin raised his voice. "I swear to you all," he said, "on all that is precious, on all that is holy, on all that is ancient, I did not kill the prince. I never could!"

"I would never have believed it," said Husk.

Padra stepped forward. "We did ask whether casting lots was the right thing to do," he said firmly.

Urchin swallowed hard. He might be able to help, even though he was only a page with no right to interrupt. As Crispin spoke up about where he had been and what he'd been doing the night before, Urchin edged toward Padra and stretched up to whisper in the otter's ear.

"Brother Fir doesn't like casting lots, sir," he said.

"How do you know that?" Padra whispered back. He bent to listen, then stepped forward.

"Husk, didn't Brother Fir have doubts about casting lots?" he demanded. "When you and the page went to collect the prince's body? Brother Fir should know."

"He did," said Husk, looking thoughtfully at Padra, then at Urchin. "Yes, you're quite right, he did; but the king gave his permission. Padra, you may have a point! Maybe the lots are wrong!"

"They must be," said a squirrel in the crowd. "Crispin wouldn't do such a thing." There were murmurs of agreement around him.

"Let's take another look at the evidence," said Husk. "Unfortunately, we don't have much."

"Call a council," said Padra. "Crispin has the right to defend himself."

A council was called, chosen from animals of the Circle. Two hedgehogs, two squirrels, two otters, two moles, the king, and Brother Fir all took their seats around the platform. Urchin chewed his lip.

"Keep your nerve, Urchin," whispered Padra. "Everyone knows he didn't do it."

The questioning began. Padra and Fir agreed that Crispin had stayed with them, watching the stars until nearly dawn. Then, Crispin said, he had looked in at the window of the royal chamber, seen the family asleep, jumped in at his own window to fetch a cloak, and gone on patrol around the south shore and the western woods. He had stopped at a stream for a drink and a wash, when he saw the flurry of animals running to the tower, and joined them.

Many animals had seen him and talked to him, but none could be sure exactly when. He had been seen racing through the wood to the tower, but a dark, smooth mole called Gloss pointed out that everybody knew how quickly a squirrel could get from one place to another. He could have murdered Tumble, escaped to the woods, and doubled back when the uproar started. And the prince's wound looked as if it had come from a sword or a dagger. How many animals carried swords?

Crispin swished his sword from the sheath. It was shining clean. But as Gloss said, no animal would commit a secret murder, then leave the blood on his sword.

A dark-whiskered otter called Tay stood up, pressing her paws on the table as she spoke. She had been an obvious choice for the council because of her great intelligence and her knowledge of the laws and customs of Mistmantle.

"We must consider the succession," she said. "King Brushen is the third hedgehog king of his line. Prince Tumble would have been the fourth. If the hedgehog line were to come to an end, the crown would pass to a captain. After hedgehogs come squirrels. To put it simply, without a hedgehog prince or princess, the next monarch would be a squirrel captain. Now. The question is, which squirrel is next in line? Crispin, or Husk?"

She frowned so that her whiskers stood out in a line. Urchin, knowing that everyone was thinking the same thing, felt sick and desperate. He wanted to say something, do something, produce evidence, prove Crispin's innocence beyond doubt, and be the rescuer of his captain. But he was only a page, and there wasn't anything he could do.

"Just so," she said. "Crispin has been a captain for just a little longer than Husk. Personally, I have always found casting lots to be an excellent way of finding out a villain." And she sat down.

"Then it may be true," said Husk. His voice shook.

"Crispin had a weapon, he appears to have had the time, and he had a reason," said Tay. "*And* he could move freely about the tower. Nobody would think anything of it if they saw him near the king's chamber."

"But nobody *did* see him near the chamber!" argued Padra.

"He's just admitted how good he is at getting in and out of windows," said Gloss.

There was more argument. Fir stood up and demanded to know the whereabouts of all the captains that night. Padra had still been with him when the death was discovered. Husk had been on duty, and various guards had seen him.

45

Urchin tried to catch Crispin's eye. He wanted to give him a look that would say *I believe you, even if every creature in the island turns against you.* But Crispin's eyes were on the council.

"Crispin, I would rather not believe it," said Husk, "but the prince trusted you. He loved you and looked up to you. If you hid behind a curtain and called him, of course he'd come."

"He loved everybody," said Padra. "He'd go to anyone."

All the time the king had sat hunched over the table, his eyes down. Now he gave a low growl.

"Crrispin," he growled. *"CRRISPIN!"*

The growl grew to a roar, and in a rage of claws and bristles, he hurled himself at Crispin. Without thinking, Urchin leaped forward to knock Crispin out of the way. He turned sharply to face the king— he couldn't raise a paw against his king, but he could come between him and Crispin—but the king wasn't there. Padra and other animals held him back. Armed guards rushed forward.

"Treachery!" roared the king.

"Your Majesty, this is madness!" shouted Padra as the guards seized Crispin.

"Crispin," snarled the king, "there was never such a foul traitor, never such an evil murderer on this island. Your presence is pollution. You are to die before the sun goes down."

Urchin heard the sharp gasp of horror all around him. Never, ever, had a death sentence been pronounced on Mistmantle. Padra and Fir pleaded with the king. Curling his paws tightly, Urchin watched

Brother Fir lead the king away from the others to the window. The priest was speaking urgently, his eyes wise and troubled.

Do something, Brother Fir, thought Urchin as Fir reasoned with the king. He won't listen to anyone else. *Oh, Heart that cares for Mistmantle, please, care for Crispin now.*

"So," said the king at last, "his blood is too tainted to be shed on our island. Let him be exiled from Mistmantle, from this day on."

"He will leave the only way he can," said Tay, "by water. We all know what that means. Because of the guarding of the mists, no creature who belongs here can leave by water and return the same way. The mists will keep him out. And because there is no other way he could return, Crispin's exile is for life. He can never return."

"Take him away!" growled the king. Urchin tried to get near Crispin, but the guards had pressed around him. He could only watch, helpless and furious, as the circlet was pulled roughly over Crispin's ears, his sword unbuckled, and his robe dragged from his shoulders.

The creatures were ushered from the Gathering Chamber quickly, because their mood was ugly. Some were raging at Crispin, spitting and growling and reaching for things to throw at him. Those who believed he was innocent were outraged and ready to fight.

Urchin had been forgotten again. He picked up Crispin's robe from the floor and folded it over his arm, with the sword, sword belt, and circlet underneath. If nobody noticed, he could get them back to Crispin.

"That traitor's robe must be burned," called Tay. "And his weapon . . ."

"I'll take them," said a mole from somewhere behind Urchin, and before he could argue, a tough little mole with the look of an old soldier had snatched Crispin's possessions from him. For a moment it seemed that the mole winked at him, but there was no time to think about that. Crispin was being hustled out of sight, and Urchin had to stay close to his captain. He wriggled his way through the crowd to catch up, following as closely as he could as the guards dragged Crispin down a flight of stairs and flung him into a guard room. Urchin tried to slip in after him, but the door clanged shut in his face. Two surly hedgehog guards stood on either side of the door, not looking at him.

"Let me in!" demanded Urchin. "I'm his page!"

"Don't care if you're his mother, nobody's going in there," said one of the hedgehogs. "He's on his own till we find a boat leaky enough for him."

"I have to stay with him," said Urchin. He was trying to think of how to trick his way in when he heard paws padding quickly down the stairs behind him and the hedgehogs saluted.

"Open the door!" snapped Padra.

"Nobody's allowed in!" said the hedgehogs together.

"Straighten yourselves up and obey orders, you pair of arrogant mud-brained pincushions!" barked Padra, but they had rushed to unlock the door before he even finished. "Urchin," he added gently, "this is not the place for you."

"But, please, I'm his page and I belong with him, Captain Padra, sir," said Urchin.

"You'll see him before he goes, I promise," said Padra. "If you want to help him now, send for Brother Fir."

"Yes, sir."

"Then find an otter called Arran. She may be near the Spring Gate of the tower; do you know where that is?"

"I think it's where the freshwater spring runs from the rocks to the sea, sir," said Urchin.

"Good lad. Tell her to get hold of the best boat she can find and prepare it for Crispin."

Urchin stood still. "I don't want to help him go, sir," he said.

Padra sighed. "Neither do I, Urchin; neither does any creature in its right mind. But all we can do for him now is give him the best send-off we possibly can. Find Arran. If anybody argues with you—or with her—send them to me."

"Isn't there anything we can do to keep him here, sir?" asked Urchin.

"Nothing, Urchin," said Padra. And for Urchin, at that point, there was only one possible future. He waited long enough to see Padra push open the door and seize Crispin in a strong otter hug, then he raced up the stairs to find Fir, delivered his message, and dashed to the Spring Gate. His own words sounded in his head—*I'm his page, and I belong with him.* He'd promised to serve Crispin. He hadn't promised to serve him only on Mistmantle.

The tower's main freshwater supply came from a spring bubbling up through the rocks. From a gate on the east side of the tower it overflowed into a stream running down to the sea, a favorite place for otters living at court. Urchin ran to the first otter he saw. She was pale-furred, like himself, with uneven spiky tufts around the top of her head. She looked miserable, dabbling her paws in the stream, and when he spoke to her she rubbed a paw across her eyes as if she'd been crying.

"Arran?" she said. "That's me. Who wants me?"

Urchin delivered his message and had hardly finished before Arran was giving instructions to every otter in sight. Urchin ran beside her to the shore, where already the otters were lining up little boats for her inspection. She swam from one to another, her paws and whiskery face appearing over the side of each in turn.

"That one's too small," she said, and, "that's too heavy for a squirrel. That's too shabby, I'm not having that. Don't any of you answer me back, he's still a Captain of Mistmantle. Any cheek out of anyone and you'll answer to Captain Padra, or what's worse, you'll answer to me. Let's see this one. Call this a boat? Oh, this is no good. Somebody get my own boat, it's the best one on the island."

Arran's own small rowboat was brought in. It was smartly painted, and the oars looked new and well cared for.

"That's the one," she said. "Kitchens next. Provisions."

"I'll do that," said Urchin. Nobody in the kitchens seemed to care about a young squirrel helping himself to nuts, fruit, and bread. He heaped food into a basket. When it was full he packed more into his bag, filled leather bottles with wine and water, took it all to Arran, and went back for more. If she thought he had packed a lot for a single squirrel, she didn't say so. They were loading the boat when he felt somebody watching him, looked up, and saw a mole standing on the shore.

It was the old soldier mole who had taken Crispin's belongings from him in the hall. This time, he definitely winked at Urchin as he waddled unevenly down the beach, almost staggering under the weight.

"Morning, Miss Arran," he said.

"Morning, Lugg," she said, and turned from the boat. "Those are Crispin's! How did you get those?"

"Nicked 'em," said the mole, grinning, and jerked his head at Urchin. "Him and me. We nicked 'em."

"Well nicked!" said Arran. "We'll stash them under the seats and behind the baskets, where nobody will see them."

"Please, Arran . . ." began Urchin.

"What is it?"

"You know Crispin didn't do it, don't you?" he said.

"Of course he didn't," she said crossly. She gave the bundled-up robe a vicious kick to jam it under the seats. "I wish I wasn't getting this boat ready. But ready it is, so you may as well tell Padra."

Padra must have ordered the hedgehogs to let Urchin in, because they opened the door for him without a word. Nobody looked at him.

Padra, Crispin, and Fir were still talking—Padra leaned against the wall with his paws folded, Fir sat on a low stool, and Crispin stood with his back to them both, looking up through a grating. Urchin caught the words "Husk," and "watch," and "possible;" then they realized he was there and stopped talking.

"Is the boat ready?" asked Padra. "Is Arran there?"

"Yes, sir," said Urchin, thinking of what he had to do next. Wistfully, he remembered Needle, Apple, and his friends in the wood.

"Then we'll get it over with," said Crispin, and as he turned from the window, Urchin's heart tightened. He had expected to see anger in Crispin's face, but there was only compassion. Blood was drying from a cut on his ear.

"You're hurt, sir," faltered Urchin.

"Somebody hit me," said Crispin. He shrugged, and held out his paws. "Urchin, I'm so sorry about this. I know you were looking forward to being at court."

"I'll still have what I wanted, sir," said Urchin. "I know you didn't do it. I'll still be with you."

Crispin gave a little shake of his ears. "What are you saying, Urchin?"

"I'm coming with you, sir," Urchin said. He knew he'd miss his old friends terribly, and he had no idea where he'd end up. But it couldn't be helped. He was Captain Crispin's page now.

Crispin almost smiled. "I wish I could have your company, Urchin," he said gently. "You're a brave squirrel. You're as loyal as a hedgehog, as determined as a mole, and as valiant as an otter. But I don't even know where I'm going. I've never been beyond sight of the island. I could be taking you to death or danger, and I won't do that."

"But I . . ."

"Urchin," said Crispin, "if you still regard me as your captain, obey my order. Stay here."

"But won't I ever see you again, sir?" Urchin asked.

"Almost certainly not, Urchin," said Crispin gently.

It was unthinkable. Urchin couldn't imagine a world without Crispin. He struggled to hold his head up and keep the tears out of his voice. "Then, have you any other orders for me, sir?" he asked. "Because they will be all I'll have of you."

"Hurry up!" shouted a hedgehog guard, and Padra silenced him with a glare. Crispin put both forepaws on Urchin's shoulders.

"Serve this island faithfully," he said. "This island needs you more than I do. Look to Padra and Fir to guide you. If you think of me, pray the Heart's blessing on me. And take care, Urchin of the Riding Stars." His paws tightened on Urchin's shoulders. "Take care!"

"I'll look out for him, Crispin," said Padra.

"Let's get it over with," said Crispin. For a moment he clasped Urchin in his arms, then Padra, then knelt before Fir for his blessing.

"Ready," he said at last, and Urchin thought he understood for the first time what was really great about Crispin. He was about to walk out with no bitterness and no hatred. He could even care about the future of a page squirrel straight from the wood.

They set off for the shore with Crispin in the middle of a square of guards; Padra, Urchin, and Fir behind them. It seemed to Urchin like a lot of guarding for a single unarmed squirrel who wasn't even trying to escape, but when they came out into the open, he was glad of it. The jeering and growling crowd took him by surprise—but at least the escort protected Crispin from the gravel, pebbles, and rotting fruit they were throwing. Some of it hit Urchin, who was too proud to duck, but Padra stood beside him to protect him from most of it. When they reached the boat, the guards stood back, and didn't seem to know what to do next. Fir limped forward and spoke to Crispin. Padra helped him into the boat and gave him the oars. Then there was absolutely nothing Urchin could do but watch and watch until at last the boat had disappeared completely into the mist; and though he strained his ears, not even the splashing of oars could be heard.

All Urchin's efforts, all his life, had made him strong and resourceful. Now he knew he would need that strength. Mistmantle was his home. It was also an island where a ruthless murderer had crept through the tower; the king was broken with grief; justice had not been done; and there would never be Crispin again. He supposed he'd go back to the wood and join a work party, but he couldn't bear to think about it.

Padra put a paw on his shoulder as they trudged slowly across the sand together.

"It's unusual for an otter to take on a squirrel for a page," he said, "and I'm a poor substitute for Crispin."

Urchin had been feeling that he would never be happy again. Now hope flared. "I can swim a bit, sir, if that helps," he said eagerly.

Padra managed a smile. "Then, Urchin, if you'd like to be my page, report to me in the morning. No—report to me tonight, and then you won't have to go back to Anemone Wood with your tail down."

"Thank you very much, sir!" gasped Urchin.

"We'll eat in the lower chamber with the rest of the court tonight," he said. They began climbing the rocks to the tower, and without a word about it, they both stopped to look into the mists. "And, Urchin," Padra added quietly, "whatever those sharp squirrel ears pick up, be careful of repeating anything. Always think twice about what you say and who you say it to, you understand? I know Crispin was innocent, and so do you. I know you're angry, and so am I. But there is danger in high places on this island. Whoever really killed the prince is still free. So, when you're around the court, keep your young eyes and ears open. If you hear anything useful, tell me. And if you get the chance to serve the king, take it. Always be true to the king, Urchin."

That evening, Urchin moved himself and his bag of belongings into a small chamber near Padra's, close to the Spring Gate. A comfortable bed had been prepared for him, but it was very unlike the treetop nest he was used to. Padra was needed to make arrangements for the prince's funeral, so Urchin hardly saw him.

The body of the murdered prince lay in state in a small coffin in the hall while animals trooped past with bowed heads, paying their respects. One of the guards was always there, standing sternly on duty. Padra took a turn himself. The king and queen stayed in their chamber, and either Fir or Captain Husk was always with them. The queen was said to be distraught with grief, weeping helplessly in Lady Aspen's arms.

Finally, not knowing what to do, his heart still aching for his missing hero, Urchin curled up in his new, strange chamber and knew he would not sleep.

CHAPTER FIVE

LATE THAT NIGHT, DARKNESS DEEPENED over Mistmantle in its grief. Captain Husk, still in his green-and-gold robe, held a glowing lamp as he stood on watch before the pitifully small coffin on the table. Lamplight glowed on the gold clasps of the coffin, on the fastenings of Husk's robe, and on the fine embroidery of the cuffs. Still and silent, he stood on guard alone until a hedgehog marched solemnly down the hall to take the next watch.

Leaving the hall with his lamp, he did not go straight to his own quarters. In the anteroom he took off the heavy robe and laid it in the chest, then crossed the hall with a solemn bow toward the coffin and walked with grave dignity down a flight of stairs.

At the bottom of the stairs, he would not be seen. He slipped noiselessly back up a neglected narrow stairway that led him to a little space, no more than a cupboard, next to the Gathering Chamber. An opening at the back, so well concealed that it could hardly be found, led down another set of stairs, darker and narrower. He was hurrying by now. A passageway came next, hardly more than a tunnel, and so small that he had to lower his head and draw in his shoulders. He turned right, left, right again, down another flight, through tunnels and chilly passageways, where his lamp gave only a feeble wisp of light and the air smelled of mold and damp. Unseen things ran and scrabbled in the darkness. Old cobwebs caught in his fur. These were ancient passageways, unknown even to the moles.

Darkness, absolute darkness. It was around him, and deep within him. He breathed it in; it smelled of death. Death, decay, and worse. It was better not to see what might be in these tunnels. The cold was like a chilling where nothing can live. Keeping his nerve, not knowing what would come at him from the dark, Husk came to the door that waited for him.

He laid down the lamp. This was not a place for light.

Fear shivered him. He pushed with both front paws at the door, and as it creaked and moved, he felt sickening terror.

Bang the door shut! Turn! Fly! But he always felt like that at the moment of pressing the door, knowing the horror of the place. It disgusted and fascinated him, but the fascination was stronger. He shut the door behind him and absorbed the sense of creeping evil.

Rough, cold stone was clammy under his paws. The smell of decay filtered into him. He could taste the smell. In the thick, deep darkness he could see no more than a gleam of slime on the rough walls, and a patch of even deeper darkness. That was the pit. Dark as a nightmare, dark as drowning, the pit yawned like a hungry mouth from the center of the floor. It was as if by being here he could feed its evil, as it fed his. He closed his eyes and reached into the greed and ruthlessness in himself.

He had first found this place when he wasn't looking for it. He had been looking for the legendary Old Palace but had stumbled on this ancient dungeon instead.

He wished he knew the story of this place. It must have a history. Its aura of horror told him that murder and despair had happened here.

Evil breathed and echoed around him, exciting and satisfying him even as it appalled him. It spoke to him of power, fear, treachery. In here, he could think clearly of how worthless the other animals were, and how unfair it was that he had to serve the king, when he would be a far better king himself. He thought of the first murder he had ever committed. As he soaked himself in the atmosphere of the dungeon, its power seeped into him until it spoke to him. It spoke to him. Words formed themselves clearly, grimly, in his head and heart. They were words of prophecy.

I will be all powerful. But the one that falls from the sky must be destroyed.

The one that falls from the sky? What did that mean? He imagined something falling from the sky. In the smothering blackness behind his closed eyes, a picture was forming. A picture of something falling from the sky—something almost white—he ached to see what it was, but it was not clear. Was it falling, or was it flying? The picture in his head was clearer now, like a reflection in dark water. Something was moving in the sky . . . coming closer . . . words were rising from his heart as another message formed itself inside him.

Fear nothing until squirrels fly through the skies.

Squirrels in the sky! That was too ridiculous! It might as well be "until the ends of the earth"! He need fear nothing, ever! He sprang up, shut the door on the swallowing pit, and laughed wildly in the dark where no living thing heard him.

CHAPTER SIX

IN THE DAYS AND WEEKS AFTER THE FUNERAL, Urchin learned more of his duties. As Crispin had promised, he learned to use a sword, as well as the less exciting things like when to bow and when not to. As a very new and young tower squirrel, he found it safest to bow to everyone. He carried messages. He learned how to serve at the table, and how to clean and polish a sword. He learned to cook fish, and didn't mind that, so long as Padra didn't expect him to eat it. He discovered that the water from the spring at the gate was by far the best water anywhere on the island, especially when it was freshly drawn. He learned to clean and care for Padra's chamber, which always smelled faintly of smoked fish. When even the moss for the bedding began to smell smoky, he threw it out and replaced it. His own bed became more of a nest, but nobody minded. He was gathering pawfuls of moss one morning when he saw Gleaner scrambling about in the high branches of a rowan tree, collecting sprays of bright red berries—but she pretended not to see him.

When the fresh moss had been piled onto the beds, Urchin was supposed to report to Padra. Padra being an otter, this was often difficult, as he could have swum halfway to the mists. More often, he would be swimming near the shores on patrol, but that could mean a long journey around the island. (If Urchin saw Padra twirling about in the water with Arran, or loping along the shore with her, he thought it best to stay back and wait.) If Padra was nowhere to be found at all, Urchin had discovered that the best thing was to go up to Brother Fir's tower and ask the priest's permission to look out from there. He could be sure of a good view, a warm welcome, and a cup of hot berry cordial on a cold morning.

As this was turning out to be one of those mornings, Urchin ran up the stairs to Fir's tower. He reached the workroom landing in time to see a roll of canvas waddling toward him on its own paws, and collide with it.

"Look where you're going!" cried Needle from behind the canvas.

"Sorry!" said Urchin. "What's that for?"

"Hold the other end and don't ask stupid questions," snapped Needle, and with a struggle they carried the canvas into a workroom and heaved it onto a long table. At last Urchin could see Needle's face, and she looked tense and troubled.

"You all right?" he said.

"'Course I am!" said Needle. "The work's really good. I sit next to a nice hedgehog called Thripple; she's helping me to learn. She looks a bit odd, but she's lovely. And Mum had the baby! A little boy! We call him Scufflen!"

"Oh, good!" said Urchin. But the trace of anxiety in her eyes told him that it wasn't exactly good.

"He'll be all right," she went on quickly. "My mum's been feeding him lots, so he's putting on weight."

"Oh," said Urchin, and his heart sank. He knew what could happen to undersize babies. "Is he very tiny?"

"Who said he was tiny?" she snapped, and her spines bristled so that Urchin dodged. "There's nothing at all the matter with him. And his paw . . ."

"What's wrong with his paw?" asked Urchin.

"Didn't say there was anything wrong, did I?" she said. Then she sat down on a bench and gave a little sigh. "I'm sorry. I know I'm not being very nice. And there isn't anything the matter with his paw, not really. It's just a teeny bit curled in. You'd hardly notice it if you didn't know."

"Maybe he just hasn't opened it out yet," suggested Urchin, to be helpful. He didn't know anything about babies, but it made sense to him.

"Yes!" said Needle, brightening up. "Yes, that'll be it! He just hasn't wanted to uncurl his claws yet! He'll be all right."

"I'd better go, then," said Urchin. "I'm looking for Captain Padra."

"Why didn't you say?" said Needle. "He just went up the stairs to Fir's turret."

Padra had been in the turret for some time while Urchin was with Needle. He often went there when he needed to think out loud, though as a sea animal he disliked heights. Instead of looking down, he stared out at the wide, gray sea.

"The work parties start earlier and earlier," Padra said. "Winter's coming, when everyone just wants to keep warm and get enough to eat. I know the work has to be done, but we managed for years up to now without animals being rounded up before dawn and heaving timber about all day." He turned impatiently. "It's far worse since Crispin went."

"Hm," said Brother Fir. "And why is that, do you suppose?"

"Either the king's still angry and is taking it out on everyone else," said Padra, "or he knows some reason why we need to do extra work and he hasn't told the rest of us, *or*"— his tail swished in irritation— "the instructions aren't from the king at all. I think this is all Husk's idea, but he couldn't get away with so much when Crispin was here."

"Hm," said Fir.

"Husk spends more time with the king than anyone else does," said Padra. "I think he's the one giving orders, but like everything else about Husk, it can't be proved."

"You are still seething about the trial," observed Fir, and was interrupted by a polite little tapping at the door. "That's Urchin's knock."

64

"Wait outside, Urchin," called Padra.

"Why should he?" said Fir, and bent stiffly to put a saucepan of cordial to warm by the fire. "Let the lad come in, have his drink, and hear what you think about Captain Husk."

"Of course not!" said Padra. "He's only a young page; we can't involve him!"

"Ah, but he already is involved," said Fir. "And too young to be left in danger, and he certainly will be in danger if he isn't warned." He turned a gaze of deep intensity on Padra. "We're not talking about just any young squirrel lad, you know."

"He has a great future, I think," said Padra.

"Oh, please, Padra!" said Fir. "Do I have to do your thinking for you? Is it something to do with that otter-shaped head? Think, can't you? After a night of riding stars, something important always happens. After the last one, the prince was killed and Crispin was exiled. But on the one all those years ago, before you and Crispin were captains, nothing dramatic happened at all. Unless you count the arrival of one lost, scrappy baby squirrel." He raised his voice. "Urchin, come in!"

Urchin hopped into the chamber, wondering why they'd kept him waiting. He bowed smartly to Fir, then to Padra.

"Heart bless you, Urchin," said Fir.

"Heart bless you, too, Brother Fir, and reporting for duty, Captain Padra, sir," gabbled Urchin.

"Oh, report for a hot drink while you're about it, what's the hurry?" said Fir, filling a wooden cup from the saucepan. The aroma of hot, spiced fruit rose from the cup, and Urchin folded his paws gratefully around it.

"Your captain has time to waste with a creaky old squirrel like me," went on Fir. "But don't get him angry, Urchin. He's still cross about Crispin's trial."

"If you can call it a trial." Padra glanced at Fir, knelt to be nearer to Urchin's level, and lowered his voice. "I think you're too young to be told this, Urchin, but Fir thinks you should know, and he's usually right. I don't know how Husk fixed the casting of lots, but I suspect he did. And he was better placed to kill the prince than anyone else was. I don't think any of those witnesses could be sure about when they saw him."

Urchin looked down into the cordial and shuffled his paws. He felt he ought to show surprise and horror, but he couldn't. It was something he had to face. Husk carried a sword. He was often close to the royal apartments. And he had taken charge of the casting of lots that declared Crispin guilty. Urchin realized now that, in his heart, he'd always known Husk could be the murderer. He hadn't wanted to believe it, but it made sense.

"All he had to do next was to get Crispin blamed and exiled," continued Padra. "With the prince and Crispin out of the way, he's next in line to the throne."

"The queen could have another baby," said Urchin.

Padra shrugged. "They say her health is almost broken, and her spirit, too," he said. "Hardly anybody every sees her, except Aspen and the maids, and Aspen may be paw-in-paw with Husk. Weevils, plague, pestilence, rot, thunder, and lice upon him, he's getting the island in his paw."

"Hm," said Fir. "And he's clever enough to get away with it. The animals will never rise against the king. They might rise against Husk, eventually, but only *if* you have real evidence against him and *if* they realize that he isn't obeying the king at all. But it will take a long time. You must wait for the right moment, Padra."

"Will there ever be a right moment?" said Padra.

"There is a right moment for everything," said Fir. "Like tides and fishing. At present, I think it is the right moment for you to give Urchin his orders. Let him finish his drink first."

"Urchin," said Padra briskly. "I want you to go to the king."

Urchin spluttered on his cordial. "The king!" he gasped.

"Every animal has the right to see the king; don't be so flustered," said Padra. "He'll be in the Throne Room. I need to know what plans he has for the winter, and whether the stores are full yet. Ask after the queen. Keep your eyes and ears sharp, and if Husk is there, watch him."

Urchin held the cup tightly. It was exciting, being entrusted with secrets like this, but something knotted in his stomach when he thought of Husk as a murderer. Still, he only had to watch him. He wouldn't be alone with him.

"Yes, sir," he said. "And, sir, my friend Needle has a new baby brother, Scufflen. I think they're worried. He's a bit small." Over the rim of his cup, he saw a look pass between Fir and Padra.

"Keep me informed," said Padra. "And when I say 'me,' I mean exactly that. Me, not Husk. Finish your drink and run to the Throne Room."

Urchin scrambled out of the window, down the wall, in through another window—it was the quickest way—and ran through the corridors to the royal chambers. At the heavy oak door of the Throne Room, he was asking the guard moles if he could speak to the king when Captain Husk himself stepped briskly from the chamber. Urchin jumped back in alarm, then tried not to be frightened.

"You're Padra's page, aren't you?" said Husk. "Fetch wine from the cellar. Bring it straight here."

"Y-yes, sir," said Urchin. "What kind, sir?"

"Tell the otter in charge of the cellar it's for the king," said Husk. "He'll know what to send. Quickly, now!"

Glad to escape, Urchin ran down to the wide, airy cellar and collected the wine—"we seem to be going through a lot of this just now," remarked the cellar otter as he handed over the bottle—and hurried back up again. Ahead of him, a squirrel who looked very much like Gleaner dashed across and jumped from a window, but so quickly that Urchin couldn't be quite sure who it was. He arrived at the Throne Room door a little breathless, was let in by the moles, and waited by the door as Padra had taught him.

Bottle in paws, he watched, remembering Padra's instructions.

Since the prince's death the king seemed to have grown old—tired, and gray at the muzzle—but he was still the tallest, strongest hedgehog Urchin had ever seen, and held his head high. A fire flared in the grate, lamps glowed on the walls, and the king's crown gleamed. His paw rested on the arm of the gilded throne, and a small table stood at his elbow with a wineglass, almost empty. Threadings on the walls glowed with color, and the floor had been freshly covered with rushes.

"Your Majesty looks tired," said Husk. "Perhaps you slept badly?"

"I never sleep well now, since . . ." began the king, and Husk nodded in sympathy. "But we have work to do. I suppose it's work parties again, is it, Husk?"

"Nothing that Your Majesty need worry about," said Husk. "With more animals, and an earlier start, we'll stay on top of the work."

The king slumped wearily in his throne. "I don't know where all this work comes from, Husk," he sighed.

"Well, I'm afraid, Your Majesty," said Husk, "it's because we let things go in the past. We've been careless, if you'll excuse my saying so, and need to catch up. We have very few weapons; we couldn't defend ourselves if we had to. Just think, if a certain squirrel—no need to name names—had organized a rebellion against you, we couldn't have fought back. Don't even think about what might have happened, Your Majesty. So we need weapons. The moles have found a very good supply of garnets. We're storing some, and trading the rest for swords."

"Jewels for swords," mumbled the king.

"So, if you would give the permission, sir?" suggested Husk, and spread out beech leaves on the table. "It can't be done without a royal warrant."

The king raised his paw heavily, and Urchin saw that he trembled. He scratched his clawmark on a leaf.

"And we need an order for the young otters, to make them work longer hours," said Husk. "All they want to do is play about in the water."

The king raised a paw, then lowered it again and sat back. He almost smiled. "Let them play," he said.

"As you wish, Your Majesty," said Husk. "Where's that page with the wine?"

Urchin stepped forward, bowed, and held out the bottle. He wasn't sure if he'd be expected to pour it himself, but Husk took it and filled the king's glass to the rim.

"It'll be a long hard winter," said Husk, putting the glass in the king's paw. "Gloss the mole says so, and so does Tay the otter. A reliable mole and the historian, they should know. If we're going to have food and fuel for the winter, everyone has to work hard."

"But they already do work hard!" said the king, and peered past Husk toward Urchin. "Who's that?"

"Padra's page," said Husk, and waved a paw at Urchin. "You can go now."

Urchin bowed awkwardly. His mouth felt dry. "I have a message from Captain Padra, sir," he said.

"It can wait," said Husk. "Stand outside the door."

"No, come here, page," said the king. He leaned forward with a new light of interest in his black eyes as Urchin stepped forward and bowed. Padra hadn't told him if he should look the king in the eyes, but it felt like the right thing to do.

"You're the foreigner, aren't you?" said the king at last. "The found thing? Shell, or Starfish, or . . ."

"Urchin, Your Majesty."

"Well, serve your captain and be true to the island," he said. "What was Padra's message?"

"I was to ask if we have enough stores for the winter," said Urchin, still looking up into the searching black eyes. "And he asked after the queen's health."

"The queen sleeps far better now that Lady Aspen looks after her," said the king.

"Lady Aspen is very glad to be of help," put in Husk.

"And Husk seems to have all the winter plans under control," the king went on. "But shouldn't we be trading for wool, not swords?"

"We're doing both, Your Majesty," said Husk quickly. He pushed a leaf toward the king and turned sharply to Urchin. "Go, and give Captain Padra his answer."

Urchin closed the door as slowly as possible. Husk lowered his voice, but Urchin still heard him.

"The weaker ones won't survive another winter, Your Majesty," he was saying. "It's sad, but the only kind thing to do is to keep culling. Should I pass you your drink? Thank you, Your Majesty, and we also need a clawmark for that little order . . . thank you."

71

Urchin had heard plenty. He was ready to dash through the nearest possible route back to Padra, but opposite him, a door opened. With a waft of perfume Lady Aspen swept down the corridor, and Urchin pressed his back against the wall to let her through. Her head was high, a yellow cloak as fine as candlelight billowed from her shoulders, and on one forepaw a bracelet of rowan berries was bright above the fur. Scurrying along behind her was Gleaner.

"Thank you, Gleaner," Aspen was saying. "I'm sure you'll be an excellent maid. Report to me this evening. And I will inform Captain Husk about that hedgehog." With polished claws she knocked on the Throne Room door.

Gleaner had caught sight of Urchin. She turned to grin unpleasantly into his face.

"You're not the only one invited to the tower!" she hissed, and whisked away.

Urchin bolted along the corridor. This time his way was blocked by a tall, broad-shouldered, and very short-furred squirrel. Urchin looked up and disliked him at once.

"Where do you think you're going?" snarled the squirrel.

"To the shore, sir," said Urchin.

"Then go the other way," ordered the squirrel.

"Yes . . ." said Urchin, and hesitated. He didn't know the name of this squirrel, and didn't want to call him "sir" again if he could help it.

"My name's Granite," growled the squirrel, and stretched out a hard, curling claw toward Urchin's face.

Urchin tightened every muscle. His instinct was to flinch, but he knew better than to show fear to a bully. The claw ran along his whiskers. In his heart he squirmed, but he forced himself to stand fast as the squirrel repeated his name.

"I'm Granite. Remember me."

CHAPTER SEVEN

URCHIN FLED FROM THE TOWER to the clean, salt air of the shore. The tide was out, and he bounded along the hard, wet sand with its debris of shells and seaweed. The row of wooden mooring posts stood clear of the water, some with boats tied up. Far out in the water, Padra and Arran swam side by side, but this was no time for leaving them alone, so Urchin jumped onto a post, balanced with his tail, and called for Padra. He had expected to see a wave of a paw, a slow turn, and a leisurely swim back, but Padra flicked himself over and swished to the shore with Arran following.

"Can I talk to you in private, sir?" asked Urchin.

"You can say anything in front of Arran," said Padra, shaking water from his fur. "But we'll go around the shore."

He led them farther from the tower. Urchin began his report at such an urgent gabble that Padra had to stop him and make him start again.

". . . so you were right: the ideas about work parties and things aren't from the king," he finished. "Or at least they are, but Captain Husk's telling him what to think."

"Did the king ask for the wine himself?" asked Padra.

"He didn't have to," said Urchin, "Husk kept filling the glass. And Lady Aspen's taking Gleaner as one of her maids, and they were talking about a hedgehog. I think Gleaner may have told her about Needle's baby brother, and she'll tell Captain Husk."

"Pestilence!" muttered Arran, and Padra's mouth gave a twist that twitched his whiskers.

"I'll see what I can do," he said. "Anything else?" When Urchin told him about Granite, he stopped and took a deep breath.

"Granite from the armory?" he said. "I always thought he was a nasty-claw thug, but somehow he got into the Circle. Then Crispin put him in charge of the armory, which was wise, because Granite likes weapons, but the armorer doesn't actually get to use them against anyone. If he's prowling the corridors, we should be worried." Then he smiled down at Urchin. "That is, I should be worried, not you."

"But, sir," said Urchin, "when they do a culling . . ."

"It's very quick," said Padra. "It's best to wait till the youngster's fast asleep, then do it so quickly they don't know anything about it. Now, I've put you in for a fencing lesson, and I hear you're learning well. Run along to the fencing master."

"Yes, sir," said Urchin, "but about little Scufflen . . ."

"I'll do what I can for him," said Padra. "That's all."

Urchin ran to his fencing lesson. If Padra couldn't save the baby hedgehog, he'd do it himself.

In the Throne Room, Husk was filling the king's glass again.

"You're right, Your Majesty," he said. "Of all the Circle animals, Granite will make the best captain."

The king frowned. "I said Tay the otter was the best, Husk," he said.

"Oh, yes, Your Majesty, but that was before Granite was nominated," he said. "Tay's a great scholar, but she's not a leader. Gloss the mole was mentioned, but the trouble with moles is that you can never be sure where they are. Padra nominated Arran, but he would. He hasn't always been wise in his choice of friends, has he? So . . ."

"Oh, I'll consider Granite, then," said the king wearily.

Husk bowed, and left the king with the half-empty bottle at his paw. Back in his own chamber with its deep-red hangings and heavily curtained windows, he laughed.

More culling would save the trouble of keeping wretched infants through the winter. There were others who needed the food. He looked forward to killing the new hedgehog.

Granite would be a useful captain. As a fighter, he was unbeatable; as a bodyguard, he would be invincible; and he wouldn't be troubled with thinking too much. He'd do whatever he was paid to do.

But I am invincible anyway, thought Husk. *I need fear nothing until squirrels fly through the skies.* Those words of prophecy had come to him in the dungeon, and could be relied on. The evil there was so powerful and it had a voice so secret that not even Aspen must know of it, but it spoke with his own voice, rising from his own center like a warped stem. Soon he would truly be king of Mistmantle, and anyone who didn't like it would be against a wall with a sword to the heart. And why stop at Mistmantle? There were bigger, richer islands to be conquered.

Gloss the mole could be a problem. He would be jealous of Granite. He was useful, but he saw too much. Best to find him a job that would keep him out of the way.

Soon there would be a splendid wedding and a feast to keep the common creatures happy. The more stupid among them had forgotten Crispin already.

Three nights had passed when, far beyond the mists, Crispin heaved his boat well up the shore, stretched the stiffness from his limbs, and fastened on his sword. He'd already landed on one island inhabited by snakes, and another where he'd been attacked by swarms of vicious crabs, and on both he'd needed quick wits and good swordsmanship to rescue himself. But this one looked better. He took an upward path through a wood of beech and hazel, eating the nuts he found on the way and following the sound of running water until he found a fresh, clear stream. He drank, washed his face and paws, and went on.

The path opened at last to a lake larger than Crispin could ever have imagined. Trees drooped over it. Reeds bordered it, and lilypads floated. Tiny islands, with a few bushes and a tree on each, stood here and there. Bubbles rose and ripples spread as fish nudged the calm surface.

"The Heart brought me here," whispered Crispin, and gave thanks.

A wild and noisy flapping made him leap backward with paw on sword hilt. White wings blurred his vision; a stinging blow to his paw sent the sword spinning far away; and Crispin found he was looking up at the furious, hissing face of an enormous white swan.

"What dare you do here, tree-rat!" spat the swan.

Crispin held his ground, but he had never been so close to a swan. Its size was overwhelming.

"I'm a stranger here, sir," he said. "Crispin, Captain of Mistmantle."

"Call me Highness! Lord Arcneck!" snarled the swan. "You belong in the wood, tree-rat! This is the mere! It is only for swans!"

Beyond the swan, on the lake, Crispin could see gray-brown cygnets bobbing between the lilypads. A sudden movement near them made him watch.

The swan was lecturing him on the laws of the island, but Crispin wasn't listening. His eyes were on that movement gliding under the water, near enough to the surface for him to see the long, strong body.

A watersnake! He had sometimes seen them at Mistmantle. They may only be a kind of fish, but they were big and strong enough to drag down and devour a young animal. Usually the otters dealt with them, but Crispin had learned from Padra what to do with watersnakes.

He leaped for his sword. The swan arched his neck to strike him, but Crispin was springing into the water.

"Watersnake!" cried Crispin, and as the frightened cygnets scattered, he flung himself on the back of the great ugly fish, leaned forward, and plunged the sword hard into the roof of the open mouth, ramming it home. As the fish reared and thrashed, Crispin clutched the sword hilt in both paws. He was still holding it as the dying fish hurled him into the air, and the swan's beak gripped his tail.

The swan dragged him to the bank and dropped him. Crispin stood up, shook water from his fur, and wiped his sword clean on the grass as the swan's neck curved over him. Its mate was chivvying the cygnets away from the great, bleeding body of the watersnake.

"Brave, for a tree-rat," remarked the swan. "If we want your service again, you will give it. You may continue to live on this island, in the wood, with the other tree-rats." It turned a sharp, hard eye toward the body. "Watersnake? It is a pike. Pike, tree-rat. What is it?"

"A pike, Highness," said Crispin. He supposed he'd get used to this. Behind him, he heard giggling. He almost turned to look, but remembered in time that turning his back on Lord Arcneck might be an unpardonable insult. So he waited, still hearing the stifled laughter behind him, until the swan had glided away and he could turn to see who was there.

A group of young female squirrels had gathered to watch. The only one who wasn't giggling stepped forward.

"Swans are like that," she said gently. "You'll get used to it. I'm Whisper. Who are you?"

On a late afternoon, Urchin was on guard duty at the Spring Gate, with the dying sun in his eyes. He was chafing his paws against the cold as Padra appeared, and put a mole on guard.

"Good news," said Padra. "Come with me."

"Needle's brother?" said Urchin hopefully.

"First things first," said Padra, hurrying on through the tower. "Husk and Aspen's wedding will be soon."

"Oh," said Urchin. "Is that good?"

"It's excellent!" said Padra. "Husk's ordering singers and robes and jewels and whatnot, so he's leaving the king alone. Quick sharp, before he gets back."

They hurried through the tapestried corridors to the Throne Room, where Urchin stayed a pace behind Padra, kneeling as Padra knelt, glimpsing the king's tired smile. Behind the throne stood Granite with his shoulders squared. Urchin's fur bristled.

"Padra," said the king, and Urchin thought his speech was slurred. "We used to patrol the shores together. You used to take the prince out in your boat! He loved the water!" A tear trickled down his face, and as he lifted a paw to brush it away,

Urchin lowered his eyes. "Is there something you want, Padra?"

"Good news, Your Majesty," said Padra. "The hedgehog baby born to Mistress Ramblen is fine and healthy, and will thrive. There's no need to cull." He looked up into the king's eyes. "A beautiful baby boy hedgehog, Your Majesty."

"If he can thrive, let him," mumbled the king, and dabbed at his eyes with a napkin. "A hedgehog baby."

"Thank you, Your Majesty!" cried Urchin, then turned hot as he remembered he hadn't been invited to speak. He felt the king looking at him, and shyly raised his head.

"Weren't you here with Husk?" asked the king curiously. "He's to be married, you know. What would we do without Lady Aspen? The queen adores her. I offered him a wedding gift, but he only wants jewels for his wife. Padra, you should marry. Loneliness is terrible. If you want to marry your otter friend, you have my permission."

For once, Padra seemed lost for words. It only lasted for a moment.

"I've no idea if she wants to marry me, Your Majesty," he said, "but I hope she can be our new captain."

The king's paws twitched. "Oh, Padra," he said. "I have already made Granite our new captain."

"Plagues, lice, and pestilence!" muttered Padra as they strode from the Throne Room. "Fleas and worms to the pack of them!"

"But we can have more than three captains," said Urchin, hurrying to keep up.

"Not with Husk in charge," said Padra.

"You saved Scufflen," said Urchin.

"Yes, I suppose so," said Padra. "Go and tell Needle."

Urchin ran to the workrooms. He wondered if Needle would still be there, but everyone seemed to be working late. She came to the door looking anxious and flustered, with bits of thread caught on her spines. Urchin told her the news and stood well back in case she tried to hug him.

"I'll get permission to go and tell Mum," she said. "I think they'll let me go, but there's so much work all of a sudden. You know about the wedding? Look at this!" She opened a door.

Urchin's eyes widened in astonishment. Lace, as white and fine as mist, was everywhere. It hung from frames and trailed across the room.

"She's going to be so beautiful!" said Needle. "But there's lengths and lengths of embroidery to do—and she's supposed to have a tiara with jewels, so the moles are all digging furiously—and we have to make a new captain's robe—they said it's for a squirrel, but he must be a tall one. And Captain Husk had already ordered new Threadings. Come and I'll show you."

Urchin followed her into the long workroom where the nearly finished Threadings hung in their frames. They were beautifully stitched, with glowing color and gold and silver thread, showing, as usual, the kings, queens, heroes, and captains of the past.

"More squirrels than anything else," said Urchin.

"I know," said Needle. "We ran out of squirrel-red wool. Captain Husk bought some more from the ships."

There were a few hedgehogs, but hardly ever a mole or an otter. Urchin went from one to the next—squirrels on thrones, squirrels with swords, squirrels in trees. There was said to be an ancient underground mole palace somewhere on the island, in the roots of a tree. It was probably only an old tale with no truth in it, but Urchin had always liked that story. The Old Palace was in a tapestry, too, but with a squirrel lord on a throne instead of a mole.

"The rocks," said Needle.

"Sorry?" said Urchin.

"The rocks," said Needle. "Mostly, I get to do the rocks, because I'm new. Thripple does the clever bits—robes and things."

"I was looking at the faces," said Urchin. "Have you noticed? All the females look like Lady Aspen. And all the males look like Husk."

CHAPTER EIGHT

FROST BEGAN TO SETTLE IN THE MORNINGS. There was frost that froze on fur and whiskers; fine white frost that crunched under paws in Anemone Wood; delicate frost that crisped the fallen leaves and sparkled on the moss. Nights were sharp and bitter, with the moon rising high above Mistmantle Tower in a clear sky. Fires were lit in hearths, and the nibbled cores of fir cones were thrown to the flames. Padra and Urchin spent long evenings with Fir.

Preparations for the wedding filled every day. Guards of honor were drilled. New cloaks and robes were made and old ones repaired. The Gathering Chamber was decorated. Stores were heaped up in the kitchens. All the talk in the woods and water, on the shores, everywhere, was of the wedding. When Husk was not in the Throne Room, the king was guarded by Captain Granite.

The night before the wedding, swords, silver dishes, and trumpets were polished until they flashed in the candlelight. Whiskers were smoothed, fur was washed, claws were trimmed. Apple came to the tower with a small pot of deep red paste made from wax and pollen for Urchin to rub on his ear and tail tips to enhance their color. Urchin thanked her, but decided against using it. He thought Needle might like it, so when Apple had gone he took it to the workrooms.

He found Needle still at a bench, and still stitching with fine white thread onto snowy silk, though she looked near to tears with exhaustion. A hunchbacked female hedgehog stood beside her, packing frothy white things into boxes. White sheets were spread over every surface, and even on the floor. When Urchin hopped in and opened the pot of red paste, Needle shrieked and curled into a ball.

"Go away!" she wailed. "Put the top back on that, *now*!"

"It's only paste!" said Urchin. This wasn't like Needle.

"Get it out!" screamed Needle from inside the ball. "Take it away and don't let it touch anything! And wash your paws!"

The other hedgehog gently stroked the top of Needle's head. Now that Urchin could get a good look at her, he saw that her face had a squashed and lopsided look that should have been ugly, but her eyes were kind.

"It's all right, little Needle," she soothed. "No harm done." She looked past Needle to Urchin, who still stood uncertainly in the doorway. "She's tired. And it's very important that we don't get any marks on the wedding clothes, so we can't have colored paste in here. Don't worry, you weren't to know that. I told her she should go to bed, and I'll finish off here when I've delivered these. I'm Thripple, I've been teaching her."

Needle uncurled very slowly. By the time Urchin returned from washing his paws, she had calmed down.

"Sorry," she said wearily. "I've had enough of Lady Aspen's wedding robes. We've still got her train to finish. Those things Thripple just packed, they're for the bridesmoles, they have to be delivered to the royal chambers. And it's all pure white. White on white on white. It hurts my eyes. And the slightest touch of a stain will ruin it, so don't bring any more sticky red pollens in here, *please*, Urchin."

"Sorry," said Urchin. "I can take those boxes to the royal chambers, if you like."

"It would be a big help," said Thripple.

Needle managed to smile. "I'll see Scufflen tomorrow," she said. "I've made him his own little robe out of leftover bits. We've all got some time off after the wedding, so I can go home and take it to him. That's the only thing about being here. There isn't much time off, and I hardly ever get to see my family and the rest of the colony. I'm looking forward to putting his little robe on him, even more than the wedding and the feast. Will you be wearing something special?"

"Sort of," he said. "Just a green cloak that's been altered to fit me." He wasn't sure, but he hoped it might have been Crispin's once. Even so, the color that suited the real red squirrels never looked quite right on him. "Are those ready to take?"

Thripple piled up boxes in his paws and warned him not to try climbing out of windows. Urchin trotted a little precariously to the royal chambers, peering past the boxes as he went. He was nearly at Lady Aspen's chambers when somebody bumped into him heavily from behind. The top box tipped, rocked, and tumbled. White silk flowers spilled wildly over the floor.

"Clumsy!" said Gleaner from behind him, and bustled past importantly. "Now, don't try to pick them up, you'll only get them dirty. Leave them to me."

"You're welcome," said Urchin.

"I'm really very busy, but I suppose I'd better do it," said Gleaner, but she didn't seem too busy to stop and talk. She stood blocking the corridor, a small phial of violet glass clutched in her paw. "Lady Aspen and I have very important things to do. I have to look after the queen tomorrow. She's extremely ill."

"Is she worse?" said Urchin with concern.

"She's very ill indeed, and Lady Aspen's most worried about her," announced Gleaner. "And as the wedding is tomorrow, I'll be looking after her because I know everything to do." She looked over her shoulder and added quietly, "You can't trust mole maids. I'll have to miss the wedding, but I don't mind. The queen needs me."

"Gleaner!" called Aspen from inside the queen's chamber.

"I'm sorry, my lady, Urchin's keeping me talking," said Gleaner, and took the remaining boxes from Urchin's paws. "I'll tidy those up presently."

"Captain Padra's regards to the queen," said Urchin, and darted away before Gleaner could tell him to run along. He wondered how Needle could stand the workrooms. He'd already seen enough of little white lacy things to last him a lifetime.

The queen, thin and haggard, lay propped up on pillows in the four-poster bed. The windows were tightly shut, and the fire made the room drowsily hot. When Gleaner carried in the boxes, the queen's eyes remained shut.

"Was that Padra's page?" asked Aspen as she bent over the queen.

"Yes, my lady," said Gleaner with distaste. "Here's the boxes from the workroom, except for the one he dropped, and here's the medicine, my lady."

"You know exactly what to do?" said Aspen.

"Seven drops in the small glass of water, if she's worse," said Gleaner. "And put away the phial carefully in your wooden box, because it's a special medicine just for the queen."

"And if you're at all alarmed about her, even if it's in the middle of the ceremony, send somebody to find me," said Aspen. "I hate for you to miss the wedding, Gleaner, but I know the queen will be in safe paws."

"I don't mind, my lady," said Gleaner.

"I suppose that page will have to be on duty," sighed Aspen. "He spoils the look of things. I find it really worrying, not knowing where he's from or anything about him. It's most unsettling. He could be anybody or anything."

The glow of having something to tell warmed Gleaner. "Oh, as to that, my lady," she said, "I don't exactly know where he's from, but I know more than most. I can tell you a secret about him."

Husk tried on his new robe and set the circle of gold on his head. Tomorrow he would wear a jeweled one, and the king had been happy to provide ropes of necklaces for Aspen.

Jewels were wealth, and wealth could buy anything. It could buy power. The work parties were grumbling about the long hours and hard work as winter set in, but a good wedding banquet would keep them quiet.

He had given orders that all animals for the cull were to be brought to him. Wise parents took it as an honor that their pathetic little brats should be put to death by the compassionate claw of the king's chief captain. But lately, too many of them had been left in the care of a guard, and handed over to Padra.

Padra was interfering, as usual. He'd even got a pardon for that weedy new hedgehog. But Padra had to learn who was in charge. In all the bustle of the wedding, nobody would question a change of orders. The baby was to be handed over. Husk felt the need to kill.

CHAPTER NINE

BEFORE DAWN, IN THE SMALL CHAMBER by the Spring Gate, Urchin wriggled farther into the sleepy warmth of his nest and squeezed his eyes shut. Padra was nudging him awake.

"Early start," said Padra cheerfully. "What about a swim before breakfast?"

Urchin curled up tightly and pulled a blanket around his shoulders.

"There's only one thing better, and that's swimming and breakfast at the same time," said Padra. "Shall I bring you a fish?"

"Fish ish ushty, sha," mumbled Urchin.

"Beg your pardon?" said Padra.

Urchin poked his head out and blinked. "Fish is disgusting," he yawned, and wriggled back down. He emerged long enough to add "sir," and hid under the blanket again.

"Be up and about by the time I come back," said Padra. "Find a nice frozen pool to shake your head in. It brightens the eyes!" With a laugh and a good-natured kick at the nest, Padra went away. There was a soft splash as he slipped into the stream, then Urchin was asleep again.

He was dreaming of a wedding banquet made up of nothing but fish when he was woken by a sharp and furious banging at the door. He had barely lifted the latch when it flew open and he was thrown violently against the wall and pinned there. Needle was screaming into his face.

"You lying, filthy, worm-ridden squirrel, what have you got to say?" she shrieked. "You and your filthy, slithering otter—I hate you—I hate you both!"

She let go with one paw to dry her eyes, and Urchin slipped free. He rubbed at his neck where her claws had scratched.

"What have I done?" he gasped.

"What have you done? What haven't you?" she screamed, pounding him with both paws. "You promised they wouldn't take my brother! You promised!"

Urchin caught her wrists to stop her hitting him. "What happened?" he said. "Tell me!"

She gulped hard and swallowed before she could go on. "They came this morning," she sobbed. "Two guards came. They brought Scufflen and my mum here, because he's named for the cull. She's up in my workrooms now, crying her eyes out and cuddling him as long as she can. So a lot of good *you* did!"

"Come with me," said Urchin. He dragged her after him through the Spring Gate as Padra was walking up the shore, shaking water from his ears. To Urchin's annoyance, he wasn't alone. He didn't even see Urchin as he was talking over his shoulder to Granite, a few steps behind him.

"I'm afraid he's a dead loss," Padra was saying airily. "He's been with me for months now, and he's completely untrainable." He waved a paw, turned, saw Urchin and Needle, and greeted them with his usual cheerfulness. "Is something wrong?"

Urchin couldn't say anything. He was too stunned. He knew he had something to say to Padra, but the words he'd just heard had knocked it out of him.

"My brother!" snapped Needle. "Urchin said you'd saved him, and now he's been brought to the tower!"

Padra's eyes flicked from Urchin to Needle and back. "Where?" he demanded.

"Workroom," stammered Urchin, trying to pull himself together.

"My bit of the workrooms," sobbed Needle.

"Show me!" said Padra, and set off after Needle at a run. Urchin followed, but Padra called over his shoulder. "Find Lugg the mole!"

Find Lugg. He didn't even know where to start looking, and all he wanted to do was find a hole in a tree and hide. He'd done his best, and thought he'd done well. He'd worked hard, obeyed orders, and learned everything Padra had taught him, or he thought he had. And that was what Padra thought of him. *A dead loss. Completely untrainable.*

He could at least have kept his opinions to himself instead of telling Captain Granite.

But maybe Padra wasn't so great. He hadn't saved Scufflen. Urchin trudged back to the tower. *Find Lugg.*

White pennants flew from every turret in honor of the day. Urchin straightened his back and raised his head. Today, he'd show them, Padra and all of them. Today, he'd make sure nobody could call him a dead loss. Then tomorrow, he'd report to Padra and say—*Please, sir, I know you think I'm a dead loss and untrainable, so I'm sorry I've wasted your time. Maybe I should go back to the wood and . . .*

. . . and what? Stack timber on boats, he thought bitterly. A long way down from being a tower squirrel.

He could take his chance with a boat and go to find Crispin! Crispin wouldn't have called him a dead loss! But all that was for tomorrow, and today, he'd dazzle them. Today, he'd be brilliant, today . . .

. . . he'd find Lugg. It was a start.

It wasn't easy. The tower mole guards were lining up as guards of honor; the wood moles didn't know much; and the ones who didn't have anything to do were pretending to be very busy and important and only said "Don't know," "He's gone," or "Push off, squirrel." Finally, scurrying along a corridor, he saw a small pair of mole paws hurrying toward him under a heap of logs. From behind the heap came a long grumble of curses.

"Lugg!" said Urchin, feeling better already.

"Who wants 'im?" said the voice.

"Captain Padra," said Urchin, and ran to lift some of the logs until he could see the graying muzzle of Lugg the mole. "It's urgent. He's gone to the workrooms."

"What's he want?" He dropped the logs and kicked them in Urchin's direction. "Captains! Too many captains if you ask me. Give us a paw. These are for the Gathering Chamber."

"It's urgent!" said Urchin.

Lugg looked around, summoned a pack of young squirrels who were practicing a wedding song, and left them rolling the logs to the Gathering Chamber. Urchin explained about Scufflen as Lugg trotted at his heels to the foot of the workroom stairs.

"Blooming stairs," he grumbled, and was trudging up after Urchin when they were pushed firmly out of the way by two squirrel guards and Tay the otter. Tay carried something bundled up in a blanket in her paws.

At the top of the stairs stood Needle and her mother, pressed together, sobbing bitterly. Padra, unconcerned at the prickles, hugged them both.

So Padra was sympathetic, but he hadn't saved little Scufflen. Urchin leaped down the stairs after Tay and the escort. Tay turned at the sound of his paws.

"Report to your captain," she ordered. "Up the stairs with you!"

Urchin had no intention of reporting to Padra. He dived out through the nearest window, ran up the wall and, guessing which way Tay would go, glancing in at one window then another, kept track of her. They seemed to be heading for the south front of the tower, where Husk's chambers were, above the Gathering Chamber.

Urchin found the small window of Husk's chamber, and peeped in. The deep red drapery darkened it, but he saw that Husk was still in there, and ducked sharply under the sill. From there he could hear the door open and Tay's commanding voice as she dismissed the guards.

"You may go." He heard the door shut. "Here he is, Captain Husk. I've doped him well with poppy distillation so he'll sleep until you have time to deal with him."

"Leave him on the bench by the window," ordered Husk. "There's no time now. Get a few more drops into him to make sure he stays quiet until after the wedding, and I'll do it then. I'd like to see to it now, but . . ."

"Blood on the robes, captain!" said Tay.

Urchin was losing his grip on the windowsill. He shuffled, and held on tightly.

"Exactly," said Husk. "Did his mother put up a fight?"

"The sister was worse," said Tay. "And Padra tried to interfere. He argued that the king had expressly commanded this one be spared, but I know the law better than he does. He was a great deal easier to deal with than that ill-mannered little hedgehog. Her spines should be trimmed."

"Never mind her," said Husk. "I should be in the anteroom. Thank you, Tay."

Urchin lost hold. He fell, scrabbled, twirled his tail, regained his balance on the next ledge he found, and dashed back to the workrooms to find Padra, crashing into Lugg on the way.

"You're late," said Lugg. "Captain wants you. Gathering Chamber." He glanced around, and whispered, "Found young 'un?"

"In Husk's chamber," Urchin whispered back. "On a bench by the window."

"Alive?"

"Yes, but they doped him."

Lugg winked. "Leave him to me," he said, and waddled away before Urchin could ask him what he was going to do. Urchin scurried off to the Gathering Chamber and found Padra running up the stairs, straightening his circlet.

"Where were you?" demanded Padra, and didn't wait for an answer. "Listen. The thrones for the king and queen are just in front of the Gathering Chamber windows. I'm on one side of them, and Granite's on the other. Your job is to stand at the anteroom door in case anything should be needed. Come and help me robe."

All the brightness the island could offer in winter had been gathered into the chamber. Ivy trailed from window ledges and spilled from vases. Shiny holly and evergreens hung in torch brackets on the walls, and everywhere was the golden brown of seed heads. Ribbons and garlands, silver and white as frost, had been brought from the workrooms, and every animal who owned a cloak or hat was wearing it. There were caps with feathers, bonnets with flowers, and all kinds of wreaths and circlets made with the greenery of winter. Urchin saw

96

Apple's bonnet long before he saw Apple. It was decorated with faded rosebuds so old that Urchin couldn't remember a time without them, but for every special day she'd added some extra trim. Today, a ring of gull's feathers trimmed it and tickled over the brim.

On a bench, a choir of small squirrels in white-and-silver robes sat squashed together, whispering and trying not to fidget. As Padra and Urchin marched down the hall, heads turned. The excited chattering faded, then rose again as they turned in to the anteroom.

Tay was helping Captain Granite into his robe. With a firm paw she smoothed the robe over his broad shoulders, and he winced.

"Some silly young animal has left a pin in here," said Tay severely, and pulled a pin from the seam as delicately as if it were something unpleasant. "Those workroom animals should be punished."

"They did have to hurry to get it finished in time, madam," said Urchin as he lifted Padra's robe from the chest. Tay swung around with such a glare that Urchin though she might hit him.

"Speak when you're spoken to, squirrel!" she ordered. "You're only a page! Can't you keep him under control, Padra? Does he know nothing?"

Urchin bent his head over the robe and bit hard on the inside of his lip. Padra and Granite already thought him untrainable, and now he'd proved it to Tay as well.

"I think Urchin only meant to warn you that you might find more pins in it," said Padra, and turned his back on Tay for a moment to flash a smile at Urchin. "Isn't that right, Urchin?"

"Yes, sir," said Urchin, glad to be rescued. He hopped onto a chair to help Padra into his robes, trying to forget about being a dead loss and remember what to do with a robe.

"That's all wrong," said Tay crossly. "Has nobody ever told that page how a robe should be worn? The collar should be higher. Which hook do you have it fastened on, Padra? The left cuff should be folded so that . . ."

"This is how I wear it, Tay," said Padra wearily. "Don't fuss. Nobody will mind."

"If the king or Captain Husk sees a captain improperly robed, they may feel it shows a lack of respect," said Tay.

"In the presence of Lady Aspen in her wedding robes, I'm sure the king and Captain Husk won't be looking at me," said Padra. He grinned wickedly at Urchin and added, "And, of course, Tay, you'll dazzle them too."

Tay only frowned. "You should have mentioned the queen," she said.

"I doubt the queen will be well enough to attend," said Padra. "Urchin, send my regards to Her Majesty."

"Tell them I am inquiring after the queen's health, and send her my good wishes," called Tay as Urchin hurried to the royal chambers. He was speaking to a mole maid at the door when Gleaner bustled over in a white apron.

"The queen?" she said. "She's not well enough to go to the wedding. I'm looking after her today. I told you last night, weren't you listening?"

"Captain Padra sends his regards," said Urchin. Gleaner wrinkled

up her nose as if Captain Padra's regards were more trouble than they were worth, but somebody called her name.

"Wait there," she said, and there was a low-voiced conversation with a mole maid before Gleaner turned back to Urchin. "Send Mistress Tay here," she said.

Tay was delighted to be sent for. She soon returned and issued instructions to everyone, including Urchin, with a "Hold that, page," and "Fetch this, page," and "Out of my way, page," until Padra politely reminded her whose page Urchin was, and sent him to put on his cloak. Finally, when Urchin felt he had been ordered about by every animal in the tower, a trumpet sounded. The wedding was to begin.

He took his place at the door. Music swelled and filled the hall, hushing the excited animals. Brother Fir took his place on the dais. In marched the king, the jeweled crown proud and high on his head, paw on sword hilt, the cloak of heavy purple velvet swinging from his shoulders. Urchin looked at him with new respect. This was a king to be proud of, not at all the way he had appeared in the Throne Room, with his speech slurred and his paw shaking.

But he strode through the hall alone. The music stopped. In an uneasy silence, Tay carried in the queen's crown on a velvet cushion and placed it on the empty chair. That, thought Urchin, must be why she had been sent for.

Husk entered next, and the awkward silence changed to roaring cheers. Urchin gazed in astonishment. Did all captains dress like that for their weddings? He supposed it must be some sort of rule that nobody had told him about. He had never before seen a captain's robe with jewels in the hem and the collar, or a captain's circlet wreathed with garnets and emeralds. But while Husk was greeted with cheering, Lady Aspen, as she appeared in the doorway, was met with hushed wonder.

Clouds of silk and the finest lace billowed around her like cherry blossom. Diamonds flashed in her fur. The wedding garland on her head sparkled, and her train flowed across the floor behind her. She was astonishingly, breathtakingly, beautiful, and every single creature in Mistmantle adored her.

At some point, Padra and Granite must have taken their places. Padra had been right. Nobody was looking at them.

In a room made hot and stuffy from the log fire, Gleaner bent over the queen as she lay unconscious among the gold and purple hangings. Her breathing was shallow, and her skin dry and wrinkled. When Gleaner took her paw, she rolled over and curled into a ball.

Gleaner wished there was somebody she could ask for help. There were mole maids about, but Lady Aspen could be scathing about them—*Useful servants, but they don't know anything and they can't learn.* Gleaner was in charge.

She was to send for Lady Aspen if she was seriously alarmed, even in the middle of the wedding. Well, she wasn't seriously alarmed yet, but she was worried. She sent a maid to see where the wedding was up to, just in case.

"You'll get better, Your Majesty," she said. "You'll soon be better." But she didn't believe it, and didn't know if Queen Spindle had heard her. The queen turned restlessly, tried to speak, and slept again.

"They're making the promises," said the excited mole as she came back. "I'll watch the queen if you want a look."

Gleaner shook her head. She knew what to do. She lifted down the violet glass phial, shook it, and mixed the medicine as Lady Aspen had taught her, counting out the drops. Then she slipped a paw behind the queen's head.

Poor Aspen, thought Urchin as he watched the wedding. Perhaps she doesn't know what Husk's really like.

Husk's circlet glittered, catching the light of the dozens of candles. It was time for the king to speak. Aspen, taking her seat, settled like thistledown.

"This has been a dark year on Mistmantle," began the king, "and the winter drains away the sunshine. But in this season of sorrow in our hearts and winter on our land, we welcome this bright day. Captain Husk and Lady Aspen have gladdened our hearts, our land, and our future. They have asked me for a favor for you all, and I am glad to grant it. You are all to have a day off tomorrow!"

There was a long, loud cheer, and hats were thrown into the air.

Urchin hoped Apple wouldn't grumble out loud about how "in the old days we had a day off when we felt like it and we didn't have to ask nobody's permission and the work still got done," but if she did, nobody heard her. When the cheer died down, and dropped hats had been picked up from the floor, the king went on.

"None of you has seen how devotedly Aspen has cared for the queen in her illness and sorrow. Lady Aspen is as wise and good as she is beautiful, and deserves all the honor Mistmantle can bring her. In her, as in all things, Captain Husk has chosen well. Without Husk's friendship, counsel, and help, I would find it a hard and lonely thing to be your king." His voice faltered, and he paused to gather himself together. "Husk is like a son to me," he finished quickly, and sat down.

Brother Fir nodded to the squirrel choir to sing. Serving lads and maids were slipping away from the hall to put on their aprons. Soon there would be feasting, dancing, and entertainment, long into the night.

From the royal chambers, Gleaner heard the music. The party must have started by now, and the feast. The mole maids had sent whispered giggling messages to their friends in the kitchens, and trays of food and wine were carried up from a back staircase. While the maids danced in the corridor, Gleaner nibbled candied walnuts and watched the queen.

Her breathing seemed slower now. Gleaner took her paw. It felt limp.

"Your Majesty?" said Gleaner. "Your Majesty?"

The queen took a long, struggling breath. Then nothing. Gleaner's eyes widened. She turned hot and cold. The next breath came, long and rasping. Then a long pause. Another rasping breath. Gleaner ran to the door and shook the first maid she found.

"Fetch Lady Aspen!" she ordered. "At once!"

The party in the Gathering Chamber seemed to be going on forever. The tables had been pushed back, and plates of little sweet things stood among the crumbs and wine stains. The young animals had gathered under the tables to eat sugared almonds and marzipan.

Urchin was wondering whether Lugg had managed to rescue Scufflen—he had certainly been planning something—but Lugg was nowhere to be seen. In the meantime he tried to look busy, as he didn't want to dance if he could help it. His dancing lessons had barely started, and he wasn't at all sure if he was getting it right. But he had discovered that dancing *with* a hedgehog was much safer than dancing anywhere near one, and that Arran the otter didn't seem to mind how many mistakes he made. He had to dance with Apple, and it took great effort not to limp as he walked away afterward. He went in search of Padra before she could ask him again. Hopefully, he would be given a useful job to do so that he could impress Padra and avoid dancing at the same time, but he realized too late that Apple was following him.

"Mistress Apple," called Padra, "you haven't danced with me all evening! You're not avoiding me, are you? Will you do me the honor?" There was the swiftest wink at Urchin. "Hold my robe, will you, Urchin?"

Urchin watched Padra heave Apple around the room. The uneasy feeling that he was being watched crept over him, and he turned to see a sleek, dark mole look away quickly. It was Gloss, who had argued against Crispin at the trial. Urchin shuddered, then forgot Gloss as he saw Gleaner and a mole guard wriggle through the hall.

They whispered to Husk, who listened, dismissed them, and strode to the throne. Something was happening. Presently Husk led the king and Brother Fir toward the royal chambers. Padra, finishing his dance with Apple, joined them, and Urchin followed, still carrying the sea-turquoise robe over both paws. He half expected to be told to stay out of the way, but Padra only said, "You may be needed in the royal chambers, Urchin, but put that robe away first. I won't need it again tonight."

Urchin carried the robe to the anteroom and laid it on the floor to smooth and fold it. With the door closed, it was as if the crowded hall was in another world. He was alone in cool stillness and quiet. A single lamp glowed.

Snow was falling, floating in thick soft flakes through the darkness. Urchin laid the robe on the floor, then went to the window and rested his paws on the sill. It was quiet enough even to hear the waves swishing gently onto the shore, and he thought of Crispin and prayed, as he always did, for the Heart to keep him safe. More than ever he missed Crispin, who always had a kind word for him.

He turned to open the heavy lid of the chest with both paws. Husk's green-and-gold robe was still in there—of course—he was wearing his new one today, his magnificent wedding robe.

Whoever had put that robe away had not done it correctly. It would crease if he laid Padra's on top of it. He smoothed it and felt the layers of creases underneath. It would have to be taken out and folded again. He held it high to shake it, and, taking care not to let his claws catch the embroidery, smoothed it down.

On the bottom of the chest, something fluttered. Urchin bent to look more closely. Three dried leaves lay there, and he reached to take them out.

If they had been scented leaves, he would have understood why they were there. They would be to keep the moths away, or make the robes smell sweet. But these were plain beech leaves. He turned them over and held them to the lamp.

There was a clawmark on each one. Crispin's.

Urchin wasn't sure what they meant, but he knew they were important. His green cloak had been stitched up hurriedly at the hem and the stitches were long and gaping. Gently, to hide the leaves without damaging them, he slipped them between the stitches into the hem. Padra must be told.

CHAPTER TEN

IN THE ROYAL CHAMBERS, the queen lay very peacefully among the deep pillows. The king held her paw. Brother Fir stood at the end of the bed, and Padra, Aspen, and Husk, keeping a respectful distance, had taken their places at the door.

Once, the queen had opened her eyes and smiled at the king. Later she had said, clearly but very softly, "Aspen." Then the slow, rasping breathing had continued and the pauses between the breaths became longer, until the next breath did not come.

Aspen stepped forward and felt for a pulse in the queen's neck. She turned to Brother Fir, shook her head, and drew back.

Nobody noticed Urchin take his place in the doorway. Something jostled his shoulder, and Captain Granite pushed past him. He looked ready to march straight up to the king, but Aspen put out a paw to warn him, and Husk whispered something in his ear.

"This will break the king," whispered Aspen.

The king raised his head. "I wish," he said, but his voice was low and slurred, "I wish I had not sent that treacherous squirrel away. When he killed our son, he destroyed her. I wish I had him here now, to tear him apart with my own teeth and claws. Wherever he is, may my curses reach him!"

Brother Fir said nothing, but held up a paw as if to hold back the curses. Husk summoned Padra to his side.

"The only question," said Husk, "is whether to tell everyone now, or later."

"The morning will be soon enough," said Padra firmly. "Let the king grieve in peace. We can announce it first thing tomorrow. Meanwhile, get the servants to clear the dishes and tell the musicians to stop playing, they'll all understand that it's time to go." He turned and noticed Urchin at last. "Urchin, come and help me."

Urchin hurried behind Padra, who murmured instructions into the ears of servants. Soon tables were being cleared, one torch after another was extinguished, and the animals, some yawning, the little ones asleep and being carried, were making their way to the doors. However well Padra organized them, it would take a long time to clear the tower.

"Find Husk!" he called to Urchin. "I could do with him here! At least find out what he's doing!"

Find Husk! Getting through the crowd to the royal chambers would be impossible, but as a page he had learned any number of back stairs and scarcely used corridors. He had turned right into a passageway that led down a stair, under the hall, and back up the other side, when he saw a squirrel dart around a corner.

It couldn't be Husk—but it looked like him. It was his shade of fur, and his quick way of moving.

"Captain Husk?" he called, but the squirrel had already vanished without hearing him. With paws at full stretch, Urchin dashed after him, and was just in time to see the squirrel turn the next corner and whisk around a door.

This time, he was sure it was Husk. He was also sure that Husk didn't want to be followed, and even more sure that he should be.

Slipping through the almost hidden opening, he could just see Husk at the bottom of a stair. Silently, he followed. The stair gave way to a passageway, and the passageway turned to a tunnel of intense darkness. Urchin listened for paws and the brush of fur on tunnel walls, and followed. If he stopped to think about what he was doing he might turn back, so he decided not to think. Just follow.

The tunnel became darker, narrow, and fusty. Urchin's night vision was good, but soon he could see only shapes and shadows, darker than the dark, as he ran. It might be best not to see. The earthy smell of underground became moldy and repellent, and the chill of the place struck deep and damp through his fur. Something sticky caught on his ears. He ran with his shoulders drawn tightly in and his head down, trying not to touch the sides. Under his paw, something squelched. Setting his teeth, urging himself to be brave, he ran on.

Captain Crispin chose me for a page. I have to prove myself.

It was colder, damper, darker. He padded on, listening for paws, straining his ears. If he lost that sound, he could be stranded in here . . .

He could be lost.

For how long? Fear shivered through him as he ran. He should never have come, and it was too late to turn back. One wrong turn, and he could be lost underground forever. In the suffocating darkness, something cold dripped on his head; unseen wings flapped in his face; his cloak caught on something. He bit his lip hard. The tunnel was smaller. Earth pressed around him.

Cold sweat broke on him. The air was foul and clammy, and the darkness so thick that he seemed to breathe it in. His paws squelched. *Keep listening.* If he turned back, he might never get out—and what if he went on? What if Husk caught him? There was nobody to hear him cry out. Nobody down here except himself and a murderer. With nausea and terror, his stomach tightened.

Oh, Heart keep me, he prayed desperately. *Oh, please, Heart hear me.* If he ever did get out, he told himself, it would make an exciting story to tell Needle. He must ignore the dark, the smell, and the cold, and only listen, taking the next step and the next. He shut his eyes—it made no difference to what he could see—and sharpened his hearing.

A door squeaked. Opening his eyes, he thought he saw the gleam of white fur on a squirrel's chest. Then the door creaked again, and it had gone.

A waft of chill, foul air made him press his paws over his mouth, but with it was something far worse. It was horror. Something evil was reaching for him, creeping on the air from that door, now rushing at him with festering decay and all the cruelty of hatred. Then he heard a sound that chilled him through every nerve, even before he realized what it was.

It was a laugh with no laughter in it, more like a shriek of despair. Husk's voice was barely recognizable, but he was laughing. Instead of joy there was cruelty, insanity, and evil in the laugh.

The hideous laughter stopped suddenly. There was muttering as if Husk were talking to himself, but Urchin couldn't hear the words. His eyes staring wide, his ears upright, his coat bristling, he backed away. The sense of horror was too appalling. Just a few steps. Then something slippery under his paw made him lose his balance, and he stumbled, scrabbling wildly at the earthen wall. It made the softest noise, but in that place of desolation it sounded like thunder. He froze, terrified. He heard steps. Captain Husk had heard him.

For a second, Urchin couldn't move—then he turned and fled, paws fully stretched, pelting wildly through unseen tunnels. A vague sense of direction told him that if he continued forward and upward, he should come out where he came in, at the back stairs beside the Gathering Chamber. He had to escape the darkness, the smell, and the suffocating evil before they caught him and trapped him forever. Somewhere, there must be light. There must be.

A faint taste of freshness on the air gave him hope. *Get out, get out, get out,* went the rhythm of his aching paws, pounding onward. His lungs hurt. The tunnel was cleaner, wider. Good. There was a flight of stairs. He could get out. The surface under his paws was firmer; he was on a floor that had been swept and cleaned. He must be in the main body of the tower by now. There should be guards around—but how could he explain himself?

It was still dark, but this was the normal, safe darkness of a chamber at night. From the distance he had run and the stairs he had climbed, he must be under the Gathering Chamber. Good. There would be a window. From there he could jump down, run to the Spring Gate, and find Padra.

A great gust of fresh air met him and he gulped it in thankfully. A window was open. He gathered himself together to jump.

But his guess had been wrong. He was one floor higher up than he thought. He jumped from a window beside the Gathering Chamber, with rocks beneath it.

CHAPTER ELEVEN

MOSTLY, THE SQUIRRELS ON SWAN ISLE made Crispin long for Mistmantle. At first, they ignored him. Slowly they accepted him, when they found he was quick at gathering and storing nuts for the winter and had a clear memory for where they were hidden. The qualities that had made him a good captain—courage, understanding, quick thinking, swordsmanship—were useful to them. But they were a thoughtless, forgetful bunch who couldn't attend to anything for more than a second or two, and Crispin yearned for real conversation, even with Apple.

The swans were still proud and distant and called him a tree-rat, but they valued him. And there was Whisper. He seemed to be truly himself when he was with her.

Whisper was different. Crispin was sure she didn't belong on Swan

Isle at all. She helped him to find his way around and learn who was who. She listened when he wanted to talk about Mistmantle, and understood when he didn't. More and more he wanted to be with her, and more and more, he was.

It amazed Crispin that he could accept the life of a woodland squirrel, with no tower, no ceremonies, and none of his Mistmantle friends. When his heart cried out to go home, he reminded himself that if he had never left the island, he would never have met Whisper. He was learning to live away from Mistmantle. But the thing that still twisted his heart was knowing that on his own island, his name was the name of a disgraced traitor and murderer, and there was not a thing he could do about it. On a summer evening, thinking of home as he watched Whisper splashing her face in a stream, he said, "Is there anything in the world that you really want?"

It was unusual for her to be flustered, but at this moment she seemed quite at a loss for words. She suddenly concentrated very hard on combing a tangle out of her fur.

"You say first," she said.

"If I could have one thing," he said, "I'd go back to Mistmantle and clear my name. And," he added, realizing that he didn't want to go there alone, "I'd take you with me."

"Oh!" she said, and bent her head farther over the tangle.

"Whisper of Mistmantle," he said, and sat looking at her. "That's what I'd like. I'd like you to be Whisper of Mistmantle."

The tangle was out now, but she was still combing it.

"Now it's your turn," he said. "What do you want?"

Slowly, she rubbed her fur dry.

"Whisper of Mistmantle," she said.

There was no priest on the island, so on a day of sunshine and sparkling water they made their promises to each other in the presence of the squirrels and Lord Arcneck. As a token of their marriage Crispin placed his gold circlet on Whisper's head, where it gleamed in her fur like a crown. Now, Crispin thought, he would be content to stay here.

She wore the circlet always. As winter gripped the island with iron gray skies, the gold shone in Whisper's fur. On a bitterly cold day, they were digging up nuts from the winter store when a cygnet came, half flapping, half running, toward them.

"Crispin!" it screeched. "Come now! *Please!*"

No swan had ever said "please" to him before. He drew his sword and, with Whisper following, ran.

The sky above the mere was gray with snow. Ice floated in the water. The younger swans had huddled together in the reeds and were making scared, hissing noises deep in their throats while a little farther out Lord Arcneck floated on the water and struggled to hold up his lady's head. She was almost underwater. Only her beak and the top of her head still showed.

Something was pulling her under. Crispin took a deep breath, and jumped.

The freezing water was so sharp that only the need to keep his mouth tightly shut kept him from crying out. Through the murky green of the mere he saw the thick twine of water weed caught around the swan's leg, dragging her under. In the bitter cold he needed both paws to draw his sword and swish it down, but the weed was too thick and strong to slice through.

His lungs were bursting. He kicked his way up to the surface and crouched on the bank, gasping with cold, his teeth chattering as Whisper hugged and chafed a little warmth back into him. The ripples he had made caused a wave that passed over the swan's head, and snow had began to fall, whole flakes that melted into the water. Snow would make the water level rise. The sword would not help him, and he threw it aside.

There was something else he could try. He rubbed at his legs, which were cramping with cold; then, his ears ringing, he dived in again.

He could no longer feel his paws, but only two stinging stars of pain as he gripped the weed. He must bite once, and hard, into the sword cut he had made. After that, he would have to kick back up to the surface before the swing-back of the weed could break his neck or fling him spinning to the depths.

Chill, stale water rushed into his mouth. He bit hard. With a lurch, the weed broke; the swan lifted free. Waves rocked over the mere; Crispin lost his grip; and as his eyes closed, he no longer felt anything, even the cold.

CHAPTER TWELVE

H E'S WAKING UP," said a voice.

It was a kind voice, and Urchin found he was warm and lying on something soft. Even with his eyes shut—and it seemed too much of an effort to open them—he knew he was safe. He could hear voices, and recognized Padra's. That was reassuring. Someone was tucking a blanket, around him. There was the crackling sound of a fire, and someone was singing very, very softly, like a lullaby. For a strange, confused moment it seemed to Urchin that his whole life had been a dream and he was now waking up to being newly born, with a mother and a place of safety. But as he became more fully awake he knew he was a page with a sharp pain in his shoulder and an ache in his left hind paw.

He knew something terrible had happened. It wasn't long ago, but he couldn't remember what it was.

A paw was slipped gently behind his head. There was a faint scent of fur and fish.

"Urchin?" said Padra. "Urchin, can you hear me?"

Urchin forced his eyes open, blinked a bit, and saw Padra looking gravely into his eyes. "Urchin, do you know who I am?"

"You're Captain Padra," whispered Urchin, and the effort made his eyes close again. But presently he found he could open them and keep them open, and focus on Padra's watching face. Urchin was lying on a soft bed of moss, and Padra was asking him if he hurt anywhere.

"My shoulder, sir," said Urchin. He tried to touch it, and winced. "And my left hind paw."

"Better than I feared," said Padra. "Can you tell me what happened at the tower yesterday?"

Urchin frowned. So many things had happened.

"In the Gathering Chamber?" said Padra.

Urchin thought for a moment. "Wedding, sir," he said. "Husk and Aspen."

"And what is the name of the captain who had to go into exile?"

He didn't have to think about that one. "Crispin, sir," he said.

"And what's the name of your young hedgehog friend?"

"Needle, sir," he said, wondering why Padra wanted to know.

"So your brain's in one piece," said Padra, and the anxiety left his face. "What happened to you?"

"Give him time, sir," said a soft voice. "Don't rush him. Heart love him, he doesn't even know where he is."

117

Urchin didn't even know how awake he was. He raised himself carefully on his right side, and a small mole held a drink to his lips. He didn't know what it was, but it warmed him and cleared his head. Awkwardly, with Padra supporting him, he sat up.

The room smelled of earth, but it was dry, pleasant, and warm. The light was comfortably dim, but from the spreading tree roots above him he could see he was underground. The crackling fire he had heard was blazing in a hearth, and beside it stood a wooden clotheshorse, where very small blankets were hung up to air. On the other side of the hearth, in a rocking chair, a hedgehog sang softly to a small bundle in her arms.

From somewhere to his left there came a thin cry, and the sound of gentle shushing. Urchin turned carefully, gritting his teeth against the pain in his shoulder as the mole maid left him and bustled over to a row of tiny nests all covered with blankets, and lifted something up. A pair of very small squirrel ears showed over her shoulder. Then he heard laughter, and saw a young hedgehog and a squirrel rough-and-tumbling in a corner.

"Quiet, you two!" said the mole.

"I'll explain all this presently," said Padra. "You first, Urchin. I want to know how you came to fall out of a window."

"Is that what I did, sir?" asked Urchin. He told Padra all he could, but his memory was blurred and confused. He could recall most of the previous day. He knew the queen was dead. He'd had to find Husk—he had seen him and followed him down a tunnel—it seemed to be a long way down, but maybe that was only a dream. A very bad dream. Darkness, he remembered that. But it wasn't just darkness. Something had frightened him so badly that he ran—he had kept running. . . .

"I'm sorry, sir," he said. "That's all I remember."

"Were you pushed?" asked Padra.

"I don't think so, sir. I was just . . . just . . ."

He turned his head because he could not bear Padra's kind, steady gaze. He could hardly whisper the words for shame.

"I was running away from something, sir. I'm sorry."

"Sometimes, Urchin," said Padra, "running away is absolutely the right thing to do. I don't blame you, and you mustn't blame yourself. What were you running away from?"

"I can't remember," said Urchin, and shut his eyes as he searched the depths in his memory. *Darkness and damp. Husk was there. Something bad.*

"I'm sorry, sir," he said. "It was pitch dark and foul, and I don't know. But . . ." Grimacing against the pain, he heaved himself forward and whispered, "Husk was there."

"You're sure?" asked Padra.

"Yes, sir." He thought hard. "Without his robe . . ." His eyes widened, and he struggled to sit up. "My cloak! Where is it?"

"Behind you," said Padra. "Mother Huggen says she'll wash it."

"No!" cried Urchin. "Nobody is to touch it!"

"All right, Urchin, I won't let them," soothed Padra. "Go on with your story."

Urchin tried again to concentrate. "I found a room with fresh air—I got away, I found a window. . . . Did I fall out?"

"You did, Urchin, but you survived," said Padra, and his whiskers twitched in a smile. "You landed on something soft."

"That was lucky!"

"Not for Apple," said Padra. "Well, a combination of Apple and snow, really. She was underneath the window enjoying the snow, and heard a thud. That was you, bouncing off the wall. Next minute, you'd squashed her into a snowdrift. But she was delighted to have been useful, and she's all right except for a few bruises. But you should rest again, now."

"I'm sorry for the other things, too, sir," said Urchin miserably. He may as well get the whole wretched thing over at once.

"What other things have you done?" Padra grinned.

"Just being untrainable, sir. I tried hard."

"*What?*" said Padra.

It was too much. Urchin squeezed his eyes shut and turned his head away.

"You told Granite I was a dead loss and untrainable, sir," he said, and tried to keep the tears from his voice.

"Oh, Urchin, my brave young page, we can't have this," said Padra firmly. "You don't think I meant that, do you? Do you want to know why I told Granite you were useless? Because Granite, now he's a captain, wants a page—and more to the point, he wants you. If he asks Husk for you and Husk gets around the king, they'll find some

120

way of taking you out of my service and into his. Do you want that?"

"No, sir!"

"No, so I'm doing my best to put him off. And I advise you to look as dim and hopeless as possible when Granite's around."

"Shouldn't be too difficult, sir," said Urchin, and wondered why he'd ever doubted Padra.

"And now, about young Scufflen," said Padra.

"I understand, sir," said Urchin. "There was nothing you could do. But it wasn't just any baby hedgehog, it was Scufflen, and Needle loved him."

"Would you like to hold him?" asked Padra.

It didn't make sense. I'm definitely not well, thought Urchin. I must have banged my head. But the hedgehog in the rocking chair stood up, still smiling down at the bundle in her arms. Not sure what was happening, or even whether he was properly awake, Urchin held out his paws. He looked down into the solemn, sleeping face of a baby hedgehog with milk around its mouth. It hiccupped.

It was a very small baby, wearing a tiny white robe that looked as if it had been made of scraps from the workroom floor. Lifting a corner of the blanket, Urchin saw the curled paw.

"Scufflen!" he whispered. The baby yawned enormously, showing a milky tongue.

"I'll find him a nest now," said the hedgehog, taking him back.

Urchin gazed at Padra with new admiration.

"You saved him!" he said.

Mother Huggen carried Scufflen to the nests. The mole was settling the baby squirrel to sleep, and another squirrel had joined the young ones playing on the floor. Urchin's heart lifted and brightened.

"This," said Padra, "is the most secret place on all the island. You didn't know I was a nursemaid, did you?"

"Do you rescue them all, and bring them here?" asked Urchin eagerly. "All the babies to be culled?"

"Not all," said Padra. "I can't save them all. Husk gets to them quickly. And some of the frail ones don't survive, but at least they're well looked after while they do live. This morning I was about to send you to find Scufflen, but you'd already done it. You told Lugg where he was, so Lugg sneaked into Husk's chamber through a mole hole, dragged the baby away, and brought him here. Can you guess what this place is?"

It was underground, in the roots. But it must be a very ancient tree, to have such complicated, spreading roots, and so strong. The ceiling was arched and vaulted with the stretching roots. The fireplace was wide and built in stone, with a mantelpiece, and in one wall was a sturdy wooden door.

"It can't be the Old Palace!" cried Urchin, and gazed about. "It's real, and I'm in it?"

"The ancient mole palace—yes, Urchin, it is," said Padra. "Did you believe it existed?"

"I always hoped it did," said Urchin.

"Most animals think it's only a legend, and we let them go on

122

thinking it," said Padra. "Those of us who know aren't allowed to tell anyone else where it is, or even that we know. There's Mother Huggen here, and Moth the mole." The mole maid waved a paw at Urchin. "She's Lugg's daughter. Arran knows, and Fir, of course. He's allowed to pass the secret on, and he told Crispin and me years ago. Husk always suspected that we knew where it was, and I'm sure he's tried to find it. When you're recovered, I'll teach you the routes to it. We bring the babies' mothers here to see them, but they have to be blindfolded, and of course they keep everything secret."

"But the babies can't stay here forever," said Urchin. "What happens when they get older?"

Mother Huggen hurried to rescue a small hedgehog that was getting a little too close to the washing.

"This one's nearsighted," she explained as she turned the little hedgehog around. It trundled away with determination and bumped into the log basket, but didn't seem to mind. "I send him to play with the moles. They're all nearsighted, so they teach him how to get along."

"You're right, Urchin, they can't stay here," said Padra. "As soon as they start to talk, we move them out. They soon forget about being here."

"I make them little mitts to fit over any bad paws or anything of that sort," said Huggen. "They look just like real paws; you wouldn't know. And we train them well, so nobody can see anything the matter with them."

"But where do they go?" asked Urchin.

"Mostly to colonies on the north or west of the island, well away from the tower, or in the middle of the wood," said Padra. "Places where nobody will ask questions about one or two extra young ones, and the parents know where they are. But I wish we didn't have to do this. There's something very wrong about this island, Urchin. There shouldn't be any culling at all."

He walked to the fire, carefully stepping over a baby squirrel, and stoked the blaze. Urchin limped painfully toward him.

"This isn't the only quiet backwater colony on the island," went on Padra. "There are groups of animals here and there, mostly near the shores or in the caves by the waterfall, living quiet lives and keeping away from the tower as much as they can. That's apart from the host of hedgehogs and moles digging for jewels, who work so hard they must have forgotten what daylight is like. You didn't know I have a younger brother, did you? Fingal. He lives in a small otter colony, about as far away from Husk and the tower as I can get him."

"Quite right, too," said Mother Huggen. "Fingal's safer that way."

"Everybody's safer that way," said Padra. The nearsighted hedge-hog was now climbing in and out of tree roots. When it met a mole head on, it curled into a ball in shock.

Padra threw another log on the fire, and sparks showered upward. "It's worse since Crispin went," he said. "The king listened to him. No wonder Husk wanted him out."

"Crispin!" said Urchin, remembering. He hobbled painfully back to the moss bed and scrabbled at the hem of his cloak.

"I was coming to show you, sir!" he cried. "I was putting the robes away, and I found these in the chest!"

The leaves were battered now, with bits broken away from the edges. But the mark was still visible.

"Crispin's mark!" exclaimed Padra, his eyes bright and keen. "Where did you find these?" He stood turning the leaves in his paw as Urchin answered.

"Have you ever seen a captain give a token, Urchin?" asked Padra.

"No, sir," said Urchin, "but I saw the king once mark a leaf for Husk."

"I'm sure he did," said Padra drily. "Captains don't use tokens much these days. Husk gets Gloss the mole to carry messages for him. I like to give my orders myself, if I give them at all. But if Crispin wanted to confirm that an order was from him, or give his approval of something, he'd send a leaf with his mark on it as a token. What you've found here may just be some old tokens."

"Oh," said Urchin, disappointed. "So they're not important, then?"

"I think they're very important," said Padra. "They may be just a few old tokens, but Crispin wouldn't have left them in the robe chest. Somebody must have collected them for a purpose."

"Or Husk got hold of one, and made copies of it," suggested Urchin.

"So," said Padra, "on the day when we drew lots . . . Urchin, I must have seaweed where my brain should be! Why didn't I see it before? I've always known that Husk tricked us that day, but I couldn't see how. He didn't take Crispin's token out of the bag at all—he must have hidden one of these in his paw."

"Or tucked it into his sleeve," said Urchin in excitement. "We—I mean, someone—should have checked which tokens were still in the bag."

"And we would have found Crispin's," said Padra.

"So these are evidence that Husk did it!" said Urchin eagerly. "If we take these to the king . . ."

"Slow down, Urchin," said Padra. "What can we prove? Husk would only say that they were old tokens Crispin left lying around, or that we copied them ourselves to incriminate him. The king and the Circle would listen to him, not us. We have to wait until Husk goes too far. He will, believe me. The animals will lose faith in him, and be ready to listen to us. Then we can move against him, and these leaves will help us to do that. But we still have to wait for the tide to turn."

"But he gets worse all the time!" said Urchin. "He's even talking about rationing the winter food! Can't we *help* the tide to turn?"

"Oh, yes, we can do that," said Padra cheerfully, "but we have to do it cautiously. If Husk thinks we're stirring up rebellion, believe me, he'll have us murdered on the quiet. Me, Arran, Lugg . . . even you, Urchin."

Urchin was about to say that he was willing to take the risk, but Padra stopped him.

"Yes, I'm sure you're willing to die for the island, but you're more use alive," he said. "We all are. Without us, there'd be nobody left to protect the others. When I show up Husk, it has to be in public, at a big, special occasion. He wouldn't be able to do any quiet knife-in-the-back stuff with the whole island watching."

"Like at a feast, sir?" said Urchin. "The next one's the Spring Festival."

Padra smiled. "Yes," he said thoughtfully. "I was thinking of the Spring Festival."

"Shh!" said Huggen, and Padra sprang to his feet with his paw on his sword hilt. Something was moving toward them through the tunnels. Urchin stepped back from the entrance, flexing his claws. But then Padra relaxed, and let go of the sword.

"Arran," he said. "I know her step."

"Ask her to marry you, why don't you?" muttered Mother Huggen.

"She'd only hit me," said Padra.

Arran appeared presently, loping on all fours as she emerged from a tunnel.

"Padra, you're on next watch with the king," she said.

"Stay here tonight, Urchin, and I'll get you out tomorrow," said Padra. "If anyone asks, I'll say you were so useless you didn't know which floor you were on, and that's why you fell out of the window. On your head, so no harm done. I'll tell Fir the truth, though. He ought to know everything you've told me. And, Urchin, those leaves could be vital. You've done bravely today. But don't put yourself in danger. I told Crispin I'd take care of you."

"I'm too old to be taken care of," said Urchin as Padra left. But it was good to be here, with the flickering fire and Mother Huggen bringing him hot drinks and creamy hazelnut porridge, and Moth hushing a baby. The small hedgehog half woke up, found its way to Urchin's lap, and fell asleep again.

"We all need to be taken care of," said Mother Huggen. "This island is full of young animals Captain Padra has rescued. Arran, will you stop and have some cordial with us? And it's time you asked Padra to marry you."

"He'd only laugh," said Arran.

Urchin wondered what Padra would do at the Spring Festival. But filled with hot porridge and warmed by the fire, he could no longer keep his eyes open. He was drifting into dreams. He managed to slur a prayer for Crispin, but he was already more asleep than awake.

CHAPTER THIRTEEN

GLEANER WAS CRYING.

She was hunched miserably in a small chair in a corner of Husk and Lady Aspen's chambers. It was a hard and uncomfortable chair, a good place for misery. She was not used to being snapped at and hadn't deserved it, so she sniffed in a corner out of the way, where somebody was sure to find her. Two mole maids came in carrying black mourning veils, and she drew a paw across her eyes.

"Still crying for the queen?" asked one of the moles.

"I think the captain was a bit sharp with her just now," said the other. The moles didn't like Gleaner, who had become Lady Aspen's darling so quickly, but Captain Husk had been bad-tempered with everyone since the queen died. It was time his wife knew about it.

"I didn't mean any harm," said Gleaner. "I knew there should be flowers by the coffin and I'd been out in the snow and ice to find something pretty, and I told him so, and he turned and shouted at me for nothing!"

"Shouted at you?" said a mole eagerly.

"Yes, he shouted that I was to stay away and leave him alone," she sniffed.

Lady Aspen glided into the room.

"My poor little Gleaner!" she said. "Still weeping for the queen?"

"Captain Husk was cross with her," said the moles, and exchanged sly smiles. Either Gleaner or Captain Husk would be in trouble. They didn't care which.

"You may go," said Aspen, and the moles curtsied and scurried away. "Never mind, Gleaner. Captain Husk has too much on his mind just now, and the whole island depends on him. Did the moles bring the veils?"

As Gleaner dried her eyes, Lady Aspen took a veil and shook out the folds. Husk had not been himself since the wedding, and she had accepted his brooding silences and short answers. It was better not to ask questions. They had never discussed the night when Prince Tumble died. It was enough to know that he was dead. And Husk had never asked her about the queen. She had cared for the queen and the queen had died and that, too, was enough. They knew each other too well to ask questions. She threw the veil over her ears and was looking at herself in the glass through a dark film of silk, when Husk came in.

"Off you go, Gleaner," Lady Aspen said, and Gleaner was glad to hurry away with a quick, hurt glance at the captain. Husk made sure she closed the door after her. There were too many small animals scuttling about the tower these days.

Had one of them been following him four nights ago, after the queen died? No, of course not. Those tunnels were always full of creatures of the dark, things that crept, squirmed, and scuttled. It was only one of those. Or had he really heard a brush of fur and running paws behind him? There was a swish and a rustle as Aspen bent to pick something from the floor, and his paw flew to his sword hilt.

"My lord!" she cried.

"My love," he said, "you startled me. It's nothing."

Long slashes of rain dashed hard against the windows of the crowded Gathering Chamber. The funeral service was nearly over, and Urchin waited to take his place in the procession. Brother Fir came first, limping. Queen Spindle's coffin, draped in black, was borne slowly from the Gathering Chamber as a choir of moles sang their low, solemn dirge and a hedgehog carried her crown on a velvet cushion. The king followed the coffin, his face grim, leaning his paw on Husk's shoulder. Behind them came Granite, with Aspen veiled in black; then Padra with Tay; the animals of the Circle; and rows of guards. Finally, when the crowd had lost interest, came Urchin as Padra's page, and Gleaner as Aspen's attendant.

"See?" whispered Gleaner. "You're not that important."

Urchin didn't mind being at the back of the procession. What he minded was the way Padra had been placed behind Granite and Aspen, in front of a chamber full of animals. It was a deliberate insult. The coffin was carried down to the vault below the tower, followed by the captains, Tay, Aspen, and the hedgehog with the crown. Nobody else. The guards saluted and were dismissed, and Urchin and Gleaner stood back to let the tearful animals shuffle down the stairs, wrap their cloaks around them, and scurry home through the pelting rain.

Urchin spotted Apple in the crowd. Her rosebud bonnet had been trimmed with blackbird feathers for mourning, and she wore a very old and battered cloak. He couldn't reach her—he had to stay at his post at the top of the stairs—but she saw him, stuck out her elbows, and barged her way through.

"Terrible business, this, terrible, poor queen, poor hedgehog, what a nice queen she were before the little prince died, it's the king I feel sorry for, poor old king, what's he going to do now? Do they give us anything to eat on the way out?"

"They're giving out drinks and biscuits at the main door," said Urchin, but as a tower squirrel, he felt secretly ashamed. The meager refreshments amounted only to watered-down cordial and plain biscuits. Tay had said it was a solemn occasion and plain food was suitable. "And not much of it," she had added. "We can't have them making a feast of the queen's death."

"Keep moving, please," called a hedgehog behind Apple, who was

132

blocking the hallway. Urchin put her paw through his arm and escorted her to the door.

Sleeting rain drove in from the sea. In the doorway at the top of the stairs, tower servants with silver trays gave out the frugal drinks and biscuits.

"I think nothing of this," said Apple, inspecting her biscuit. "There's not going to be rationing, is there?"

"I don't know," said Urchin. He'd heard those rumors, too, and hoped they weren't true. Sea air, long hours of work, and sword practice made him hungry. "I hope not."

"Looks like they've started already," grumbled Apple. "Don't see how they expect us to do all that work, not with rationing. All this extra work, with never a decent meal inside us. And they can't expect the young 'uns to go without, nor the very old 'uns, neither, and anyway they don't eat much, them old 'uns."

This analysis made surprisingly good sense to Urchin. It might sound sensible to the king, too, if only somebody could get near enough to tell him. Apple licked the last of the biscuit crumbs from her paws.

"Can't afford to waste nothing, not if they're going to start counting out the hazelnuts after this," she said. "Suppose I have to go. I miss you, you know."

"And I miss you, Apple," he said, and bowed. As a page he'd become used to bowing to almost everyone and everything. Then he kissed her cheek, a little awkwardly.

"You've turned out good, I'm proud of you, proud of you," she muttered, and rubbed her eyes as she turned to go.

Maybe it was because the stairs were wet with rain, or maybe she couldn't quite see clearly. Apple's balance had never been good. One second, she was saying good-bye to Urchin. The next, she was tumbling head over heels down the steps with a trail of "ouch!" and "oof!," gathering speed until she rolled at last to a halt beyond the foot of the stair. The hat rolled a little farther, leaving a few loose feathers and a squashed rosebud. Urchin dashed down after her just as the royal party were leaving the vault and walking solemnly round the corner of the tower.

Apple had landed far enough from the stair to be directly in their way. She lay still, panting, as if she had to wait for the world to stop spinning as King Brushen, Husk, and Aspen drew nearer.

Heat rose in Urchin's face and crept down his paws. With any luck, he thought, a hole in the stairs would appear and he'd drop through it, or there might be a bird big enough to swoop down and carry him off. But he had to help Apple, even if it did mean getting in the way of the procession and being the laughingstock of the whole island.

Before he could reach her, Lady Aspen had slipped from her place. She darted to Apple's side and helped her to sit up.

"Poor squirrel!" soothed Aspen. "Are you hurt? Don't try to stand." Padra was approaching, too, but she waved him away as Apple stammered her thanks.

"Don't be alarmed," called Aspen. "I'll take care of her." She looked up to see Urchin, who had caught the hat before it could blow away. Remembering his training, he had placed himself on the seaward side to protect them from the driving rain.

"You're Padra's page, aren't you?" she said. "Thank you, but we can manage without you. Off you go, now. Report to your captain."

Apple was getting her breath back. "He's my little fosterling, him, my lady, he's my Urchin, I brung him up, my lady, least we all did, all of us in the wood, but mostly me, my lady, please, he's a good squirrel, I'm right proud of him, my lady."

Stop it, thought Urchin as his claws curled with embarrassment; please, please, stop it. Aspen was looking at him with a new interest.

"Is that so?" she said, and smiled warmly. "I can see you'd be proud of him. And how kind of you to take care of the little foundling!"

"Yes, well, it were me that foundled him," said Apple. "He were all washed up on the shore, all wet and cold and scrappy, may the Heart love him missus, I mean my lady, sorry, my lady." She was standing up now, and able cautiously to let go of Aspen's paw. "I can get home now, thank you, my lady."

"No, no, you must come with me," urged Lady Aspen. "Come to my chambers. Take a little wine. On such an afternoon I need company." She looked about her. "Gleaner, bring Apple's hat and carry it with great care. Apple and I shall have a cozy afternoon together. Urchin, report to your captain!"

Urchin didn't have a choice. He bowed again as Gleaner took Apple's hat with a gleam of triumph. Padra didn't particularly want to be reported to and had no orders for him, so he went to meet the Anemone Wood animals on their way out. Shaking ears and whiskers against the rain, they asked him how he was getting on at the tower, and what Padra was like to work for, and was the food good. Sooner or later they all got around to the same question—*Are we going to have rationing? Is it true?* Then, *There's no need for it. You'll tell Captain Padra that, won't you? Can you tell the king?*

Urchin said he'd do what he could, though he didn't know what that could be. These animals were his family, and he couldn't bear for them to go hungry through a long winter. Not even Crackle, Gleaner's old friend, who was hopping up to him with a timid little smile, as if she wasn't sure whether or not he'd be pleased to see her. She wasn't sneering at him the way she used to in the old days.

"You look very smart, being a tower squirrel," she said. "Is Apple all right?"

"Lady Aspen's looking after her," said Urchin.

"And Gleaner," said Crackle, pouting a little. "Gleaner won't talk to me now. She won't have anything to do with me, not now she's a tower squirrel. Sometimes I have to deliver nuts and herbs to the tower and I see her, but she's too busy and important to talk to me."

"Never mind," said Urchin. It was all he could think of.

"I don't," she said. "I don't mind a bit about her. But do you think there might be any work for more tower squirrels? Do you think they want anyone in the kitchens? Or the workrooms? Or cleaning, or anything?"

"I'll tell you if I hear of anything," he said, feeling sorry for her. He didn't have the heart to tell her that the tower wasn't a happy place to be just now, with the king broken in despair and Granite, Gloss, and Tay never far away. He wondered where Aspen had taken Apple and wished, for Apple's sake, that he could have stayed with her.

In Lady Aspen's sitting room, Apple didn't even try not to stare. She had never imagined that any room could be like this, with velvet curtains hanging from heavy gilded rings, embroidered cushions, chairs—even the chairs had padded seats, worked with embroidery! Surely they weren't for sitting on! A rug lay on the floor, and Apple took care not to step on it. A great gilded mirror hung over the fire, and Apple, about to ask why that squirrel was staring at her, realized it was herself and shut her mouth. The hazelnuts in the bowl were tossed in spices and something she supposed might be orange peel, but oranges were something she rarely saw. Gleaner poured the wine and took her cloak to dry.

"You look better now," said Aspen, and appeared not to notice as Apple heaved herself awkwardly into a chair. The wine was a rare treat for Apple, and sips of it warmed her down to her claw tips.

"It's very nice, my lady," she said. "I'll send you some of my apple-and-mint cordial, that's nice, too, not so nice as this, my lady, but it's good, and I'd like you to have some, Lady Aspen, my lady."

"I should be delighted," said Aspen smoothly. "Tell me all about Urchin. You must be proud of him."

Apple loved to talk about Urchin. Aspen let her go on drinking wine, eating hazelnuts, and talking, then suddenly interrupted.

"The shore?" she said. "You found him on the shore?"

"Yes, my lady, all cold and wet and a sorry little scrap, all washed up on the shore. I reckon he came out of the sea, my lady."

"And how did he get in there?"

"Dunno, my lady. Fell off a boat, I suppose."

"Yes," said Aspen. "He may have fallen off a boat. I seem to remember hearing somewhere—I can't remember who told me this, my dear, and I may have misunderstood—that he came from the sky."

Apple coughed on a hazelnut. "What? I mean," she added hastily, "beg your pardon, my lady; sorry, my lady; please my lady. No, whoever told you that, they got it wrong. I found him, and he definitely got washed up. It was a night of riding stars, my lady, and I'd gone out looking for one, and there may have been things dropping out of the sky all right, bits of star, my lady, but not no squirrel."

"Of course," said Aspen graciously. "What a silly idea!"

"He fell out of a window once if that's any help," said Apple hopefully. "The night of your and Captain Husk's wedding, my lady, what a beautiful wedding, my lady. I were down on the shore, I must have got a bit lost going home, and anyway, the snow were that beautiful, anyway, our Urchin drops out of a window. Nearly flattened me. Good thing I was there, and there were all that soft snow."

"How did he come to do that?" wondered Aspen.

"Dunno, my lady. Must have been lost, or something."

"We were generous with the wine that day," said Aspen thoughtfully.

"Not, not my Urchin, he wouldn't have got drunk, and anyway he didn't smell of it, my lady," said Apple. "He didn't smell too good, mind you, I mean, my lady, smelt all fusty as if he'd been somewhere not very nice, but he hadn't been drinking no drink, my lady."

"Well, I have enjoyed your company so much!" sighed Aspen. "But I have kept you far too long. Your cloak is still wet. Wear one of mine." She lifted the lid of a chest and selected a dark green wool cloak.

Apple gasped. "Ooh, no, my lady . . ."

"Keep it as a gift," said Aspen. "I insist. I have so enjoyed our afternoon. Gleaner will show you out."

When Apple had settled Lady Aspen's cloak around her broad shoulders, pulled her hat over her ears, and been escorted away, Aspen settled herself in the window seat. She looked down to the shore, turning the silver bracelet on her forepaw while she tried to fit together the pieces of the Urchin puzzle.

Urchin should have been left to drown. Whatever he was, he was alien to Mistmantle, and the way he stood out in a crowd was unsettling. As for Apple, she should have been culled at birth.

Apple didn't know about Urchin falling from the sky, but Brother Fir himself said that he had. Gleaner had been eavesdropping on the night . . . on that particular night, the last night of riding stars, and she had heard Fir and Crispin telling Urchin about it. Why hadn't they told Apple? And what was this about Urchin falling from a window, smelling fusty? What had he been up to? There were too many unanswered questions about the freak squirrel.

She turned and turned the bracelet. Husk thought Urchin would be a good page, if he weren't so pathetically devoted to Crispin and Padra. And the only reason Padra was still on the island, still alive, and still a captain, was that Mistmantle would fall apart without him. For the moment they still needed Padra, but she didn't like his page at all.

She sent a mole maid with a message, and in no time, Gloss the mole slid like a shadow to her door. She dismissed the maids and went to speak to him in the doorway. Apart from well-trained females who knew their place, moles really did not belong in chambers.

"Gloss," she said, "I have some work which will suit you excellently. I want Urchin the page watched."

"I'm already detailed by Captain Husk to watch someone else, my lady," said the mole politely.

"You don't have to do the watching yourself," she said. "Simply find somebody who can. Bring reports to me."

"Yes, my lady."

When he had gone she sat down wearily on one of the embroidered chairs, sighed, and closed her eyes. Everything should be easy from this point. The animals would be kept working too hard and eating too little, by the king's law. What sort of king would make such laws? A king driven mad by the deaths of his wife and son. And kind

Captain Husk would give them a magnificent Spring Feast. Who would they love the best?

It should be simple, but she felt uneasy about Urchin. He was dangerous; too strange, too unpredictable, showing up when he wasn't wanted, capable of wrecking everything without even trying, and much too helpful to Padra. She would have him watched and not trouble Husk, who had been having sleepless nights lately.

She crossed to the mirror, smoothed her fur, and fluffed her ear tufts with a tiny brush. Then she took the bracelet from her forepaw and, to see how it looked, placed it on top of her head, between her ears.

"Queen Aspen," she whispered to her reflection.

CHAPTER FOURTEEN

URCHIN WARMED HIMSELF BY THE FIRE in Padra's chambers.

"We need to catch the king alone," said Padra, thinking aloud, "preferably at a time when Husk hasn't filled him up with wine so he can't think straight."

Urchin preferred his own room, but he had come in here to light the fire which was now flaring brightly in the hearth. Padra's room was plain and soldierly and smelt of smoked fish, and there was always a damp cloak steaming on a clotheshorse, but Urchin enjoyed his company. They were toasting acorn bread (for Urchin) and fish (for Padra) on long forks beside the fire. Padra gazed into the flames as he turned the toasting fork. They always talked softly these days, as Padra was sure Husk had spies everywhere. The crackling and spitting of the fire was a useful way of covering speech.

"I think that's cooked, sir," said Urchin.

"Mm," said Padra, and drew the fork from the fire. "Pleasantly charred. You really should try a bit, Urchin."

"No thank you, sir."

"How can anyone not like fish?" Padra blew softly on the silver and gold scales, to cool them. "If it comes to rationing, you'll be glad to eat anything. At least the otters won't be hungry. There's always plenty of fish. But don't worry, Urchin, it won't come to rationing."

"Good," said Urchin, and nibbled at the acorn bread.

"Apart from anything else, where would we get food for . . ." He left the question unfinished and licked his paws, but Urchin knew he meant the nursery. "We need to get the king to make a ruling against it, one that Husk can't change. Look out for an opportunity, Urchin."

They were still eating and licking their paws when somebody knocked at the door.

"Mole," said Padra. "You can always tell from the sound. Comes a long way down the door, moles being short little chaps."

Urchin answered it. "Hello, Lugg!" he said.

Lugg marched into the chamber and saluted. "Littl'un brought for a culling, sir. Baby girl otter, sir. Funny-shaped tail. Captain Husk nowhere about, sir."

"Is that so?" said Padra energetically, and buckled on his sword. "Well, there's no need to trouble Captain Husk about this, is there? Where is she? I'll take care of her, and go down for a swim afterward. Don't stay up for me, Urchin."

Urchin was about to ask if Padra had any orders for him, but Padra was already out the door. It was a good thing the baby had been brought when Husk wasn't there . . .

When Husk wasn't there.

He ran to the door. "Lugg!" he called.

"That's me," said the mole.

"Where's Captain Husk?"

"Dunno."

"When will he be back?"

"Dunno that, neither."

"Captain Granite?"

"Armory. Drunk."

"Is anyone with the king?"

"Dunno. Lady A sometimes sits with him."

Padra should be the one to do this, but he wasn't there. Urchin knew he should be allowed to see the king—any animal should. He just didn't want to risk getting everything wrong. He considered for a moment, rubbing one hind paw against the other, and said, "I'm going to see the king."

"Good for you," said Lugg.

"I might not be allowed near," he said. "Husk always has guards posted."

"I'm a guard," said Lugg gruffly. "If the king needs guarding, I'll guard him. Leastways, I'll guard somebody, even if it's only you. Come on, young 'un."

Urchin cleaned his whiskers, washed quickly in the spring, and pattered upstairs and along corridors with Lugg marching behind him. The stairs and halls grew wider; the corridors became brightly lit and were hung with Threadings; and Urchin felt the tingle of nervousness in his paws. Long before they reached the Throne Room, he saw the door open; and hobbling out came the reassuring figure of the priest.

"Hello, Brother Fir!" called Urchin, feeling more confident already. But there were wet, streaky marks on Fir's white tunic, as if something had splashed it, and he was wiping water from his face. Urchin sprang forward.

"Brother Fir!" he exclaimed. "What happened to you?" Fir limped toward him, not looking at all worried, sniffing at his wet paws.

"Hm," he said. "Life is full of new experiences, don't you think, Urchin? Nobody ever attacks a priest. Completely forbidden. None of them do. Goodness knows what they think would happen—nobody ever tried it to find out."

"You were attacked?" exclaimed Urchin.

"Oh, no. Didn't I tell you? Nobody attacks a priest. It was only a cup of some drink or another, and I daresay the king threw it to miss. Most of it did. He always used to be a very good shot, so I think he was aiming past me. However, he was shouting 'Out of my Throne Room, priest,' as it hit the door."

"Might be a bad time to see him," remarked Lugg.

Fir stopped licking thoughtfully at his paws. "You wanted to see His Majesty?"

"I was going to, sir," said Urchin, and spoke softly. "Padra wanted to talk to him about rationing without Husk there, but Padra's been called away, so I was going to do it. But if the king's angry, he should be left alone."

"No, no, Urchin," said Fir. "He's angry with *me*. If you kneel and talk to him politely, he'll be perfectly happy to hear you. But don't say a word about Husk. Don't even mention him, and certainly don't question his judgment. I did, and that's when the king threw the"—he licked a claw with a frown of deep thought—"some sort of spiced drink. Yes. Go now, Urchin. Heart keep you. I shall go to pray for you. And to take this wet tunic off. Hm."

It was only as he waited outside the Throne Room door that Urchin realized he had no idea what to say. He was still trying to work something out when the hedgehog guards finally let him in, and he stepped forward into a wall of heat that took his breath away.

The fire in the grate roared, leaped, and crackled up into the chimney. Every window was closed. At the far end of the room, the king had slumped forward on his throne, his chin on his paws, his eyes on the floor. Urchin bowed, then knelt.

"I'm Urchin, Padra's page, and I would like to speak to Your Majesty, please," he said.

The king did not answer. He raised his eyes to Urchin, then looked back to the floor.

"May I speak, Your Majesty?" asked Urchin. The king still didn't speak, but he didn't refuse permission, so Urchin went on, though he wasn't even sure if the king heard him.

"Your Majesty, I know this is a terrible time for you," he began. "I don't like to bother you, but my friends in the wood are very worried, and they want me to talk to you for them."

The king said nothing. Urchin went on.

"Your Majesty, it's said that there's going to be rationing through the winter. The Anemone Wood animals are really worried. So's everyone, I think."

The king gave himself a little shake. It was a long time since an ordinary animal had come to him like this, simply and trustingly. He had forgotten how much he enjoyed the company of simple creatures. It was good that this young squirrel page felt able to talk to him.

"They can't go hungry, Your Majesty," said Urchin, hurrying in case Husk arrived. "The very young ones can't live on short rations because they're growing fast; the working ones need all their strength; and the old don't eat much anyway, and it's cruel to deprive them when they've worked hard all their lives. We don't need rationing. We had a good nut harvest in the wood, there's fruit in the stores—and honey—and there's plenty of trade, so we needn't go short of anything. We all love you, Your Majesty, and if you order rationing, we'll obey you. But all my friends that I grew up with and my foster mother and everyone, please don't make them go hungry. I know you don't want that."

There was a long pause. Urchin, his heart racing, wondered if the king was about to call the guards and have him thrown out. But the king leaned forward and looked down at him with interest.

"I remember you. The foundling," the king said, and smiled. "What if we were to run out of food before the Spring Festival?"

"We won't, Your Majesty. We never have," said Urchin, hoping he was right.

"Captain Husk says we will," said the king.

This was dangerous. Not a word against Husk.

"Captain Husk . . . um . . ." he stammered desperately, then inspiration struck. "He's so busy serving Your Majesty, maybe he doesn't have time to keep accounts of ordinary things like food supplies. It's too much for him to do."

"That may be true," said the king thoughtfully.

"My captain could be in charge of the food supplies," offered Urchin brightly. Then he wondered why he had said that, and how he could explain it to Padra.

The king was frowning. Urchin's stomach churned. He must have stepped over the line, and any minute now the king would throw something. Anxiously he watched the king's paws, but they stayed folded.

"Padra?" said the king thoughtfully. "I always thought he was a bit of a plodder, as captains go. Padra the Plodder, Urchin! But it's a job for a plodder. I'll do as you suggest." He said nothing for a while and Urchin waited to be dismissed, but then the king said, "You haven't had anything to drink, Urchin. Nor have I. Husk usually leaves wine somewhere."

"I don't want any, thank you, Your Majesty," said Urchin quickly. He'd rather not encourage the king to drink.

"What do you like to drink, Urchin?" asked the king.

"I live by the Spring Gate," began Urchin, "so—"

"Water straight from that spring!" exclaimed the king, and for the first time his face brightened. "You lucky squirrel! It's always stale by the time I get it." He gazed past Urchin, and his eyes misted. "My dear queen Spindle loved that spring water. We used to meet there, long ago, when she was not much older than you are."

He covered his face and Urchin waited, not sure what to do. Then suddenly he knew exactly what to do and went to speak to Lugg, who still waited at the door.

"Please fetch His Majesty some water from the spring at the gate," he said. "Freshly drawn."

Lugg hurried busily away. The king raised his head.

"That was thoughtful, Urchin," he said. "And while we're waiting for the water, open the box on the shelf over the fire and take out a leaf."

The box was full of dried beech leaves, and Urchin took care not to let them blow away in the draught from the fire. He offered a leaf to the king.

"Take this to Padra," he said, and extending a sharp, shaking claw, he scored his mark into it. "This is my authority to take charge of food stores. And another leaf."

Urchin fetched one. The king marked that one, too.

"This is for Anemone Wood," he said. "It is my pledge to the animals that there will be no rationing, on my word of honor." He sighed deeply. "My dear queen would not have wanted rationing."

Presently there was a padding of paws and a few splashes as Lugg brought the water. The king sipped, closed his eyes in pleasure, drank deeply, and called for more.

"This reminds me of being a young hedgehog," he said. "Take a drink, Urchin. I want that water sent every day. I feel clearer in my head than I have for months. Why is it so hot in here? Open a window! And tell me more about Anemone Wood!"

It was a long time before the king dismissed him. Bright with eagerness to share the good news, Urchin pattered back through the corridors with Lugg.

Not far from the Throne Room, he stopped. His nose twitched. There was a fusty smell. He couldn't remember what it reminded him of and wasn't sure he wanted to, but it troubled him. It cast shadows over the day.

"Come on, young 'un!" called Lugg, and Urchin was glad to hurry after him and leave that nasty smell with its odor of creeping evil. He was about to bolt back to Padra's chambers and tell him what had happened, but then he remembered Brother Fir hobbling away in his wet tunic. Perhaps he'd better go and make sure Fir was all right. It was the sort of thing Padra would want him to do.

He found Fir kneeling by the fireplace in his turret room. The stained tunic had been sponged clean, and he was draping it over a stool near the fire to dry.

"Are you unharmed, Brother Fir?" asked Urchin anxiously. The priest looked around with a twinkle in his eye.

"It would take more than a little wetting to do me any harm," he said. "I seem to have survived most things over the years. But I think I need a little drop of hot cordial, and someone to share it with." He took the little saucepan that was warming at the edge of the hearth, and poured steaming cordial into two wooden cups. "And I have wanted to talk to you, Urchin."

He pushed the wet tunic across the stool to make room for Urchin, who sat down. Fir heard the story of what had happened in the Throne Room, then he sipped a little cordial, and began.

"Padra did tell me, you know, about your extraordinary adventures"—he lowered his voice to a whisper—"the night the queen died. But I would like to hear it all from yourself, and particularly about the underground place where you followed Husk. Quietly, Urchin."

Urchin told him. It wasn't easy to talk about, and he couldn't remember much. The fear and the sense of evil in that place came back to him like a bad dream as he spoke. But he told Fir all he could, and at the end, Fir simply said, "and I suppose you have no intention of trying to find the place again?"

"Certainly not, sir!" said Urchin.

"Quite right," said Fir. "You mustn't. Well, well, run along to Padra and tell him all you've been up to. Keep out of Husk's way."

After Urchin had gone, Fir knelt for a long time, gazing into the fire, deeply thoughtful. So that was where it was.

It was a story known, as far as he could tell, only by himself and the king. It was a story from far, far back, before the moles had ruled the island and built their palace. It was the story of a squirrel king who hated the Heart and loved hate, destruction, and power. Any creature who opposed him was dragged underground to be killed and thrown down a pit, or thrown down alive; and the place of these murders was said to be infected by fear and horror. It had been sealed up after the evil king's death, and soon nobody knew where it was. But Husk must have found it.

"We have ignored it too long," Fir murmured to himself. "Too long. If Husk found it, so can I. And I must. It must be prayed in. And it needs to be blessed with light. Candles. Hm. I need candles."

He would need strength, too. He closed his eyes and prayed. There would be a hard battle for Mistmantle, and this was his part in it.

As Urchin was leaving the Throne Room, Husk reached the end of the corridor. He paused to lean his paws against a windowsill, and tried not to shake.

It had been a long day, that was all, with so much to do. He had needed to go back to the dark dungeon and the pit to renew his strength, and now his paws were grimy and cobwebbed. He'd need a wash before he went to the Throne Room.

He heard scurrying paws in the corridor. Some nuisance, some sharp-eyed twitch-nosed animals who couldn't let well alone. He pressed back into an alcove, hidden by the shadows. From the royal apartments came a guard mole—one of Padra's cronies—and the freak squirrel. He was coming to hate that little page.

By the time he reached Padra's rooms, Urchin had forgotten about the moment of fear in the corridor. But to his great disappointment, Padra wasn't back. The chamber was lonely and silent. Urchin made himself a nest of cloaks and moss by the fire, wrapped the precious leaves in his own cloak, folded it into a pillow, and settled down to wait. For a long time he lay awake, gazing into the fire, reliving his meeting with the king. He slept at last, but lightly, and every swish of the waves outside disturbed him. When he dozed again, something seemed to scuttle about in the dark.

Crabs sometimes got in here, being so near the shore. And beetles. That was all. He was more than half asleep. And as Urchin slept by the Spring Gate, somewhere in the darkness of the tower, in the high corridors overlooking the sea, there was a scream.

Lady Aspen leaped from the silken-draped bed and ran to open the bedchamber doors. Guards were running through the corridors.

"Leave me a lamp and return to your posts," she commanded. "My lord had a nightmare, that is all." With the lamp in her paw she glided back to the bed, where Husk was sitting upright, his fur stiff with bristling, his eyes wide and staring.

"He's there!" he whispered.

Aspen shook him gently, and he shuddered. His fur was damp with sweat.

Husk knew he was in his own bed, but the nightmare was still there. He felt the deathly cold of it. If he shut his eyes, even only to blink, he saw it again. In his nightmares the dead Prince Tumble crawled out from the darkness and scuffled through the tunnels that led to the dungeon, covered in dust and cobwebs, bloodstained, turning his head in the dark, sniffing for him, seeking him out. . . .

He dared not shut his eyes.

CHAPTER FIFTEEN

THE DOOR OPENED AND SHUT QUICKLY. Urchin was suddenly awake, sitting upright on his nest as Padra came in, shivering, with sand in his wet fur.

"Still here, Urchin?" he said. "You shouldn't have waited."

"I had something to tell you," said Urchin. It was a bitterly cold morning, so he pushed logs onto the fire and prodded it with a poker. While he made breakfast, he told Padra everything he had done the night before, leaving out the bit about "Padra the Plodder." Padra grinned and occasionally said "You did what?" and "Cheeky little rodent!"; but now and again he would put a claw to his lips to remind Urchin to speak quietly. Finally, Urchin put the king's leaves into his paw, and Padra turned them in delight.

"Well done, you cocky young ear-twitcher!" he said. "It could have gone disastrously wrong and I suppose I should warn you never to do such a thing again, but I'm impressed. I should give you my sword and circlet now, but they wouldn't fit you. You've made more work for me, you know, putting me in charge of the stores."

"Sorry, sir."

"I don't mind! Husk will think it'll keep me out of mischief. It won't, because I'll bring in Arran to help. And you can trot back and forth to the wood now and again to keep a check on the stores there. Give you a chance to see Apple and your friends. But wherever you go, keep your eyes and ears sharp." He lowered his voice. "Were you followed last night?"

"I don't think so, sir."

"I was," said Padra. "I think it's that slithery mole."

"Gloss?" asked Urchin.

"Sh!" said Padra sharply. "I led him a dance and shook him off by going through water, and I even did that the long way around. And stayed late, and came back through water, which is why I'm so late. Or so early." He yawned. "And so tired. But I'll . . ."

"There was someone here last night!" said Urchin, and his fur bristled with fear as he remembered. "I heard something. Scuffling. I woke up a bit, but I thought it was just a crab."

Padra slipped down to all fours and examined the floor, his nose and whiskers twitching as he searched and sniffed. Finally he stood up, called for Lugg, and glanced around outside before drawing him in.

"Lugg, were you in here last night?" he asked.

"No, sir."

"Some mole was," said Padra. "Mole tracks." He examined his bed. "Moles have been through this, too. Arrange a guard on this chamber, day and night."

"Yes, sir."

"Urchin," said Padra, "where did you keep the king's leaf tokens last night?"

"In my cloak, sir," said Urchin. "I slept on them."

"Good lad. That's what they were looking for. Husk probably got back from wherever he was—I'd give a good night's fishing to know where that was—and came back to find the king with a clear head, absolutely determined to refuse rationing, and sending out tokens to prove it. He probably sent a mole to search these rooms in the hope of stealing the tokens before we could spread the good news—which we must, sharpish."

Urchin, too, bent and inspected the floor. Now that Padra had pointed it out, he could see the faint empty prints of mole paws. It was unsettling to feel that he wasn't safe in Padra's own chambers.

"Can I look at my own room, sir?" he said.

A few shreds of moss had fallen from his nest, and the satchel he sometimes carried had been put away a little too neatly. He bent to examine the floor, as Padra had done.

"That's enough," said Padra softly. "They don't have to know that we're on to . . ." He stopped and listened with paw on sword, then flung open the door with a broad smile.

"Fir!" he cried. "Brother Fir, you should have sent for me. I would have come to your turret—you shouldn't be laboring up and down stairs."

"Hm," said Fir. "Very kind of you, young Padra, to remind me of my great age. However, squirrels are generally good at climbing, though we wouldn't expect an otter to realize that, would we, Urchin? But Urchin is too young to bother with stairs. He nips in and out of windows and runs down walls."

"And thinks I don't notice," agreed Padra. "Fir, have you had breakfast? I hear the king's been throwing things at you."

"Hm," said Fir when he had heard everything. "I'm actually rather pleased that the king threw that drink. Most of it hit the wall. Best place for it. Sleeping draft. Hefty one."

Padra's whiskers twitched into a frown. "This is serious," he said. "Sleeping drafts! Can't we stop her?"

Fir held out his wrinkled paws to the fire. "No, we can't," he said. "I had a word with Lady Aspen. She made no problem of it. She said she makes the king's drafts herself. Following the deaths of his wife and son, he's been very distressed and sleeps badly, so of course she offers him sleeping drafts at night. He knows what they are, and drinks them gladly. She even offered me the recipe, quite needlessly, of course. I knew how to make the things before Aspen was a chubby little bobble with burrs in her fur and sticky paws, but I don't use them. Best not to. And if the king has Husk topping off his wine all day and the good lady tucking him up with a sleeping draft at night . . . Hm, His Majesty's royal brains aren't his own."

"It's worse than we feared," said Padra.

Fir stood up. "Make your move soon, Padra," he said, and his voice was no more than a whisper. "Urchin has done well for us. Follow it up. And take care." Before he left, he gave them both his blessing.

"May your hearts be open to the Heart that made you," he said as they knelt. "May the Heart nourish you in all that is good."

"You will need it," he added as they rose. "You will need all the strength the Heart gives you."

Arran was put in charge of the food stores as Padra's deputy. There were some strange happenings in the early days—berries were spilled, beech nuts were found to be damp, and flour went missing—but within a week she had the stores well guarded, and had personally chosen every single member of her staff. It wasn't difficult. Plenty of animals knew how their babies had been saved from culling, and who to thank for it. Padra and Arran could count on their loyalty, and most of the otters would serve her faithfully because she was one of their own. They all agreed that, if ever it came to a row, they'd rather fight on Arran's side than against her.

Aspen was worried. Husk still had nightmares. When he learned that Urchin had outwitted him, his fury had lasted for days. And now there was a continuous chain of squirrels running up and down the

Throne Room with nothing better to do than to carry fresh spring water.

On a morning when Granite had taken the king to visit the graves, Husk and Aspen met Gloss in the Throne Room. Of course, Husk did not sit on the throne. He stood tall and straight in front of it, paw on sword hilt, with Aspen beside him. Gloss slipped noiselessly into the room, and Husk's gaze was as cold as the winter sky.

"You were told to watch Urchin," he said. He was quiet and dangerous.

"Excuse me, my captain," said Gloss smoothly. "My lady only told me to find someone else to watch the foundling squirrel. I myself have been shadowing Captain Padra, as you ordered, and have had both their rooms searched."

"And found nothing!" rasped Husk. "What do you have to say?"

"Only," said Gloss sweetly, "that I have served you well in the past."

Husk knew it. Gloss had served him very well, almost too well. He knew too much.

"You have served excellently," said Husk. "You have been well rewarded, and you will be rewarded again. Have you learned anything about Padra?"

"Otters have unnatural habits," said Gloss with distaste. "I can follow him so far—he seems to head for the far side of the wood, or perhaps the west shore—but sooner or later he always slips into water, and I lose him."

"We need an otter to track an otter," said Husk. "Very well, Gloss. Leave Padra to me. Watch Urchin. When your eyes close, make sure somebody else watches him. Now, go."

The mole bowed politely, and slipped away.

"Slimy as an otter," said Husk. "Nasty, creepy beast. But we need him. His eyes are poor, but he has the hearing of a bat and can smell out a worm at a hundred paces. I need an otter to spy on Padra, and there can't be many we could trust. The brainless beasts think they're heroes."

"Dear Tay would do it," said Aspen.

"She's a lot older than Padra," said Husk. "And she's more interested in law and ancient history than in splashing around streams and all that ottery stuff. But we'll see." He opened the door and called for a guard. "Send me Tay," he ordered.

Aspen took a nut from a dish and nibbled daintily. "We can't possibly enforce rationing now," she said.

"No," said Husk, and smiled unpleasantly. "We must make the best of things. If everyone has plenty of food, who will get the credit for it?"

She smiled back at him. "You will!" she said.

"And if there isn't enough, it's the king's fault," he said. "Or we could blame Padra the Pathetic." He laughed a wild, high laugh that made Aspen bite her lip. "At the Spring Festival, they must see that everything good on this island is from me, and everything bad is from the king."

"How easy!" she said, to reassure him.

"But if the Spring Festival is to be the turning point," he said, "two things must happen. Firstly, the king must appear to be so broken with grief that he is half mad, and cannot go on being king."

"And secondly?" she asked.

"Secondly," he said, "Padra is to be publicly disgraced and arrested."

There was a tap at the door. "Mistress Tay," said the guard, and Tay strutted into the room on her hind legs, smoothing her dark whiskers.

"I need an otter I can trust," said Husk abruptly. "I need Captain Padra observed."

"Difficult," she said. "Not the sort of task to which I am accustomed. But whether you could entrust it to any other otter—that's really very debatable indeed."

"Will you do it?" demanded Husk.

Aspen moved in front of him, stepping softly, her voice gentle and persuasive.

"Captain Husk is most concerned," she said. "We have reports of Padra going at night to the far side of the woods near the west shore, but without a powerful swimmer he can't be traced farther. He may be up to something most disloyal. Even a plot against the king—who knows? He was very friendly with a certain squirrel we prefer not to mention."

"West of the woods?" said Tay. "That's interesting."

"Yes," said Husk impatiently. "You're an expert on the old stories. Do you believe in the Old Palace? Do you believe it exists?"

"I believe it may, Captain," she said.

"He knows," muttered Husk. "Padra, Crispin. I'm sure they knew. Wouldn't tell me, of course, but I'm sure they knew. I'm sure that's where Padra's going, and if he's going there, it's because he's up to something. Something he doesn't want me to know about."

"I see, sir," said Tay. "Well, sir, all I can say is that if you will offer me the task, I will undertake it. Anything I can find out about Padra, I will."

"I want evidence against him," growled Husk. "Evidence that can be brought to the Spring Festival. Evidence that will get him arrested."

"It will be a great pleasure to find it," said Tay with dignity. "And a privilege."

"And," purred Aspen, "if it happens that Padra can no longer be a captain, we will need a new one." She tipped her head to one side, looking up at the top of Tay's head as if she were measuring it for a circlet. "We understand each other, Tay."

Returning to her own dark chambers, Tay brought to mind everything she had ever heard about the Old Palace in the tree roots. Then she went to look at the Threadings—the oldest and most faded Threadings, made long, long ago in the days when some very old creatures claimed to have been told about the Old Palace by their grandparents, who said they had seen it.

This could be exciting. Perhaps Padra really did know. And if he did, why did he go there?

Goodness knows why he was a captain. A pleasant manner, an

ability to befriend anything that swam or walked, a bit of organizing and swaggering—anyone could do that. She had been passed over.

Captain Tay. Lady Tay. Lady Tay would do nicely. If she could only discover the Old Palace and disgrace Padra, she could have any title she liked.

CHAPTER SIXTEEN

THROUGH THE WINTER, Urchin was a little less at court and a little more in Anemone Wood. With Padra in charge of food supplies, there were plenty of reasons for going there. There were nuts to be brought from the wood, and butter, cheese, dried fruits, and fish to be delivered. Sometimes, Needle went too. She knew that Scufflen was safe somewhere and that it was something to do with Padra, and that was enough for her.

The more Urchin and Needle went to the wood, the more whispers spread around the island. Animals were telling each other that culling and work parties were a lot more to do with Captain Husk than with the king, and it was Captain Padra who fought for the interests of the ordinary islanders. As more families were affected by the culling law, more parents were led, blindfolded and in secrecy, to the nursery in the Old Palace where Mother Huggen and Moth the mole maid cared for their rescued babies. Now and again a new young animal would suddenly come to play with the others in the wood or by the shore. Everyone was careful not to wonder where it had come from, or whether it had a trace of a limp. They knew.

In the darkness of burrows and tunnels it was whispered that Crispin's trial had not been all it seemed. And if Crispin hadn't murdered the prince, who had?

Urchin went to the Throne Room whenever he could, but usually Husk, Aspen, or Granite would be there. The best time to speak to the king was early in the morning, when the sleeping draft was wearing off and the wine had not been brought. From midmorning there was always a flagon and a cup at the king's side, with another bottle ready when the first was finished. So every morning at breakfast time, Urchin would fill a bowl with water bubbling from the spring and run up the stairs so the king could drink it while it was fresh and new.

Usually, though, he didn't get past the guards. They would ask politely for the water and promise to give it to the king, but Urchin doubted that it ever reached him. An announcement was made from the tower. Captain Padra was managing the food stores so remarkably well that all the animals were exceptionally healthy for the winter. That meant that they could do more work, which was good for them and kept them warm. They must start an hour earlier in the morning and finish an hour later at night. They could work faster. They could carry heavier loads. The king was said to be considering culling the old as well as the young. There were poor old animals whose bones ached and whose lives were dull, and it was cruel to expect them to cope with cold, dark winters, harsh winds from the sea, and scorching summers. And the younger animals would then not have the burden of caring for them.

On one wild, rough night, animals were huddled in nests and tunnels in the tower, the shores, and the woods. They warmed cordials and told old stories. Some complained about Captain Husk, some about Padra, and some even said that the king was at fault. He was a good king, but grief had turned his mind. Nobody blamed Lady Aspen for anything. She was kind and gracious to common animals, and had cared so dearly for the queen. Just to look at her and hear her sweet voice was a delight for tired hearts and minds.

In the nursery, Moth aired blankets and spooned porridge into milky mouths. Huggen knitted and stitched and made little mitts, as lifelike as real paws, to hide deformed limbs. The nearsighted young hedgehog was being taken for a little tour of the tunnels by a group of kindly moles. His real name was Hoppen, but he was so determined to learn everything he was taught, and so affectionate and eager to please, that they changed it to Hope. Arran, visiting them that night, pointed out that he was old enough to leave the nursery. But he had become something of a pet, and they were reluctant to see him go.

"He's awful fond of his mum," said Huggen as she knitted. "They call her Thripple. She doesn't get here often, but it's not her fault. They make her work such long hours at the tower. She's an excellent, neat-pawed hedgehog; she works on the Threadings. He does so miss her."

"Poor little thing," said Arran. "How's the new otter?"

The new baby otter lay sleeping on the hearth. "She's doing lovely," said Huggen. "Nothing the matter with her that we can't put right with love, warmth, and good feeding."

"Padra's bringing her mum tonight," said Arran. "I must get back now. It's not good for Padra and me to be away from the tower at the same time."

"Ask him to marry you, why don't you?" said Moth.

"He'd only laugh," said Arran.

As the wind howled and beat about the tower, Husk scrambled from the bed and felt for his sword. The hedgehog was coming at him again—Prince Tumble, who wouldn't stay dead—he was coming nearer. . . .

"Get back!" he yelled hoarsely. "Get back, get back, get back!" Aspen was trying to tell him something, and he pushed her away.

"He's here!" he croaked. "He's here! Get away!"

"Nobody is here," she said calmly. "Go back to sleep."

It took him a little time before he knew he was awake. Only a nightmare, but real enough to drive him wild with terror. Aspen was taking the sword from his paws.

Unable to stop shivering, he found a cloak and wrapped himself in it. Then he knelt by the deep glow in the hearth, where the embers still gave a little heat.

"Shall I give you something to help you sleep?" asked Aspen.

"No," he said. "I don't want it."

"The draft I give to the king," she said gently, "is not the draft I would give you."

"I don't want it," he said again, and stayed crouching by the fire. His spies had told him that the common animals were saying Crispin was innocent. If they weren't all so stupid and inferior, they would have worked that out long ago. But nobody would blame *him*. He'd stabbed so expertly and so cleanly that there was no trail of blood. He'd carried out enough cullings to know how to do that. He'd cleaned his paws and sword on moss, and burned the moss. There were no witnesses. He'd disposed of all the tokens he'd made of Crispin's clawmark.

Or had he?

Of course he had. He must have done.

The wind moaned like the crying of an infant, like the mourning of a queen. He did not want to sleep. If Aspen only knew the nightmares he had, she would not try to make him sleep. Worry nagged at him. He would have no peace until he had been to the anteroom by the Gathering Chamber, and looked in the robing chest.

There was not a trace of a leaf. He shook out the robes to make sure, inspecting his own very carefully, turning the cuffs inside out.

He tipped up the velvet bag. Not one of the forged tokens remained. He was safe.

The tide was out. Padra swam far from the shore by moonlight until he had to come inland, then ran, fast and low, to a dry cave. He wriggled through until he could hear the scuffling of paws inside and the hissing of low otter voices.

"Nothing to worry about," he whispered. "It's only me, Captain Padra. I'm here to take you to see your little daughter. Are you ready? We'll go overground, then through the water, and I'll have to blindfold you. Trust me. And don't make a sound."

Wrapped in her dark cloak, in the shadow of a fallen tree, Tay remained perfectly still and watched. Once or twice she lost sight of them, but there was the occasional smooth, swift movement as Padra and a young female otter slipped in and out of the river. At the point where the stream ran underground, she lost them. If her theory was right, they were nowhere near the Old Palace, but a long upstream swim could bring them to a network of tunnels. If all she had learned was true, most of these tunnels were too narrow for a full-grown otter. There was only one big enough, and that one ran northwest through water.

She could follow no farther. She doubted she could manage the swim, and the risks of Padra noticing her were too great. But she had learned enough. On such a cruel winter night, her triumph warmed her. She had worked out the site of the Old Palace. Her name would be remembered. They would weave Threadings about her. Lady Tay the otter, who rediscovered the Old Palace.

And who was that otter with Padra? Some common shore otter who had no business to be there. If Padra had been told where the Old Palace was, he should have kept it secret. He had betrayed his trust. And what was he doing there that meant he had to slip out under cover of a winter night?

He could be preparing a rebellion. Treachery! And that otter with him wasn't his girlfriend. But Tay was remembering something. It was another piece of the puzzle. The last baby brought for culling had been an otter. A baby female otter. She remembered that, because Husk had been absent, and Granite had been furious to learn that Padra had attended to the culling. The more she thought, the more she understood.

She should go straight to Captain Husk, but Husk did have a way of taking all the glory for himself. This was *her* triumph. For the moment, she would be very cautious about how much she told him. Husk would get his evidence at the Spring Festival, as he wanted. Not before.

Fir was up late, too, stretched on the floor of his turret room in prayer. If the worst was true, Mistmantle needed the Heart, and he needed courage as never before. Finally, when Mistmantle slept, he took a lamp in his paw and a basket of candles on his arm and limped slowly down the spiral stair. The worst must be faced. The place of wickedness must be blessed.

Urchin woke up early in the morning, wriggled out of his nest, and looked into Padra's chamber just in time to see the captain flop onto his bed and fall asleep. He spread a warm cloak over him and slipped away to draw a bowl of spring water and patter up the stairs to the Throne Room, but Captain Granite guarded the door.

"Spring water for the king, sir," said Urchin.

"Leave it with me," ordered Granite, but the king's voice rose past him.

"It's Urchin! Let him in! Urchin, are the spring flowers out in Anemone Wood yet? Fetch some more water for Captain Husk!"

Urchin glanced past Granite long enough to see the king looking bleary-eyed, with Husk in front of him. Husk turned sharply.

"Oh, please do!" said Husk, taking the bowl, and Urchin scampered back to the spring. He was back as quickly as he could, with more water, but the door was shut and Granite glared down at him.

"Take that away," growled Granite. "It's not wanted."

There was no point in arguing. Urchin scurried away down the corridor, found a window where he could empty the bowl, and remembered just in time to look down.

"Oops," he said. He'd nearly drenched Brother Fir, Needle, and a young squirrel with spring flowers in her paws. Brother Fir looked up.

"Come and join us!" called Fir. "It's a lovely morning! Spring's here at last!"

Urchin had recognized the other squirrel. It was Crackle from Anemone Wood, who had wanted to work in the tower.

"Hm!" said Fir as Urchin joined them. "Is that water for us? Jolly good. Needle and I have just taken a long walk and had a most interesting talk about Threadings. And we met our little friend here in the wood."

"Urchin, you look all grown up," said Crackle shyly. "All groomed and everything, and you walk differently."

"Do I?" he said.

"You're becoming a true tower squirrel," said Fir. "This delightful young squirrel has brought flowers from the wood for the king."

"Oh!" said Urchin. "He was just asking me about those. He wanted to know if they were out yet."

Crackle gasped. "He asked *you*? You've seen him?"

"Then," said Fir, "if the king is asking about the spring flowers, we must take them to him before they wilt. If I go with you, my dear, you'll be allowed in." And he limped up the stair with Crackle clutching her flowers beside him.

"What's Crackle up to?" asked Urchin.

"She's not up to anything," said Needle snappily. "I met Brother Fir this morning in a corridor—he was looking at some Threadings, and I wanted to talk to him because I was worried. Husk wants the new

Threadings ready for the Spring Festival; and we're all working so hard to finish them, we're not getting enough sleep, and we make mistakes. They're all those new Threadings with the kings and queens looking like Husk and Aspen. Brother Fir and I went for a long walk and we met Crackle, and she was crying. Since Gleaner came here, she doesn't have a friend."

"I'm not surprised," said Urchin.

"Don't be like that!" she snapped. "She only used to be spiteful because she was trying to stay friends with Gleaner. And when Gleaner honors the wood by setting her paw in it, she just boasts about Lady Aspen. Crackle's trying hard to be my friend—she's much nicer than she was. And we're so desperate to finish the Threadings, she might get a job in the workrooms. I should be there now. If I'm late, I'll be in trouble. Good-bye, Urchin."

"I'm going to the wood tomorrow to see Apple," he said. "Do you want to come?"

"What have I just told you?" she said. "I haven't time!" And she trundled away.

Urchin went back to the Spring Gate to find Padra awake and eating a fish. As he opened the door, Padra looked past him.

"Lost your shadow, then?" he remarked.

"Shadow?" said Urchin.

"Gloss," said Padra. "He's never far from you. He's so sly, he'll double-cross himself. Now, while we have a moment . . ."

He opened the door, looked both ways, put his ear to the ground to listen for moles, and finally, with a claw to his lips, knelt in the hearth. The ashes were barely warm, and he spread them in a pale dust across the hearth.

"I wanted to take you along these tunnels myself," he whispered, "but there might not be the chance, not if we're both being watched. So here it is." He drew a few lines and circles in the dust. "That's the place we both know about," he said, and Urchin, knowing he meant the Old Palace, felt his heart quicken with excitement. "There's the tower. I can't put in every single tunnel, but these are the main ones."

Drawing and whispering, Padra sketched the plan of the tunnels. Urchin watched intently. There was an entrance in Hollybank Hill and another under the bank at the east shore, and one through the stream, but not possible for squirrels. Urchin hoped he'd remember, but it was complicated.

"And here," said Padra. "If you follow it long enough, this tunnel should come out under the tower, but I don't know exactly where. I've never followed it all the way along. Take a good look at it."

When Urchin had looked, Padra stood up before the hearth. "Now," he said, "without looking, tell me the nearest entrance from the north rocks when the tide's out."

"Sandstone Bank," said Urchin promptly. "But, sir, why do I have to know this?"

Padra knelt and looked earnestly into Urchin's face.

"We don't know what's going to happen in the future, Urchin," he said. "If they watch me even more closely, or if I'm arrested—yes, I know it's an unpleasant thought, but it could happen—I won't be able to go the the Old Palace anymore, and you may have to go for me. More to the point, you may need a place of safety yourself or for your friends. So you need to know this."

"Yes, sir," said Urchin. Suddenly, danger seemed very close and real. His fur bristled. He wanted to say "Don't get arrested, sir," but it seemed silly, so he didn't.

Padra went on asking questions until he was satisfied that Urchin had remembered it all, and finally said, "Keep reminding yourself of this. It should be written on your heart and mind. Keep it secret, and never forget it." Then he swished his tail, and the only map of the routes to the Old Palace was a pile of ashes.

CHAPTER SEVENTEEN

I**N HIS OWN CHAMBER, HUSK SHOOK WITH ANGER.** When the door opened, he jumped. Aspen glided in.

"You left the king alone," she said. "He's distressed."

"I had to calm down," he said, spitting out the words in a low, tight voice. "Brother Fir brought in some little common squirrel with a paw full of weeds. We had important matters of state to discuss, and now the king just wants to talk about poppies and spring buds. Fir takes too much on himself, just because he's the priest. Padra's wretched page put him up to it. He's dangerous."

Aspen inspected her reflection in the mirror. "He could have an accident," she said. "He could trip over something, or stumble into something, or fall out of something . . . yes!" She turned with a smile of inspiration. "He falls out of things. I'm told he makes a habit of tumbling out of the sky."

Husk froze. Ice was in his spine. His nerves prickled. In a second he had hurled himself across the chamber to grip her by the shoulders, and she staggered against the wall.

"*What do you mean?*" he gasped.

"My lord!" cried Aspen.

He gathered himself together. "My dear," he said, "pardon me. I am so sorry, so very sorry. Please—are you hurt? Please, tell me exactly what you mean about 'tumbling out of the sky'?"

"If you are quite sure you want to hear," she said reproachfully, "it's simply something Gleaner told me. She overheard Brother Fir telling him about the day he was found."

"That dense squirrel found him," said Husk, but he was trembling.

"Apparently not," she went on. "Apple thinks she found him, but Brother Fir and Crispin . . ."

"*Crispin?*"

She gave him a stern look, and went on. "They found him first, and they saw him fall from the sky into the sea. I asked Apple about it and she denies it, but I think Brother Fir's and Crispin's memories are more reliable than hers. However, she did remark that Urchin had fallen from a tower window, on the night of our wedding."

"He did *what?*"

"I can't imagine how he managed it," she said. "Maybe he just had no idea where he was."

178

Husk turned so she could not see his face. He returned to the window, leaning his paws on the sill as he tried to breathe deeply and calmly.

"Send for Gloss," he said. By the time the mole slid into the room, he had gathered himself together.

"I have watched the squirrel," said Gloss. "I know more about him than he knows himself."

"I don't doubt it," said Husk grimly. "I want him dead. At once. It must look like an accident."

"Is that all?" said Gloss. "Consider it done. He intends to visit his foster mother in the wood tomorrow, and I know exactly the route he will take. There are all manner of tunnels on the way. It's amazing that nobody ever falls into them." He bowed, and left the room.

Aspen took Husk's paws. "Hold on," she said. "We're nearly there. Leave the king to me. Urchin will soon be dead. Tay will have Padra arrested. We will have a magnificent Spring Festival."

She called for Gleaner, who arrived surprisingly quickly. "Make sure nobody disturbs me this morning," she ordered. "I have the king's sleeping drafts to prepare."

Gleaner bowed and trotted importantly down the corridor. "Nobody is to disturb Lady Aspen," she said bossily to every animal she met. She was about to take up her post at the keyhole again when she caught sight of Crackle.

"What are you doing here?"

"I'm visiting Needle," said Crackle. She was lost and looking for the way out, but didn't like to admit it.

"Oh, her," said Gleaner, and couldn't resist a smirk. "Well, I know a certain squirrel friend of hers who needs to look out."

"I don't want to hear it," said Crackle, but Gleaner wanted to tell it. She pressed close to Crackle, whispering, the way they used to when they were best friends.

"Between you and me," she said, "and I wouldn't dream of telling anybody else, and you have to keep it our secret—Urchin's going to get what he's been asking for. And about time, too. I'm always with Lady Aspen; I can't help overhearing what she and Captain Husk say to each other. Urchin might have one fall too many!" And with a knowing wink, she pursed her lips and ran away.

CHAPTER EIGHTEEN

URCHIN WAS WOKEN EARLY THE NEXT MORNING by the clanging
and beating of hammers from somewhere near the tower.
Whatever it was, there was no point in trying to go back to sleep. He
packed a satchel, ready for his visit to Apple later that morning, and
slipped from his chamber, looking around as Padra had taught him, in
case he was being followed. Reporting to Padra, he found the captain
trying to sleep with his paws over his ears. Presently he muttered
something and pulled moss over his head, but he soon gave up.

"A deaf mole couldn't sleep through that lot," he said. "Let's see
what's happening. Plague on it, I've fallen asleep wearing my sword."

The noise came from the side of the tower nearest to the wood. On
the level ground beyond the rocks, animals were building scaffolding,
sawing and hammering at posts, poles, and planks. Squirrels ran up

and down, hedgehogs hammered, otters fetched and carried, and moles scurried about looking busy.

"What's this?" said Padra.

"It's for the Spring Festival, sir," said a breathless squirrel. "To hang the Threadings and the awnings and that, sir. Look! The grand table goes in the middle up on the rocks there, and the Threadings hang behind it and around it so that everyone can see them, and there's a canopy to go over the top, sir."

"I always thought that Threadings were for indoors," remarked Padra. "Still, it can't do any harm. I only wish I'd been informed." A shadow fell over them, and they turned to see Captain Granite.

"*I* was informed," he growled.

"Oh, that's all right then," said Padra cheerfully and clapped him on the shoulders. "Urchin, we'll have breakfast before you go to see Apple. Granite, would you like to join us for some fresh fish?"

"No, thank you," said Granite grimly.

"No, I thought you wouldn't," smiled Padra. "Oh, here's Captain Husk coming to inspect the work."

Husk was striding down from the tower, a rich cloak thrown around his shoulders. When a hedgehog ran up to speak to him, he turned sharply and seemed irritated. But then he was smiling, looking interested, talking to the working animals, encouraging them. Urchin was glad to follow Padra back to the tower.

Husk did not usually come out this early, but he didn't want to go back to sleep. The king had been obstinate, demanding spring water and wanting to go out and meet the animals. It had taken half a bottle of spirits and one of Aspen's drafts to quiet him.

Husk still saw Prince Tumble in his nightmares, but now he saw Crispin, too. Exile had been a mistake. Crispin should have met with an accident, as Urchin would.

"Your shadow isn't here this morning," said Padra to Urchin, back in the safety of his chamber. "I'll tell you what's going to happen at the Spring Festival."

Paws pattered toward them. "No I won't," sighed Padra, and threw open the door.

"Hello, Needle!" said Urchin, springing up; but he couldn't help being irritated. Padra had been about to tell him something important. "Oh, and Crackle."

Needle scurried in, looking anxious and urgent. Crackle pressed timidly beside her.

"We're sorry to interrupt, but we've got something important to tell you both," said Needle. "At least, Crackle has."

"You tell them," said Crackle, and glanced up shyly at Padra. Urchin just wished they'd get on with it and go.

"Gleaner was showing off to Crackle," said Needle quickly. "She was dropping hints, and said Urchin would get what he'd been asking for. 'He'll have one fall too many,' she said."

Urchin's legs felt a bit shaky. There had always been danger, but now it was close, and it was meant for him. Padra sat on the floor and took Crackle's paw.

"Is that right?" he said. "Is that exactly what Gleaner told you?"

"Yes, sir," she said shyly.

"Good squirrel," said Padra. "You've done well to tell me. Don't be afraid. Go to Brother Fir and tell him what you've just told us. I'll call a guard to go with you."

When she had gone, he checked the corridor, closed the door, and leaned against it.

"'One fall too many,'" he repeated softly. "Gleaner waits on Lady Aspen. I wonder if Husk and Aspen know you fell from the sky? It adds to your strangeness, and they don't want anything or anyone on this island that puzzles them. Much too dangerous. This is serious, Urchin."

"Fell from the sky?" said Needle.

"Brother Fir wisely kept it quiet, and so will we," said Padra firmly.

"I'll be all right," said Urchin, trying to be brave.

"Not if you stay here, you won't," said Padra. He paused and looked for a long time at Urchin before he spoke again. "Urchin, you've given them too much trouble. You've come between Husk and the king. You're my page. You look different, and you have a mysterious past. They want you out of the way. I'm sorry. You'll have to go."

"Where, sir?" asked Urchin. He hoped he hadn't understood.

"As far as possible," said Padra.

"Into hiding, sir?" said Urchin. "Maybe in the Old Palace?"

"Too risky," said Padra, and looked so unhappy that Urchin felt sorry for him. "If they're determined to find you, they will."

"And if I stayed in the Old Palace they'd find the little ones, too," admitted Urchin.

"There's only one thing to do, and I hate it," said Padra. "You've been an excellent page. And a great friend. But if you stay on the island, Husk will find you."

Urchin had felt that this was coming. It was as if everything inside him had turned as gray and cold as a winter sky.

He remembered the day Crispin left, and how he had planned to go with him, even though it would mean leaving everyone else he knew and loved. But now he would go alone. More than ever, he knew how much he owed to Padra. He had been a captain, father, older brother, friend, guide, protector. He would have to leave Padra.

"Must I?" he said.

"You might be able to return one day," said Padra. "We've never been sure whether you truly belong here."

"Yes I do, sir!" cried Urchin, hurt.

"Yes, yes," said Padra hastily. "You're one of us, of course you are. What I meant was, your parents must have come from somewhere else. So you should be able to get back through the mists."

"I don't belong anywhere else," said Urchin. "I was born here, or at least, I think I was. Sir, I don't think I could bear it, never coming home again."

Padra gripped his shoulders. "There are tunnels under the sea," he said, "or the moles say there are. Long and dark, but they're a way of traveling without going by water. You might come back that way. If there was a ship in just now I'd stow you away, but we'll just have to fit up a boat, the way we did for Crispin. You won't go hungry."

"Should I wait until nightfall?" asked Urchin hopefully.

"Nightfall could be too late," said Padra. "We'll launch you from the north shore, where you won't be noticed. Everyone's busy."

"But I was going to see Apple today!" Urchin exclaimed. "She's expecting me, and I can't let her down!"

"I'll go," said Needle. "I'll tell her—what shall I tell her, Captain Padra?"

"Tell her the truth, and swear her to secrecy," said Padra. "It's a risk, but we can't let her think you'd just disappeared."

"I've got presents for her," muttered Urchin, hoping to stretch out his last hours on the island.

"I'll take them," said Needle promptly, and Urchin glared at her.

"You'd have to get time off work," he argued.

"Captain Padra can see to that," said Needle.

Urchin turned to Padra. "They'll notice I've gone," he said. "Then what will you say?"

"No problem," said Padra. "From what Gleaner told Crackle, Husk has given instructions for your death. When you disappear, he'll think they've been carried out. If the islanders notice you've gone, they'll suspect him of your murder, which is good. Urchin, I don't like this either, and if the islanders didn't need me, I'd come with you. I'll row you out as far as the mists myself, then give you the oars while I swim back to shore, yes? I don't know much about the lands beyond the mist, but I'll tell you all I can."

Urchin was thinking of Crispin. It was reassuring to know he was out there somewhere.

"If Crispin's still alive, I'll find him," he said, and the thought of Crispin encouraged him. "I'm not just going to save myself, sir. I'm going to find Crispin. And when I've found him, I'll find a way to bring him back. There must be some way." But he thought of the vastness of the sea and its storms, and the little boats the otters used. Curling his claws, suddenly feeling very small beside Padra, he looked up and said what he would not say to any other animal, and would rather not say in front of Needle.

"I'm afraid, sir."

"So would I be!" said Padra. "But we have to do this. Before anything else, I'm taking you to Fir. Do you want to take the shortcut up the walls?"

"No, I'll walk," said Urchin, who didn't feel like running up a wall. The climb to Fir's tower, with Needle plodding behind, had never seemed so long. When they reached the workrooms, Needle stopped.

"I have to go to work now," she said.

"I'll come for you presently," said Padra.

Needle wriggled a bit. "Take care, Urchin," she said awkwardly.

"Thanks for being my friend," said Urchin. There wasn't much to say after that.

Fir's turret felt as if it had been prayed in. There was something about the stillness in the air. But Fir seemed to have changed. His face seemed more deeply lined than ever. He stood up slowly, stiffly, as if he carried a weight of sorrow and everything took a great effort, and Padra put out a paw to help him. But there was a depth in his eyes, as if he were older than the bedrock of the island, and knew more than any of its legends could tell.

"Urchin, check under the window boxes for spies," said Padra. It seemed a bit extreme to Urchin, but he obeyed his captain while Padra told Fir what had happened.

"Yes," said Fir sadly, when he had heard the story. "Yes, he must go. Hm! I suppose we should feed him." He poured water and cordial into a saucepan. "Now, Urchin of the Riding Stars, there are things you need to know."

Urchin sat down to listen, and Fir gave him an apple.

"Firstly, I'll tell you what I told Crispin before he went. I know a little of the islands. Most of the trading ships come from the northwest, and there are large, well-populated islands that way, but a long way off. The nearest ones are to the southeast, so row around the island, keep the tower at your back, and row a straight line. Give him a sail, Padra; he may not be strong enough for all that rowing. Any ship you see, any otters you meet, any island where you land, ask for Crispin. Search till you find him. And the other thing is this. Mark it well."

"Yes, sir."

Brother Fir took Urchin's paws in his. His old face warmed into a smile so kind, so deep, so wise, and so gentle that Urchin could only gaze. In the simplicity of the plain chamber, with a breeze floating in through a window, Urchin felt the holiness of the place reaching into him.

"You will come to us again, Urchin of the Riding Stars. You were sent to us on a momentous night. Mistmantle is your destiny. You will come back to us. I don't know how. But we will see you again."

Urchin forgot about being a tower squirrel and flung his arms round Brother Fir, pressing his cheek against the rough white tunic.

"Oh, my young hero," soothed Fir. "All heroes feel like this—they do, you know." He looked over Urchin's ears at Padra. "Padra, I suggest you find young Arran and ask her to arrange the provisioning of a boat. No mean rations. Honey biscuits. Spice cakes. Walnut and herb bread. Butter. Oatcakes and cheese. Apples—oh, whatever it is that this brave adventurer likes. And if you know what young Crispin likes, put that in too, because I've no doubt Urchin will run into him. And while you're at it, ask her to marry you."

"She'd only hit me," muttered Padra as usual as he ran down the stairs. When he had gone, Fir smoothed Urchin's ears, then sat him down with a cup of cordial. Urchin didn't feel that he wanted anything, but it was hot and strong, and he felt better by the time Padra came back.

"Let's get it over with," said Padra. "Give him your blessing, please, Brother Fir."

Urchin knelt. He felt very calm now that he knew he was about to

189

go. Fir's voice was as old as a threadbare cloak, but it rang with authority as he held a paw over Urchin's head.

"May the Heart keep you, Urchin of the Riding Stars," he said. "May the Heart guide you, guard you, nourish you, enlighten you. And may the great love of the Heart bring you safely back to Mistmantle."

The boat was prepared, well furnished, with oars and a sail, though Urchin hadn't practiced using the sail and hoped he wouldn't need to. Food, water, cordials, and cloaks were neatly stacked.

"Look after Apple for me," said Urchin to Padra.

"Remember all I told you," said Fir.

"And wear this," said Padra. From under his cloak he produced the small sword Urchin used for practice, with its own belt and scabbard. "Use it only if you must, and remember all you've learned. If you do strike, strike quick and clean."

"Thank you, sir," said Urchin. "And thanks for everything." It would be best now to go quickly and get it over, but Padra suddenly caught at his shoulders.

"You can't go alone," he insisted. "I can't do this, Urchin—you mustn't be left alone when we get to the mists. Somebody has to go with you."

"No, sir!" said Urchin, though he would have been glad of a friend. "That would be putting another animal into exile!"

"I'll find Lugg," said Padra. "He can look after himself." He slipped into the water and swam swiftly away. Urchin watched until he was out of sight, then turned to Fir.

"Will you push the boat out for me *now*, please?" he asked.

Brother Fir's nose twitched.

"Please, Brother Fir," said Urchin. "And Padra was going to row me as far as the mists, so I haven't said good-bye to him properly, so will you say it for me? Tell him I'm sorry for disobeying my captain, but he mustn't send Lugg. Lugg can't be spared from the island. And he has a family. He has to stay." He sprang into the boat. "Now, please, Brother Fir. Before I change my mind."

Urchin would remember these moments all his life. The dip of the boat as it bobbed into the water. The cry of a gull. A tear shining on Brother Fir's kind, wise face. A starfish on the sand. A sea urchin. The smoothness of the oars, creaking and dripping; the glint of sunlight on the water as he squinted over his shoulder to get his bearings. The tang of salt on the air. A fish gliding away under water. Steadily, stroke by stroke, he was nearer to the mists.

He reminded himself that he did not come from Mistmantle. Fir had said he could come back. He pulled steadily at the oars, though soon the mists clouded his vision and he could no longer see the pale gold rising of Mistmantle Tower. He shut his eyes and rowed on.

He hoped he was heading southeast, but he could see nothing but mist. The wake was straight, as far as he could tell, but the mists grew closer and whiter until he could hardly see even that. It was encouraging to think that if he emerged at night, he could navigate by the stars—Padra had taught him the stars—but he was losing track of time. He wrapped himself in a cloak and wondered what his friends on the island were doing. Needle, Padra—no, he mustn't think of them. It made his eyes sting.

He tried singing to keep his spirits up, but in the white wreaths of mist his voice sounded thin and lost. He prayed silently inside himself, instead. Tiny diamonds of vapor clung to his fur and whiskers. He wondered about who his parents were and what they'd do if they could see him, and hoped they'd be proud of him. He mustn't feel sorry for himself; he mustn't wish he'd waited for Lugg.

The mists seemed like a weight. The effort of rowing grew heavier. Behind his closing eyes he saw a squirrel, a female, pale like himself . . .

He was falling asleep. He must have been rowing forever. He shipped the oars and lay down to snatch a few minutes of rest, but he was soon deeply asleep. Night drew in and grew cold, and the boat drifted on. And as Urchin slept in the drifting boat, Gloss slipped out from behind the food stores and crept toward him.

CHAPTER NINETEEN

IT WAS ALL VERY WELL FOR SQUIRRELS. Urchin could run through woods, scurry up and down walls, and jump over brooks with a heavy satchel over his shoulder and not even notice it was there. Needle took the bag filled with cakes, biscuits and cheese for Apple, impaled it firmly on her spines, and trundled through the forest.

Much as she loved her work, she was glad of the morning's freedom. The hours of work grew longer and longer, and her paws were sore. Thripple, the kind and rather ugly hedgehog who sat next to her, had given her salves to put on her paws to heal them. They helped, but lately the work had been so hard that even Thripple's salves could not altogether heal the cuts and scratches. In the spring morning, she felt sorry for the animals in the workroom. The buds were fresh and green. Poppies and daffodils were springing up. She ran on through the wood, scenting the rising hyacinths, hearing the stream, picking up notes of birdsong, watching a blackbird gathering twigs for a nest. At the foot of the beech tree she scrabbled about for the nuts Apple liked, unearthing a few worms and beetles, too, which she ate. The stream gurgled invitingly, and was deliciously cool and fresh when she drank from it and splashed her paws.

On the other side of the stream, the cushions of moss were as springy as waves and as green as caterpillars. When she came this way with Urchin, he always took this stretch at a jump, while she trotted round to the shallows and waded across. Sometimes she jumped it, but her jump was always a dumpy thud compared to Urchin's.

But Urchin wasn't here today to compare to. Wistfully she thought of him, alone in a small boat on the friendless sea. He'd like her to do that jump for him. She adjusted the package on her back, retreated a few paces to get a good run, and leaped across the stream. The dry moss gave way under her paws. In sickening terror, she fell, faster and faster, too fast to save herself, hearing her own voice screaming—but her scream was lost in the deep shaft as she scrabbled helplessly at the earth.

The sharpness of her spines catching on the earthen walls slowed her fall, and by scratching and clinging, she managed to dig her claws hard into the soil. With all her strength she clutched, gritting her teeth, pressing her back against the earthen wall behind her, but she was slipping. She tried to climb—but even lifting one claw was enough to send her slipping farther down. Bracing herself, she tried again, but she fell so far that the daylight above her was now nothing but a dot of white.

But this time, she had fallen to a tree root which had grown out into the shaft. It wasn't much, but it provided a thin ledge where, so long as she didn't panic, she could balance and keep from falling any farther. She tried again to climb up, but again, she fell. She wondered if she could climb down in search of a tunnel entrance—but if she fell again, how far would it be? And what was underneath? Rock? Deep water? What if she went down and down into blackness and earth, and there still wasn't any mole tunnel? She might never be able to climb back up.

"I'll stay on this ledge," she told herself sensibly. "Somebody will find me."

She took a deep breath and yelled for help, but her voice sounded pale and scared, and she couldn't tell how far it would travel. She tightened her claws. She could be here for hours before anyone found her. Days, even.

Nonsense, she told herself firmly. *Pull yourself together, hedgehog.* Somebody would notice she was missing. Padra would. The hedgehogs in charge of the workroom would go to him demanding to know why she wasn't back, and he'd send a search party, and they'd find her. He'd come looking for her himself. Padra was like that. Afraid of falling, she wriggled to get a better grip, and prayed that Padra would come soon. He'd come. He'd hear her, he'd see where the moss had fallen in.

It never did that when Urchin landed on it. Yes, Urchin was light—but surely, if there was a tunnel underneath, somebody would have fallen in before now?

And then she suddenly felt very shaky, and had to brace herself harder. This wasn't an old mole tunnel. Tunnels didn't go straight down. This trap had been made for Urchin. To be left here would be terrible, and to be found by Husk's claw thugs might be worse. She felt sick.

Was there a sound? She strained to hear. Yes, there was a rustle. Then paws, lots of paws, on the other side of the earth wall. She had opened her mouth to shout for help when she decided it would be safer to wait and find out who it was.

There was the dragging of a tail, and the slap of paws on earth. An otter! *Please, Heart, let it be Padra!* There were small, busy paws, too, mole paws. But when the otter began to speak, Needle's hopes sank.

"Attend to me, now," said the otter sternly.

It was Tay. Wretched with fear, sick with disappointment, Needle gripped the root and stayed silent.

Cramped from his long wait behind the stores, Gloss stretched himself and raised a claw over the sleeping figure in the moonlit boat. He had brought a sword, concealed on a black belt with a black scabbard, but a claw would do it. He could kill Urchin now and return by tunnels, taking one of Urchin's ears to prove he had done it. But it would be better to stay hidden and let Urchin lead him to Crispin. Then he could kill both, and return with an ear from each.

But he might not return. Why settle for being Husk's assassin when he could find another island and become king in his own right? Squirrels thought themselves so superior. Crispin might be on an island in need of a king. And if there was a way back to Mistmantle, he could return through tunnels with an army of moles at his back, and conquer it. Then Husk would have to run errands for him, and Aspen would kneel at his paws and beg for her life.

He would not kill Urchin yet.

Urchin woke to drizzling rain and a gray sky meeting a gray sea. No sign of land, and no way of knowing if he had drifted off course. Unlike the previous day, when he hadn't felt like eating much, he was hungry, and by the time he had breakfasted on walnut bread, beech nuts and black-currant cordial, the sun was breaking through. A light breeze was in the air. Urchin sniffed at the wind and wondered which way was southeast. With a lot of struggling, he hoisted the sail and let the wind carry him. This felt good. He was Urchin of the Riding Stars, Urchin of Mistmantle, Urchin the Adventurer, following the quest for his hero alone with his sword at his hip. He only hoped he was going the right way.

When at last the sky began to darken, he thought at first that it was nightfall. But nightfall did not come in like this, with heavy clouds rolling low and growling in the sky. He pulled on a cloak as the wind teased and pushed at him, and the first big raindrops drove into his face. He pushed the stores farther under cover, crouched low in the boat, and waited for the storm to pass.

But it would not pass. The wind was a bully, slashing cruel rain in his face, tipping and pushing the boat, tossing waves to soak him. Arran had left a bowl in the boat for bailing out water, and against the buffeting storm he bailed furiously. A gust caught the sail, flung the boat about, tossed her, rocked her, punched her, and tore at the sail as he fought to bring it down; and a second gust flung him to the bottom of the boat. Struggling to stand, he was thrown off his paws again, and by clinging to the mast, saved himself from being hurled into the sea. Tucking in his head, he kept down, down, waiting for the fury to pass because it must pass; but whether he and his boat would survive it was more than he knew. With rain dashing into his face and the sodden cloak flapping about him, he tried to look for land, but through sheets of rain he could see nothing, and was helpless.

"Plague and pestilence!" yelled Urchin as he clutched the mast. The boat was completely beyond his control. She was the plaything of the wild wind that laughed as it tore at her. Icy water was in his fur, in his paws, in his eyes, slopping in the bottom of the boat. He had to bail it out, but his paws slipped, and he fell into the water he was bailing. He tried to think of all he'd ever learned about boats, but nothing Padra had said, nothing anybody had said, could prepare him for this wild sea that wanted to swallow him forever.

Nobody would know what had happened. Crispin and Padra would never have news of him; Apple . . . Falling in the sloshing water, his teeth chattering, Urchin knelt and tipped his head back against the rain.

"Heart!" he yelled. "Can't you see me? Won't you help me! Won't you do something?"

He wouldn't be beaten. He bailed with such strength and determination that he didn't notice the wind easing. The rain became lighter. Slowly he realized that the fierce, wild rocking had stopped. He could raise his face without being blinded by rain, and the darkness around him was not storm, but night.

He staggered to his paws, dropped the cloak in the puddle at the bottom of the boat, and rummaged in the stores for another to dry himself on. Then he sat on the rowing bench, shivering, looking up at the sky. The clouds had cleared. He could see a few stars. He steered southeast and followed his course until he fell asleep. As he slept, two otters swam, ducked, and bobbed up again on either side of the boat.

"Nice craft, this," said one. "I've seen one of these before."

"On Swan Isle," said the other. "Yes. Very like this one." She reached up inquisitively to look into the boat. "Same sort of creature, too. One of those tree things."

"Yes," said her mate. "One of those. A what's-its-whiskers. *Sorrel* or *Cirrel* or something. Funny color, what I can see of it. What's it doing here?"

"Maybe this one's going to Swan Isle, too," said the she-otter. "But he's a long way off it, and drifting off course."

"Shall we give him a shove?" said the other. "That sorrel thing on Swan Isle's a nice chappie; I got talking to him one morning when he was paddling about in his boat. He said his best friend was an otter."

"Is that right?"

"Yes, from Mistmantle, apparently. Asked me, if I ever got there, to take a message to a Captain Padra; but Mistmantle's a hard place to get to."

Urchin turned in his sleep. "Captain Padra, sir," he muttered, and his eyes half opened and shut again. The otters looked at each other and nodded.

"Come around the stern, then," said the he-otter, and together they propelled the boat steadily and smoothly through the night seas until, with a last gentle push, it ran aground on the shores of the island of swans. The otters smiled, nodded to each other, and swam away.

While it was still dark, Gloss left the boat. He swam to the island and began to search, far from the shore.

Dawn woke Urchin. He was stiff from sleep and aching with cold.

"Ouch," he said, sitting up to rub life into his chilled limbs.

"Land!" he exclaimed, and with a lifting heart he whispered thanks into the sky. He surveyed the island, saw nobody about, then jumped into the shallow water and heaved the boat ashore. He reached in for the driest cloak he could find and wrapped it around himself, turning sharply as he heard a rustle behind him.

He stared, blinked hard, looked again, and shook his ears in case this was a dream. But it was real, and it was wonderful.

"Captain Crispin!" he cried.

Needle ordered herself not to be afraid. Frightened animals trembled, and if she trembled she would almost certainly fall off the ledge. She had to be small and still, and listen. The scuffling of paws had stopped, but now she heard weapons clanking, which was worse. She strained to hear Tay.

"Attend to me, moles," announced Tay. "It is enough for you to know that I have discovered a site where a certain person—a certain person of high rank, who ought to know better—I might say, a certain otter—is carrying out highly illegal and unsuitable practices."

Needle couldn't quite hear her next words, only some muttering between two moles. One asked, "What's she on about?" and "She means Captain Padra's up to something," answered the other. But her next words were clear, and chilled Needle to the bone.

"There are various ways to this place," said Tay. "I will send you in the appropriate mole tunnels, while I take the otter route. Do not enter the place until you hear my signal. I will cough twice. Then we storm the site and arrest whatever we find there, however young, however innocent it looks. Arrest them all and bring them to the tower."

No, no, thought Needle. She must mean the place where Scufflen's hidden. No, no.

There was more clinking of arms; then the tramping of paws faded into the distance. Needle clenched her claws. She was in danger; the hiding place was in danger; and she could do nothing. When the moles had been silent for some time and she was about to take the chance of crying out, she heard a movement close by.

This time, there were young voices. Moles, mostly. One of them giggled.

"Come on," said a kind voice. "You're doing fine. Keep going."

"He's as determined as a mole," said another; then, "I smell hedge-hog!"

"That's me," said a very young hedgehog voice.

"No!" called Needle. "It's me! I'm Needle, and I'm stuck!"

There was a pause, then some whispering among the young animals. She picked up her own name, and Urchin's, and somebody said, "Scufflen's sister." Then a mole voice was raised, a pleasant female voice.

"Stay put. We're digging through." There was a lot of scraping and scratching, then, "Ouch!"

"Sorry," said Needle. "My spines are stuck in the earth. They're a bit sharp."

Presently a paw appeared, digging a hole through the wall. Soon, the hole was just wide enough for Needle to squeeze through. Cautiously, with a lot of "Ouch!" from the moles and "Sorry!" from Needle, she shuffled from the ledge into the safety of a freshly dug tunnel, face-to-face with a small mole maid.

"I'm Moth," said the mole maid, and nodded toward the two other moles with her. "And Jig and Fig: they're sisters. And this is Hope."

A very small hedgehog snuffled nearsightedly in Needle's direction.

"A very good morning, Mistress Needle," he said politely.

"It won't be if we're not quick," said Needle, and in a rush she told them all she had heard.

Moth nodded to the other moles. "You two get Hope to a safe burrow," she said. "If we go by a secret way, we can get to the nursery before Tay does. Needle, come with me."

She vanished so that Needle lost sight of her and had to follow the sound of racing paws. Behind her, she heard the hedgehog explaining hopefully that his mummy worked in the tower and he could go to her, and the moles gently explaining that the tower really wasn't a safe place for him just now. Then there was only the long gallop through the tunnels, Needle's heart pounding harder and harder as she ran, her legs aching, her chest hurting, a stitch gripping her side. She followed Moth down the tunnels, scrabbling upward, gathering pace on the way down, twisting, following the darting mole in and out, squeezing through tiny entrances until she suddenly found herself in a well-lit room. After the dark tunnels, she had to blink and turn away until her eyes adjusted, but Moth was already gabbling out their story to Arran the otter, who stood up on her hind legs and clapped her paws.

"We're about to be raided," she announced briskly. "They mustn't find us, and they mustn't find any sign of us. We'll go by the water route. No arguments, no tears. You'll get your paws wet, that's all. Pick up everything; burn what we don't need. Sort out the babies. If it can walk, lead it; if it can't, carry it. Look sharp!"

Everyone ran to obey. Mother Huggen bundled up blankets and food. Arran kicked nests into a jumble of moss. The fire was quenched.

"We can't take the water jars," said Arran with a frown.

"Excuse me," said Needle, "but does it matter if they know Padra's been here? There's no reason why he shouldn't be. It's only hiding the babies that's against the law."

"Well thought of!" said Arran. "That means we don't have to carry absolutely everything. Just don't leave anything babyish. What's your name?"

"Needle," she said.

"Oh!" Arran nodded at a nest. "That one's yours."

Needle had been too caught up in the escape to think of her brother. But there he was, and he was awake! Bright-eyed, he peered from his nest, his nose twitching. Needle picked him up.

"And as we go to the tunnel, walk backward, sweeping the floor," ordered Arran. "No pawprints."

Standing on an upturned boat, Padra gazed out to sea. Urchin should not have gone alone and he blamed himself bitterly, but it was too late now. He slipped into the water and thought over his plans for the

Spring Festival. Only two days to go. It was his chance to challenge Husk, and everything depended on whether the animals of Mistmantle would rally to his side. He had to convince them. With Lugg and Arran, a few very young animals, and a pawful of dead leaves, he had to save the whole island. The future of Mistmantle lay with him, and he felt intensely lonely.

He turned in the water, reluctant to go back to his own rooms. Without Urchin, they would feel as empty as hunger.

Tay coughed loudly and strode into the Old Palace. A column of moles tore in, swords raised, and stopped.

"It's empty," said one.

Another kicked the hearth. "Someone was here," he said.

"There's water in them jars," said another. "But that just proves somebody's been here. Might be Captain Padra. So what if he was?"

Tay dropped to all fours. She inspected the floor, the ceiling, the corners. She sniffed, scraped, and peered. The moles seemed more interested in standing back to gaze at the twisted roots all round them.

"Babies," muttered Tay. "They were here. I smell babies. You're all dismissed. And nobody is to mention this place, at all, ever. You are all pledged to secrecy, on pain of punishment."

The moles trudged away, grumbling. Tay sat down with her head on her paws. For years, she had dreamed of finding the Old Palace.

Was this all there was? A big, empty room with nothing to it but a few old tree roots? And she had shared it with a lot of gawping, idiot moles.

Padra had certainly been rescuing young animals, she was sure of that. Somehow they must have been warned of her coming, and escaped. But there must be evidence. Sniffing, running back and forth, she searched.

CHAPTER TWENTY

As Crispin clasped Urchin by the shoulders and stood back to look at him, Urchin struggled to identify exactly what had changed in Crispin. He no longer wore his circlet, and his coat was not so well brushed as it had been. But that wasn't all. Something of the brightness had left his face. He had lost the sharp-eyed look and the ready-for-anything air that went with being a captain. Urchin hadn't really noticed it before, but he noticed now that it had gone. He hoped he didn't look disappointed. After the first joy of seeing him, Crispin frowned.

"Why are you here?" Crispin demanded. "They haven't sent you away, too, have they? What's happening?"

"I came for you, sir," said Urchin. "And because I had to, but . . ." Then he realized how much had happened since Crispin left Mistmantle, and how long it would take to tell. "There's a lot to explain," he said. "And I've brought your breakfast, sir."

He unpacked walnut bread and honey cakes and explained all that had happened on Mistmantle. When Crispin first tasted the bread, his eyes closed. He became so silent that Urchin thought he'd gone into some kind of trance, but then he opened his eyes, sighed deeply, and said, "I'd forgotten how good this bread was. It tastes of home. I wonder where Whisper went? Go on, Urchin, I'm still listening."

Urchin went on, and they were interrupted only once when a bright-eyed female squirrel arrived and Crispin sprang up, held out a paw for her to join them, and offered her walnut bread. Urchin noticed firstly that she was very pretty and wore Crispin's circlet, and secondly that Crispin looked more like his old self when she was there.

"This is Whisper," he announced, drawing her forward. "Without Whisper, I would have forgotten who I am. Whisper, this is Urchin."

"The one Crispin found in the sea?" said Whisper. She had a soft voice and a warm smile. "I've heard about you."

"Come and have breakfast, Whisper—find out what real food tastes like," said Crispin. "Urchin, I would have drowned in a frozen mere if not for Whisper."

Whisper shrugged. "It was Lord Arcneck who fished him out," she said. "Crispin had just rescued Lady Arcneck from drowning when she was being dragged under by the weeds."

"And Whisper revived me and took care of me when I was more

dead than alive," insisted Crispin. "But go on with your story, Urchin."

Urchin finished his story. "Padra's planning a move against Husk at the Spring Festival," he said. "But we want your help. I didn't search for you just to escape, sir—we need to find a way to get you back. I know it's impossible. But we have to *make* it possible."

Crispin looked out to sea. "If I'd been a better captain, this might not have happened," he said. "I should have seen what Husk was doing and stopped it. I thought I'd learned to live without Mistmantle. Mistmantle!"

He gazed as if he thought he could see the island if he looked hard and long enough. "I was becoming used to living in exile," he said. "But seeing you, hearing about it, tasting the food—I'd even drink Apple's appalling cordial if I could go home. Oh, I beg your pardon, Urchin, I forgot she was your foster mother."

"That's all right," said Urchin. "I never drank it if I could help it. I used to pour it down mole tunnels when she wasn't looking. The moles didn't like it either, sir."

Whisper laughed, and Crispin tilted his head to look at her. "Would you come with me to Mistmantle?" he asked.

"Of course I would!" she said as if it were a silly question.

"There may be tunnels," said Crispin, "but not necessarily big enough for squirrels, and they'd be far below the seabed. I don't know the networks, or how you breathe down there. And it would take too long. I wish there were a priest here. If we all prayed, the Heart might find us a way through the mists."

"I'll pray, sir," said Urchin eagerly.

"We all will," smiled Crispin. "And while we're at it, we can just sail at the mists and see how far we get. They might let us through somehow. 'Those who belong here can leave by water, but they can never return by water.' Maybe I don't belong there any longer, so I can get back! It's worth a try!"

"But you do belong there, sir!" said Urchin.

"Well, before we do anything, I should take you to Lord Arcneck," said Crispin. "He's the Swan Lord. I'm bound to his service, so if I do leave, I'll need his permission."

"But you're a captain of Mistmantle, sir!" said Urchin.

"We're not on Mistmantle," said Crispin.

"I'll stay with your boat," said Whisper, and sprang to the prow where she perched like a figurehead. "Some of the wood squirrels would ransack it, given the chance."

"Thank you, Wh—" began Urchin; then, remembering how to address a captain's partner, corrected himself. "Lady Whisper."

"Yes," said Crispin, with a bright smile. "I'd forgotten that! You're Lady Whisper! Come on, Urchin!"

Urchin walked at Crispin's side to the lake, smiling because he could still hear Whisper's laughter. Probably, he thought, she was laughing at the idea of being "Lady Whisper." He found he was thinking about his mother, and imagining that she might have been like Whisper. He hoped so.

Crispin asked several questions about how many animals would rally to Husk, and what was in the armory, and who appointed the guards. Urchin answered to what he did know and admitted what he didn't, realizing how much he had learned in his few months as a page. From above them came a deep, steady beat, and a draft. Urchin looked up and ducked. He couldn't help it.

"Lord Arcneck," said Crispin. "The Swan Lord. He's circling the island. The swans have a very high opinion of themselves and their own importance, and as this is their island, they expect—"

From the beach below them came a shriek.

Leaping down the hill, swords drawn, Crispin and Urchin reached the shore. Whisper lay absolutely still where she had fallen, one paw thrown out as if she had tried to defend herself, the circlet still on her head. Crispin flung himself down and raised her head as he searched for a pulse and listened for a breath, but there was no life left in her. As Urchin fastened both paws around his sword hilt, he saw a sleek shadow leap from the boat.

"Crispin!" Urchin yelled, and sprang forward. There was a terrible snarl from Gloss, a flash of Crispin's sword, a blaze of blood—then there was only darkness and confusion as wide white wings covered them all, knocking Urchin onto his back and hiding Crispin and Gloss from him.

The wings lifted, and he jumped to his paws again. A swan, huge, white and terrifying, stood above him, with the helpless mole in its beak, shaking him like a rag. Finally, the swan dropped Gloss's body on the sand and nudged it over with his beak.

Urchin stared. That orange beak looked as long as his own arm from paw to shoulder. The neck was thick and strong as a snake, and the feathers were magnificent. When the proud head turned toward him, he bowed without thinking.

Crispin, his teeth bared and his fur bloodstained, was looking down at Gloss's body. Urchin couldn't tell whether Crispin's sword thrust had killed the mole before the swan had broken its neck.

"Sir," said Urchin nervously, "are you . . ." He stopped. He couldn't say, "Are you hurt?" Of course Crispin was hurt. It burned in his eyes, it raged in the shaking of his paws. It was so real and raw that Urchin felt it himself.

"Are you wounded?" he asked, but Crispin took no notice. The swan turned fierce eyes to him.

"Tree-rat!" it said. "What tree-rat are you?"

"I'm Urchin, sir," he said. "Crispin's page."

"Page? Page? What is a page?"

"His servant, sir."

"Then serve him!" snapped the swan. So Urchin took seawater to wash the blood from Whisper and Crispin. Then he fetched a dry cloak from the boat because he thought Crispin might need one, though he hardly seemed to notice Urchin folding it around his shoulders. And even though Urchin knew Whisper was dead and could feel nothing, he thought she looked cold, so he brought a blanket. There were crumbs of honey cake on her fur, and he bent to brush them away.

"Don't," said Crispin, but he took the blanket and spread it over her.

The swan tossed Gloss's body away. "How came this vermin?" it asked.

Urchin swallowed hard.

"I'm afraid he must have been in my boat, Lord Swan," he said miserably. "I didn't know." And he wondered how Crispin could ever forgive him for carrying Whisper's death to the island.

The swan stretched its neck and raised its wings.

"*You* brought this foul murderer?" it rasped.

Urchin bowed his head and wished that wretchedness were a thing he could die of. If the swan struck him dead, he deserved it. "Yes, sir," he whispered. "I'm sorry. I didn't mean it."

Crispin looked up from Whisper's body. "No, my Lord Arcneck," he said. "Urchin did not bring the mole. He came to seek my help for his island, and the mole came by stealth, with evil intent. It's not your fault, Urchin, not at all. Gloss would have been looking for me, and he saw a squirrel with a circlet . . ." His voice failed, and Urchin waited until he could go on. "Tell him what's happening at home, Urchin."

Urchin told the swan all he had just told Crispin. Crispin wasn't listening. He knelt on the shore, cradling Whisper's body in the blanket.

"Vermin," said the swan at last. "Crispin, you have served me well. If your island is riddled with vermin, I permit you to return and destroy them." And with a power that took Urchin's breath away, it spread its wings and rose into the air.

Urchin wasn't sure Crispin had heard Lord Arcneck at all. He knelt as if pain had turned him to stone, and Urchin wondered what to do.

Whisper ought to have flowers. He could see pink sea-thrift and coarse-stemmed daises nearby, and hopped away to gather some. Crispin had still not moved when he came back.

"Flowers for her, sir," Urchin said awkwardly.

Crispin gave a brief nod, and Urchin knelt shyly to put the flowers in Whisper's limp paws. Crispin folded her claws around them.

"Leave us," he said. "I'll do everything else."

"Yes, sir," said Urchin, and though he wasn't sure if it was the right thing to say, he had to say it. "Sir, I hope my mother was like her."

Crispin nodded again. "Go, Urchin," he said hoarsely, and Urchin hurried away, understanding that Crispin wouldn't want anyone to see his tears. He found a hollow in a tree root and huddled there alone, rubbing a paw across his eyes when they blurred. Perhaps this was the worst at last. After this, nothing could feel worse.

When he felt he had left Crispin alone long enough, he pattered back to the shore to find him. Something was moving among the beech trees, and his paw was on his sword hilt before he realized it was Crispin.

In a clearing, Crispin had built a neat mound of sea-washed stones, gray and green, smooth flint and dull pink. On the top lay the circlet.

"I had to build her a cairn," said Crispin, laying a bunch of sea-thrift beside it. "It marks her place. And the circlet—it's hers and it should be there where it can be seen; but I hate to think of anyone taking it away."

"I think you should keep it, sir," said Urchin. "Look after it for her. And, sir, you should have it with you when you go back to Mistmantle, because it would be like taking her back with you."

"No, Urchin, it wouldn't," said Crispin.

"I mean as near as you can get to it, sir," said Urchin, wishing he hadn't spoken in the first place. He thought of something all Mistmantle squirrels learned from an early age. Fir and Apple had taught it to him. *Even the Heart that made Mistmantle had to break with love for us. That is how it gave us the mists. But it does not stay broken. The Heart still beats, still loves, still holds us. A true heart survives the breaking.* But he couldn't very well say it to Crispin now. He wandered miserably back to the bay, where a swan floated, bobbing a little with the lifting of the waves. Two more flew overhead and settled as gently as petals on the sea, circling each other, proud and graceful as sailing ships. And Urchin, pausing to perch on a rock, gaze at the swans, and admire their size and strength, saw a possible hope.

There was a way home.

CHAPTER TWENTY-ONE

WHO NEEDED SLEEP? Husk hurried past the chambers where tower squirrels lay curled in their nests and beds. Only fools and infants needed sleep. This would be his day, and he watched impatiently for its coming. It would be dry and fine. A great day. *His* Spring Festival.

A dais had been built on the rocks, with awnings behind and above it. Space in front had been cleared for the entertainers, and the tables for the feast would be in a semicircle to face it. On the dais would be a throne for the king, with more modest chairs for himself, Aspen, Granite, and Padra, and a high table. It was a shame to include Padra, but it wouldn't be for long. The order of speeches was to be Granite, Tay, Padra, then himself—but after Tay's speech, there would be no Padra.

Splendor was the thing that mattered. He had gone to great trouble to ensure that the Threadings were rich and gilded; the high table would be hung with deep gold brocade velvet and decorated with flowers; and robes would be worn. Swords, too, just for show; and the throne would be decked with purple velvet. The creatures would have to be impressed by all that grandeur. It would make the king look ridiculous.

Husk was especially pleased about the king. Ultimately, no interfering priest or goody-goody squirrel had been able to help him, and now the great King Brushen was thoroughly wretched and broken. He could hardly mutter a sentence without tears, or listen to a choir without falling asleep. If he'd been drinking, he could hardly walk in a straight line. Most of the animals hadn't seen him since the queen's funeral. They wouldn't like what they'd see today.

Husk's wedding robe was spread across the chest in the bedchamber. It was too early to dress, but he needed to touch it once more, and press its jewels against his cheek. He had a storehouse of jewels now, for trade, for payments, for bribes, and for himself. Jewels would buy anything.

Sharply, he looked over his shoulder. Was he being watched? Followed? Couldn't be too careful. Expecting Aspen to be asleep, he slipped silently into the bedchamber, but he found her awake and perched on the edge of the bed, grooming her ear tufts with the little ebony brush.

"The king has spent a restless night," she remarked thoughtfully. "He was asking for me. I took him the spring water he likes, with a little tincture in it to calm him."

"Didn't he have a sleeping draft last night?" asked Husk.

"Oh, no!" Her dark eyes widened. "Brother Fir was concerned about the sleeping drafts the king was having. Brother Fir is the priest, after all. So I didn't give the king anything last night to help him sleep. Unfortunately, it's left him in a terrible state this morning." She turned the large brown eyes on him. "He's a very sad sight."

Husk shook his head slowly in admiration. "You think of everything," he said. "What would I do without you? Should I have a bottle of wine placed before him at the high table? He might like a drink during the entertainments."

"And a flask at his hip," said Aspen. "I'll keep it filled up. And what about you, my lord? Have you slept?"

"I don't need to," he said, and turned away. Urchin, who had disappeared so suddenly and conveniently, was part of his nightmares now. And still the bloodstained prince scrabbled his way through fusty darkness toward him. . . .

It was better not to sleep.

Padra was up early, too, climbing the stairs to Fir's turret, where Brother Fir knelt in such stillness that Padra was content to close the door quietly and watch him, drinking in his serenity. Presently he moved to kneel beside him and realized that Fir had been aware of him all the time, for he reached out to place a paw on his head in blessing. Padra's heart reached out to the Heart that beat for Mistmantle, kept it, loved it, enfolded it, and nourished it, and as he did so, the first rays of sun filtered through the window. At last, Fir and Padra rose and looked down from the turret.

In a bay half hidden by the curve of the shore, a row of little boats had been pulled clear of the tideline. Some had been turned upside down, to drain them or dry them for painting.

"They're in the green one," whispered Padra. "I daren't go there myself, in case I'm watched, but that's it. A bit closer to the tower than I'd like, but it's only temporary, and it means I can get a message to Huggen quickly if I need to."

"Hm," said Fir. "Bless them." He raised a paw toward the distant boat.

"Our animals are ready and at their posts," said Padra, still whispering. "They all know what to do. We stay alert during the entertainment and the feast, then I just have to keep my nerve during the offerings and the speeches. Lugg, Arran, and a few of the faithful ones will be on the lookout, in case Husk and his claw thugs try anything. When I make my speech and show Husk for what he is, we count on the animals rallying to me. It all depends on that. The Anemone Wooders and the otters will be with me. But if it comes to a fight—and I hate the thought of Mistmantle animals shedding one another's blood—Husk's animals will be better armed."

"It should not come to that," said Fir. He shook his ears. "That excellent otter in charge of food stores, does she look after the candles as well?"

"Candles?" said Padra. "I've no idea." From respect, he didn't ask why Fir wanted candles when the whole future of the island was at stake, but he found the question irritating. "I'll go down and see what Husk is up to. Don't stop praying, Fir. And pray for Urchin: the Heart alone knows where he is and what's happening to him. I still expect to find him two paces behind me, waiting for orders."

The sun rose higher on a fair, bright day. From their colonies all over the island, the animals gathered: families with their infants carried or led by the paw, little knots of young females whispering together about the males while the males showed off, and pretended not to notice them. Elderly creatures leaned on the shoulders of the young. Young tower animals, like Needle, who had been given the day off, ran out to meet their friends and families. Even the kitchen workers, who were still busy, popped out for a moment in their aprons to greet their friends. They would be allowed to join in the celebrations. Only adults worked in the kitchen on feast days, taking turns to join the fun.

Emerging from the woods, they gasped. The young ones stared in breathtaken astonishment. The old stopped saying that feasts these days were nothing like feasts in the old days, and shook their heads slowly in wonder. All of them wondered and whispered about the great generosity of Captain Husk.

From every turret of Mistmantle Tower, pennants fluttered in the wind. Banners hung from windows. A cloth of purple and gold had been spread over the throne, with a canopy high above it. All around it were splendid new Threadings. The feast had not yet been spread, but fresh, white cloths covered the tables, garlanded with spring flowers and branches. Most of the young squirrels ran into the treetops for a good view, and a few climbed onto the scaffolding and were sharply ordered down again. Then they all fell silent.

The chattering stopped. There was no more wriggling, no more staring up at the pennants. The trumpeters—two hedgehogs, two squirrels, and two otters—all in red tunics, marched from the tower with silver trumpets flashing in the sunlight. They formed a guard of honor and played a fanfare. Two guard moles saluted.

Four hedgehogs with gleaming fur led the procession. Then came Captain Granite and Captain Padra side by side, one in green and gold, one in sea-turquoise and silver. Sunlight shone from their circlets. But a moment later, nobody was watching them at all. The crowd gasped.

The gasp could have been for Husk, or for Aspen. Aspen, with a pale gold cloak drifting from her shoulders and a ring of spring flowers on her head, looked even lovelier than on her wedding day, and Husk was magnificent. In his shining circlet and gleaming robe, striding out into the spring morning with his head high, his sword at one hip and a dagger at the other, he looked like a lord. He looked, the animals whispered to each other, as if he should be King of Mistmantle.

At a signal from Husk, the captains and Lady Aspen turned and knelt. Everyone knelt. King Brushen appeared in the doorway, and Husk and Aspen rose quickly to take his paws before he could fall.

The crowds cheered for their king, but it was a dull cheer. It was embarrassing to see him like this. His shoulders drooped, his feet shuffled, his spines stood out at all angles. His eyes were bloodshot beneath the crown, and his face bleary. His paws trembled. But Husk and Aspen, alert to his needs, held his paws and helped him gently to his throne. They were followed by Tay and Brother Fir, but hardly anyone noticed them. Closer to the animals, slumped in his throne, the king looked worse than ever. Then, to the great relief of all the animals, the entertainments began.

And those entertainments were wonderful. Hedgehogs recited their poems with drama and tension. Comical hedgehogs fell over one another until the small otters were rolling over the grass laughing. Otters played on pipes and turned spectacular somersaults. Moles juggled with berries and gave glittering demonstrations of fencing. But the squirrels outshone the rest, singing, dancing, leaping, twisting, balancing, and somersaulting, all with dazzling speed and twirling of tails. Mole maids moved through the audience with little cups of wine and delicate biscuits, all with the compliments of Captain Husk and Lady Aspen, and all agreed that Husk and Aspen knew how to give a truly magnificent festival. Then, at a signal from Padra, a young squirrel took her place on the stage and sang so sweetly that the excited crowd calmed. Every creature listened in fascination, and some wiped away tears.

"Enchanting!" exclaimed Aspen, leaning forward in her seat. "Who is she?"

"Her name is Sepia, my lady," said Padra. "An exceptional talent. I was lucky to find her."

"Sweet," said Aspen. A choir of very small squirrels followed, and two or three of them danced.

"Delightful little things," said Aspen, putting out a paw to help the king, who had fallen asleep and was about to drop off the throne. Husk moved behind to heave him up. "His poor Majesty," whispered Aspen to Padra. "He drinks too deeply. It helps him forget his grief."

As the animals watched the entertainment, Husk watched the audience. They were enjoying the festival enormously. It was good. The king had nodded off again. Let him be.

Tay's attention was not on the entertainment. It was not at all her sort of thing, and she still had vital work to complete before the speeches. Absolute living proof of what Padra was up to was still needed. She looked past the crowds to the shore where little boats were lined up. From her high seat on the dais, she could see all the way to a green boat upside down at the end.

Something moved. It was a tiny movement far away, and she wasn't sure what, but whatever it was, it was in the wrong place. Sometimes crabs or toads sheltered under the boats, but even a tiny glimpse told her that it was not a crab or a toad.

She narrowed her eyes and looked more carefully. The boat had been propped up a little on stones at one end so that it did not quite touch the ground. Why leave a gap?

She kept watching.

The smaller animals were becoming restless, eyeing the tables hopefully. The sun was high. It was time for the king to announce the beginning of the feast, but he was slumped in his throne with a glazed look on his face.

Padra stepped over to Husk. "One of us will have to announce the feast," he said. "The king can't."

"Of course His Majesty can!" said Husk indignantly. He rose, offered a paw, and led the king in tottering steps to the edge of the dais. Rage seethed in Padra.

"Oh, the king's mantle is too heavy!" said Aspen in concern. "Let me take it. Help me, Granite."

In view of the watching animals, Aspen and Granite lifted the robe from the king's shoulders and straightened his crown. There he stood, a confused, disheveled hedgehog, with a crown and no robe; and everyone could see that he no longer carried a sword. He wore a silver flask at his hip instead.

"Anmals of Mismannel," slurred the king, "here we gather a . . . th . . . Summer Festfal."

"Spring Festival, Your Majesty," whispered Husk.

". . . Heart brought safely through anerr win . . . winner. We praisa

Heart, we give thangs. The feast is . . . begin!"

Feebly, he clapped his paws. Husk helped him back to the throne, and the feast began.

The animals, bustling and chattering, found places at the long tables as servants processed from the tower with bowls and baskets, plates and platters. There were round cakes of nuts, pies and pastries, and every kind of bread the island could provide; vats of soup, bowls of crisped seaweed, whole fishes, honey cakes, biscuits, and cheeses from faraway islands; butter, cream, and berries. Fruit was piled high, glowing with color. Crumbs stuck to whiskers, paws grew sticky, juice dribbled onto fur.

As loyal as a hedgehog, as determined as a mole, as bright as a squirrel, as valiant as on otter . . . Padra repeated the old saying to himself as he excused himself from the high table. He found Arran, who was giving orders to the serving moles.

"Don't let them give the hedgehogs too much wine," he told her. "We're depending on their support."

Arran snatched up empty flagons from the table, looked around, and saw Needle. "Needle!" she called. "Get a couple of friends and fill these at the spring." She turned to Padra. "I'll tell the staff to water down the pear wine."

Needle, with a flagon in each paw, waited until Arran was out of hearing range.

"Captain Padra, sir," she said, looking up a little shyly. "Excuse me, may I ask something about Arran, sir?"

"Yes, what about her?" said Padra, surveying the crowd.

"If she asked you to marry her, would you *really* laugh?"

"*What?*" said Padra. He laughed, and stopped suddenly. "Why do you ask? Is that what she says?"

"Um . . ." But Needle felt she had said enough. She found Crackle—they were friends now—and they scuttled off together. Padra sent for Lugg, and Tay watched the boat.

The infants from the Old Palace had been moved, for the time being, to a place of safety on the shore. It was cramped, but they were happy to build sand castles, and a party was underway. Moth and Mother Huggen wore their best frilly aprons and flower necklaces. Arran had smuggled in generous supplies of food and drink from the feast, including soft puddings and mashed-up fruit for the very small ones, and a good supply of worms and grubs as many of the animals couldn't manage anything richer. Moth, eating a dainty elderflower pastry, lay by the gap between boat and sand to see all she could of the festival. Mother Huggen, spooning lemon-cream porridge sideways into the mouth of a baby hedgehog, smiled kindly at her. Occasionally a small and inquisitive otter would wriggle free from the others and push its shiny black nose under the boat, only to be pushed firmly back by Moth or pulled by Mother Huggen.

"You go out to the festival for a bit, young Moth," said Mother

Huggen. "They'll all drop off to sleep, now we've fed them. You go and have a bit of fun."

"I'd like that," said Moth. "I'll go when I've finished this pastry."

Gleaner stood on duty behind Aspen's chair. She wasn't needed much, but she wanted to be seen with Lady Aspen.

When Aspen gave her the king's flask to fill from the decanter in the Throne Room, she scampered off with it at once. Lugg the mole popped up suddenly in front of her.

"I'll do that, miss, thank you, miss."

"But it's . . ."

"The king's, miss, to fill up. Leave it to me, miss. Captain's orders, miss."

Gleaner supposed it would be all right. Even empty, the flask was heavy. Now she had a chance to slip to the tower and style her ear tufts like Lady Aspen's.

Lugg hobbled away purposefully toward the spring and met Needle and Crackle staggering back with slopping flagons in their paws. "Is that fresh spring water?" he said. "Let's have some."

Aspen hardly noticed the guard mole bringing the silver flask back. She was cleaning up the black-currant juice the king had dribbled down his chest.

"Young squirrel asked me to bring this," said Lugg. "Heavy for her."

"Poor little Gleaner," said Aspen. She fastened the flask to the king's belt, and went on cleaning him up.

It would soon be time for the speeches. Tay slipped away. In law it was possible for a king to be replaced if he could no longer rule. King Brushen could be deposed, and Husk put in his place. But Padra would oppose it, so evidence against him was vital.

Quickly and quietly, she loped across the rocks and scrambled down to the shore. The boat was completely unguarded. Wriggling low into the sand, Tay pushed her nose under the gap and saw what she had hoped to see.

A hedgehog in an apron bent over a row of nests. Basins, blankets, balls of wool, and knitting needles were stacked neatly on the sand. A small squirrel wearing a bib sat up in a nest.

"It's Padra, Padra, Padra!" it squeaked, and Mother Huggen turned with a smile that changed to horror.

"Oh, dear Heart!" she shrieked, and stammered desperately. "I—I—I wasn't expecting company, Mistress Tay!"

"No," said Tay. "But you were expecting Captain Padra." Before Mother Huggen could move, she shot out a paw and snatched the squirrel from its nest, holding it tightly by the paw. "So this is Padra's nursery!"

"No, mistress, it's my nursery," said Huggen firmly. "And excuse me, mistress, but if you don't let that squirrel go at once, I'm afraid I'll have to bite you."

"Bite an otter of the Circle?" said Tay. "This animal is evidence. So is this one," she added, snatching Hope the hedgehog. "This boat is crawling with deformed creatures who were meant for the cull. You're all under arrest. There's no point in trying to escape. The guards will be here in two minutes. I'm taking these two as evidence."

She wriggled backward, but to her great surprise she found difficulty in moving. There was something the matter with her hind paws.

Tay wriggled more, and turned her head, trying to crawl out from the boat with a squirrel in one paw and a hedgehog in the other. She just had time to see a small mole maid tying her hind paws together with a frilly apron before the baby squirrel bit her. A blanket was wedged between her teeth; another was over her head; and she was trapped.

CHAPTER TWENTY-TWO

NEEDLE, WHO HAD WORKED LATE INTO THE NIGHT, struggled to stay awake during the speeches. The offerings of gifts to the king had been made, and now Captain Granite was speaking in a boring drone as if he had learned his speech by heart and didn't understand it. Hedgehogs had curled up to rest. Some of the moles had slipped away down tunnels. Otters basked in the sunshine, and even the squirrels were yawning. This wouldn't do. Padra needed them to be wide awake.

"King Brushen has been a great king . . ." droned on Captain Granite. Needle shuffled from her place and wriggled through the crowds.

"Ouch!" said a mole.

"Ooh!" said a hedgehog.

"Sorry," said Needle, but she wasn't. It was useful to be so sharp. She wove her way through the animals, jostling and prickling everyone she met. They didn't like it, but it kept them awake. Over a mole muttering "Tell that hedgehog to sit down" came the dull voice of Captain Granite.

"When King Brushen can no longer bear the burden of being our king, we can rely on Captain Husk. Sadly, this time is very near."

Needle stared in astonishment and looked around to see if the other animals were as shocked as she was. Some were staring with open mouths as if they ought to protest, but didn't know what to say. But others were nodding in agreement. They'd seen how ill the king was. It was only reasonable to let him abdicate. Husk would be a good king. Come to think of it, King Brushen hadn't been all that good. He'd given them work parties and culling. He would have rationed the food if Captain Husk hadn't stopped him. And wouldn't Lady Aspen be a lovely queen?

Many more animals seemed hardly to have noticed. They were too bored, or snoring on the tables.

Granite sat down. There was some polite clapping of paws and a hiccup from a sleeping baby otter.

A hedgehog stood up and announced, "Mistress Tay to speak next."

There was a long pause. "Mistress Tay?" he said again.

Guards scuttled about, looking for Tay. Animals suddenly realized that something interesting was happening, and sat up. Someone was sent to the tower to find her, but Tay still did not appear.

Needle stretched up on her hind paws to see the dais. Husk and Padra sat, absolutely calm, with nothing on their faces but polite interest.

Inside, Husk seethed with anger. This was not what he had planned. Tay had promised evidence that would have Padra arrested for treason on the spot. The king would be distressed, so he would be taken gently back to the tower with Brother Fir to look after him. Then, with all of them out of the way, Husk only needed to claim the crown, and the animals would give it.

Padra hoped he looked perfectly calm. He had no idea what had happened to Tay. He suspected that this was part of Husk's plan, and that Tay would suddenly stride up to the dais claiming that he'd murdered somebody, or tried to burn down the tower. He remembered telling Crispin to keep his nerve. Now he told it to himself. Guards were reporting back to Husk, but none of them had news of Tay.

"I see," said Husk thoughtfully, and leaned over to talk to Padra. Granite moved in closer. So did Fir.

"What can we do?" said Husk. "Padra can't speak until Tay's had her turn. I'm afraid we'll have to cancel your speech, Padra."

"But, Captain Husk," said Fir mildly. "You can't speak until after Captain Padra. So it seems that none of you can make a speech."

"Perhaps we should send the animals home," said Husk. He had looked forward to his triumph, but it could wait for another day.

"Without your speech?" said Fir. "Dear, dear me! How could we? They're looking forward so much to hearing you, Husk. Padra won't take long, will you, Padra?"

Padra had slipped down from his chair. He knelt at the king's paws and looked up into the sad, puzzled face of the king he still loved, and still served.

"Your Majesty?" he said.

"His Majesty is not well," said Aspen quickly. She offered him his flask, and he drank deeply.

The king looked down and saw Padra's kind face smiling up at him. The cold water helped to clear his head. *Padra the Plodder. Good fellow.*

"Do you command me to make my speech now, Your Majesty?" said Padra.

"Speech? Of course I do, Padra!" said the king, and raised his voice. "I command Captain Padra to speak!"

Husk snarled very softly. Padra walked to the front of the dais. Needle, watching from the front of the crowd, was aware of a shuffling behind and around her. The Anemone Wooders were moving to their places.

"Good creatures of Mistmantle," said Padra, "Your Majesty, Lady Aspen, Captain Husk, Captain Granite, Brother Fir. I won't keep you long, and I promise not to bore you."

There was no chance of being bored now. Since Tay had failed to appear, the animals had woken up. Something was going on.

"Some years ago," began Padra, "when the culling law was first established, a small squirrel was carried to the tower. She was very tiny, hardly feeding at all, and struggling to breathe, and there were those who thought she should be culled. Crispin, Fir, and I made the point that the squirrel had been born the day before the culling law was made. The king agreed that only animals born after that date could be culled. If she had been born a day later she would have been killed, but she lived. Today, she sang to you. Her name is Sepia."

A murmur ran through the animals. Husk growled.

"Since then," said Padra, "it has concerned me that some very noble animals were too eager to cull. If culling is the king's law, no animal should be culled without his express command."

Husk's eyes were fixed on Padra's back. He stamped his hind paw on the dais.

Padra nodded to Arran, who stood in front of the dais. She carried the new baby otter in one paw and in the other, wriggling a little and poking his tongue out, was Needle's brother Scufflen. Needle's spines bristled with tension.

Oh, Heart, Heart, Heart, she prayed silently. *Protect him, protect him.*

She found she was holding her breath. Padra gently took Scufflen from Arran's paws, smoothing the spines that were not yet sharp. He knelt beside the king.

"Your Majesty," he said. "This animal was condemned to death simply for being small, with the slightest curling on a hind paw. And the otter, she's not deformed at all, but an order was given for her death."

The king bent over Scufflen, picked him up, sat him on his knee, and smiled down at him. His eyes were wet.

"Oh, Heart love 'im!" said Apple's voice from the crowd. There was a little laughter and a murmur of approval.

"Your Majesty," said Padra, raising his voice. "Did you order the killing of these animals?"

"Certainly not!" growled the king.

"The poor king cannot be expected to deal with every little culling!" exclaimed Aspen.

"Little culling!" said Padra handing the animals back to Arran. "Is the death of an animal a little thing? If the king does not command them, who does?" He rounded on the crowd. "Do you know who does? Shall I tell you? All this culling is Captain Husk's idea, not the king's! The harsh work parties, too—do you think that idea comes from the king? These are Husk's orders! The king appears before you today, wretched and pitiable, because that is how Captain Husk has made him! You think you've had a fine feast because Husk provided it, but Husk wanted to ration your food all winter. Arran the otter has managed the food stores; that's who you should thank for your feast!"

The animals were all on their hind paws. Ears twitched; eyes were bright. A ring of hedgehogs and otters had gathered around the dais, closing very gradually round Husk and the king. Needle edged closer to Arran.

"What would you have eaten if the food had been rationed?" went on Padra. "What could you find? Beech leaves?" He whirled around to face Husk. "Would animals have eaten beech leaves, Captain Husk? Is that why you stored them? Beech leaves, like the ones we used for the casting of lots, when Crispin was found guilty of murder?"

The king struggled to stand. Lady Aspen leaped up.

"The king is distressed!" she cried.

"The king is angry," said Padra. "Arran, stay with him, please."

"Easier said than done," muttered Arran. "I've got my arms full of babies. Needle, hold that." She pushed Scufflen into Needle's paws, and gave the little otter to its mother. Followed by two hedgehogs, she climbed onto the dais, with a withering glare at Aspen.

Padra raised his voice above the snarling animals. "A beech leaf bearing Crispin's mark was taken from the bag," he said. "Captain Husk took it upon himself to draw the lots. Some weeks later, on the night of Husk's wedding, more beech leaves were found in the chest where our robes are kept. These, too, had Crispin's mark!"

Needle found she was holding Scufflen too tightly. Very gently, the two hedgehogs took Husk's paws and held on to them. There were hedgehogs on either side of Aspen and Granite, too. Claws curled. Teeth were bared. Husk's face was set, tight and terrifying with rage.

"How did they get there?" demanded Padra. "Had they somehow fallen in? It's easily done!" He slipped a paw into the cuff of his robe. "It's easy, isn't it, to slip leaves into a cuff, or out again! That token wasn't in the bag, was it, Husk? It was in your cuff!" And as he held the leaves high, the whole community of Mistmantle stared up at them. It was as if they were seeing a vision.

The growling rose louder, but Needle found she was breathing more easily. Padra had done it. It would be all right.

Padra held up a paw to keep the crowd from rushing forward, but his other paw was on his sword hilt. He knelt before the king.

"Your Majesty," he said, "I call for the arrest of Captain Husk."

"Arrest Husk!" roared the king.

Husk's hind paw beat on the dais again. The hedgehogs led him away. With a swish, Granite drew his sword—then from the back of the crowd came a shriek; a cry rang from somewhere else; the dais trembled; and the battle began.

CHAPTER TWENTY-THREE

WHERE DID THEY COME FROM? Moles poured from tunnels; squirrels sprang down from trees and up from rocks; there were otters and hedgehogs among them, and with battle cries they swarmed to the dais. Everywhere, sharp swords whirled and daggers flashed; but, more than that, there were such helmets and breastplates as had never been seen on Mistmantle. Scattering the woodlanders, the attackers rushed for the dais. Under Lugg's command, Padra's hedgehogs stood firm, their needles bristling, their swords high. Needle pressed Scufflen's head down and ran, covering his eyes and ears as best as she could to keep the cries of war from him. Through the shouting and clanging of weapons she heard Fir's cry of "treachery!" and Padra's of "Look to the king!" Running, she reached the sandy soil near the dais, ducked behind a rock, and put Scufflen down.

They had known Husk wouldn't go without a fight. That was why the hedgehogs had been ready for action. But there were so many rallying to Husk's side from every direction, and so well-armed! Steel flashed and rang; teeth and claws were bared; there were snarls and squeals, roars and cries; sand and dust billowed into the air as animals fell. There was no sign of Husk on the dais, but Padra and Arran held their ground, fighting back to back as Padra's and Granite's swords clashed together. And where was the king?

Lugg and the hedgehogs fought furiously, but the tide of armed moles came on. An otter who looked a bit like Padra was hurling stones toward them, but he had to stop as they mingled with Padra's supporters. Soon the moles would be on the dais, and all those sharp blades would rush at Padra. Desperately, Needle looked up. The spectacular awnings and Threadings around the dais were rocking with the surge of battle. She could use those. She looked wildly about her. Crackle and Sepia were pressed together in terror with their paws wrapped tightly round each other. A few small choir squirrels and the teams of acrobats watched, too, huddling together.

"Crackle! Sepia!" called Needle. "I need you here! *Faster!*" She stamped her paw as they crept nervously to her. "Look! We need to gnaw this scaffolding. Then we can bring everything crashing down on the moles as soon as they get on the dais!"

"But what about Captain Padra?" said Sepia.

"We get him off first! Come on!"

"I'll help!" said a small choir squirrel, and another, and another.

Crackle tried to tell them they were too young, but the acrobats were already racing up the scaffolding. A large hat with roses on it seemed to be swimming through the fray, and presently Apple was on the scene, hurling pebbles at the attackers. When she ran out of ammunition, she joined in the gnawing at the scaffolding. Other young animals, seeing them, struggled through the battle to help.

Padra and Arran had been pushed to the edge of the dais. Twice Granite had tried to force Padra over it, and Padra had pushed him back. Needle saw Granite heave his sword in both paws, ready to crash into Padra's skull; but Padra struck out with all his strength to parry the blow, staggering back a pace before finding his balance again. A mole leaped at him, but with a swish of his tail he hurled it flying from the dais. The Threadings would fall soon, but it might not be soon enough.

"Somebody help Captain Padra!" yelled Needle, but in the rage of battle she couldn't tell if anyone heard her. "Why is it always up to *me*?" Gritting her teeth, she struggled to climb onto the dais.

"What you doing?" called Apple.

"Give me a shove!" said Needle, and with a heave from Apple, she was on the dais, brandishing her spines at any mole that came near her as she darted forward, grabbed Granite's ankle in both paws, and bit with all her might. There was a howl and a kick from Granite, and as she rolled backward, she saw a squirrel leap from a Threading to sink its teeth into his shoulder. Armed moles were on the dais, then more of them.

But the awnings were ready to fall. Needle leaped down.

"Shake the scaffolding!" she gasped.

"Shake the scaffolding!" shouted Apple.

"Padra, Arran, Lugg, jump!" she yelled.

"Padra, Arran, Lugg, jump!" bellowed Apple as the scaffolding rocked.

With a cry of "Mistmantle, jump!" Padra and Arran hurled themselves from the dais. At the other side, Lugg and the rest of their supporters sprang and scrambled to safety as the scaffolding creaked and folded. Awnings and Threadings swung, swayed, and collapsed, lurching like a wild sea, as underneath them the trapped animals kicked and hacked.

Padra was already on his paws. "The king!" he shouted.

"The tower!" panted a hedgehog. "We tried to fight our way through to His Majesty, but Husk had him surrounded by guards and dragged him into the tower. Don't know where all his troops came from, sir."

"I think I do," said Padra, getting his breath back. "Who's in the tower?"

"The king, Husk, Lady Aspen," said the hedgehog. "Brother Fir, I think, but I'm not sure. Some of the servants and Husks's guards."

Padra looked up at the tower. Against the late afternoon sky, it stood as beautiful as sunset and as hard as diamond.

"They'll have every tunnel and entrance well guarded," he said. "But we should be able to take it by storm."

There were cries and curses from behind him. Swords were hacking through the fallen Threadings.

"Have that lot trussed up and put in—oh, hang it, we don't have the use of a dungeon," Padra went on. "A cave, then, well guarded. Or a burrow. Arran, Lugg, take some reliable creatures to see to it."

There was still some fighting going on below the dais, but it seemed that most of Husk's supporters were either trapped on the dais or back in the tower. The wrecked Threadings rose and fell as the moles trying to escape became more and more tangled.

"Well done, everyone," said Padra. He grinned down at the swarm of young animals gathered around him. "The collapse of that scaffolding has just saved the whole island. It certainly saved me. Whose idea was it?"

"It were 'er, sir," said Apple with a jerk of her head at Needle.

"They all helped," said Needle.

"Needle," said Padra, "you are one of the heroes of Mistmantle, and we will honor you forever. You will be in the Threadings."

"We'll need new Threadings," remarked Apple.

Needle's eyes filled with tears. She tried biting her lip; she tried pulling her face straight; but she couldn't help it: the tears would not be held back, and she sobbed wretchedly.

"I know, I know," said Padra sympathetically, and held her paws. "You've never been in a battle before. It's all too much. Cry all you like, it's nothing to be ashamed of."

"It's not that," snapped Needle through her tears. "It's the Threadings! We worked so hard—we were proud of them!"

Padra drew himself up and rubbed his sore shoulder. It had been badly jarred in the fight with Granite and felt injured, and his right hind paw had been gashed by a mole's sword.

"Time for the tower, then," he said. He climbed onto a rock and clanged his sword against a fallen helmet for attention.

"Animals of Mistmantle," he called, "loyal and true, faithful hedgehogs, bright-hearted squirrels, brave moles, valiant otters—will you rescue your king? Are you with me? At my word of command, otters to the Spring Gate! Hedgehogs and squirrels to the main stairs! Moles to the tunnels! Are you ready? For Mistmantle! For the king! For your families! Storm the tower!"

"And me with my best hat on!" muttered Apple.

Needle put Scufflen into Apple's arms. "Please take him to my mum," she said. "I'm going with Padra."

The charge Padra led was wholehearted and furious, but every tunnel and window was guarded. Rocks were hurled, and arrows sleeted down from the battlements.

"Fall back!" called Padra, not wanting to risk lives for a struggle he couldn't win. "Fall back!" But as he called out and ran backward across the rocks, a window opened.

"Captain Padra!" Aspen was calling down from a window, her paws on the sill, her head high. "Go to the windows of the Gathering Chamber. Captain Husk seeks to parley with you."

"It's a trap, sir," said Needle.

"You shouldn't be here," said Padra. "You're too young for this."

"I'm a hero of Mistmantle, sir," Needle said, "and she's setting a trap."

"That's a chance I have to take," said Padra. "If Husk really does want to parley, it's a sign that he knows he's losing. Don't worry, I've got an army at my back."

Determined not to limp, he made his way to the rocks under the Gathering Chamber windows. Armed animals followed him.

"Husk!" shouted Padra, because he would no longer call him captain. "Come to the window!"

Another window opened, and animals gasped in terror. Husk's face was fierce with wild, dangerous delight, as if he treasured this hour. He looked as if he couldn't wait to kill. He certainly didn't look sane.

"Padra the otter," he said, and laughed. "Padra the Plodder. Plodder the Otter, Otter the Plodder. Have you come to beg for mercy?"

Padra rested a paw on his sword hilt. "I come," he said, "to demand that you hand over King Brushen and Brother Fir to my safekeeping, and surrender the tower."

"And if I don't?" sneered Husk. "Will you go back to your baby-minding?"

"If you don't," said Padra clearly, "you may choose to call yourself King of Mistmantle, if you want. But whose king? Your supporters are dead or prisoners. Not one of us will ever call you king. All we can call you is murderer and traitor, and every one of us would die to defend this island from you. Only we don't intend to die. We will live on a free island, under our true king."

"Your true king?" smiled Husk, and it was a terrible smile. "Do you want to see your true king?"

He disappeared from the window. Needle tried telling herself that everything would be all right, but it didn't feel all right. And when Husk came back, she wanted to cry.

The king wore no crown and no robe. His paws were tied to his sides; his fur was roughened; and his eyes were bloodshot. Husk and a guard heaved him harshly to the open window, and for a sickening moment Needle thought they would throw him down.

There was a rasp as Husk drew his sword, and a shriek of dismay from the animals. If Padra had not held out a paw to hold them back, they might have surged at the tower at once and been ruthlessly cut down. But they stayed still, their breathing taut and shallow, as Husk put the blade to the king's throat.

"Come any nearer," he said, "and the king is dead. And then I shall be king by right of law. Who can challenge me? And it's no good trying to sneak in through a tunnel. They're all guarded. The slightest stirring of any intruder, and the king dies. And then we'll let Brother Fir out of his lonely tower so he can crown me."

"Is Brother Fir held prisoner?" asked Padra.

"No, not at all," said Husk over the king's shoulder. "He loves his turret room. And he can come out as soon as he agrees to crown me. I won't surrender, so you'll have to. Poor Padra, you can have until dawn to proclaim me king. I know it takes you a long time to think and understand. Till dawn, Padra. I can hardly wait. It will be a long night."

CHAPTER TWENTY-FOUR

PADRA SURVEYED THE BATTLEFIELD. There were prisoners to be guarded, the dead to be buried, wounded and grieving animals to be cared for, and guards to be posted. Needle, wanting to be useful, took him a flask of water.

She found him by the remnants of the dais with the young otter she had seen in the battle. Whoever he was, he was battered, bruised, and grinning.

"No more heroics, Fingal," Padra was saying. "I know you've been brave, but you could have been killed. Go and get your wounds washed. Never mind that I'm your brother, I'm your captain—so do as you're told."

Needle gave Padra the water, which he offered to Fingal first. A few squirrels were still chewing the scaffolding because, they said, it tasted nice. Some of the young ones were making nests from it, and the work of her own paws was being shredded by a baby mole. A hedgehog was eating the fringe. Needle tried not to look anymore.

"Please, sir," she said as Padra drank, "where did all those moles come from?"

"Mercenaries," said Padra, and offered her the water. "We don't have that many moles. Husk must have arranged all this long ago. He knew he couldn't count on enough support from Mistmantle animals, so he's been smuggling in moles on trading ships and bribing them with jewels. It all makes sense. That's why we've been trading so much, and he's been storing up treasure. And that's why he wanted to ration the food, so he could keep his secret army well supplied. They were all ready in tunnels, waiting for a signal. Did you notice, he beat his paw on the floor? That was the signal. One to be ready, two to attack. It's all very clear now."

"Like knowing the answer to a riddle," said Needle. "Once you know it, you think it's obvious, but it isn't really."

"Crispin would have worked it all out weeks ago," said Padra. "I always knew I had seaweed where my brain should be. But Husk wasn't ready for Mistmantle to fight back so fiercely." He smiled down at her, making her glow with pride. "He certainly wasn't ready for *you*, and he didn't expect a siege. There's still hope." He stood up and grimaced as he put his weight on his wounded paw. "Here's Moth!"

The little mole maid bustled across the rocks toward him. She looked pleased with herself.

"Moth," he called. "Are all the young ones safe?"

"Oh, yes!" she said confidently. "But we're not very comfortable stuck under that boat, especially with our prisoner. She takes up a lot of room."

"Prisoner?" said Padra.

"Yes, sir, would you like to come and see? And please will you tell us what to do with her?"

A few strong animals helped Padra overturn the boat, and Mother Huggen seized the paws of any infants likely to run away. Basins and plates had been tipped across the floor, and somebody had spilled porridge.

"Heart love us," said Padra. "It's Tay!"

From the sand, Tay glared up at him with all the dignity she had left. It wasn't much. She had been tied and trussed with whatever Mother Huggen could find—knitting wool, thick trails of seaweed, and, of course, Moth's apron. A fluffy pink blanket had been stuffed between her teeth and fastened as a gag. There was porridge in her fur.

"She's been a lot of trouble," said Mother Huggen severely, as if Tay were a very naughty child. "She's been thrashing about in a tantrum and knocked over all the basins and spilled the porridge—that's why we had to tie her up so much. I'd be most grateful if you'd take her off my paws, Captain Padra."

Padra turned to his helpers. "Mistress Tay," he said, "is a distinguished otter, a scholar, and a lawyer, and came near to being made a captain. Treat her with respect. Untie her, use another upturned boat for a prison cell, and guard her well. When we take the tower, she'll be escorted to a cell there."

He bowed low, hiding the twitching of his whiskers. "Mistress Tay, I'm sorry for this indignity," he said. "But I suspect you have brought it on yourself." Then he bowed abruptly to Huggen and Moth, and strode away before they could see him laughing.

"I suppose the little ones can go home now," said Needle, left with Mother Huggen. "Nobody's going to cull them now."

"So that's that," said Huggen. "No more secret nursery. No more babies. Home. And quite right, too."

"I've lost Hope," said Moth suddenly.

"There's no need for that, my dear!" said Huggen.

"No," said Moth, "I mean *him*! Hope! All the rest of them are accounted for, but not Hope the hedgehog!"

"Oh, bless him," sighed Huggen. "What can we do with him? No doubt he's gone off looking for Thripple, his 'beautiful mother,' as he calls her."

"I know her!" said Needle. "But I don't know where she is."

"Goodness only knows," said Huggen. "And he's not safe to be out on his own!"

"He can do tunnels," said Moth.

"He still bumps into walls," grumbled Huggen. "We'll have to start a search. But I daresay he'll be all right. There's something about that one. The Heart protects the helpless, I suppose."

In the bare Gathering Chamber, daylight was fading. Aspen sent Gleaner to light the lamps.

"And take a message to all those at guard duty," she said. "Tell them Captain Husk and I are proud of them. There are fewer of us now, but that means a greater share of treasure. Have food and wine sent to them."

"Yes, my lady," said Gleaner. "Please, my lady . . ."

"Yes, Gleaner?" said Aspen.

"It's all Padra's fault, isn't it?"

"Yes, Gleaner."

Gleaner trotted importantly away, trying to glide as gracefully as Aspen. It was Padra's fault. If he'd just let Husk take over, none of this would have happened.

Aspen turned to Husk with an impatient swish of her robe.

"Why don't we just kill the king now?" she asked.

"Because then we'd lose everything," snapped Husk. "Padra would storm the tower."

"What if he does?" she said. "We'd win."

"We might not," said Husk. The king was sagging in his arms, and he pushed him roughly up against the window. "Stand up, you. Our losses in the battle were greater than we expected. Granite should have finished Padra off; then they wouldn't have a leader. They should all have done as I said, all along. I've always said that. It's true."

He stared down at the shore. The tide was coming in. Padra's supporters had camped high, away from the shoreline, close to the tower. None of this would have happened if everyone had simply done as he wanted. He knew best.

He was the first son of his family, or at least, the first son who mattered. There had been a feeble brother who had died at birth, and a feebler one who had managed to live. But he had never been of any use. He was an embarrassment to the family and the colony. Husk had tried to explain that to his parents, but they wouldn't listen; so it had been up to him to push the miserable cripple over a cliff.

Killing the priest would be satisfying, but it was too unlucky. Besides, he would want Brother Fir to crown him. The priest would come to his senses.

There was a tap at the door. Aspen drew the small dagger she had fastened at her waist.

"Can I come in?" said Gleaner's voice, and presently she hurried in with a basket on her arm. "I brought some food."

"Thank you, Gleaner," said Aspen, replacing the dagger. "And, Gleaner, the king can't reach his flask. He may want a drink from it now and again."

"Yes, my lady," said Gleaner. She took the flask and held it to the king's lips. Whatever was in it, it didn't smell as strong as the spirits Aspen had been giving him, but she didn't like to mention it. She was frightened of Captain Husk.

"Does he never sleep?" said Padra. Looking up through the gathering twilight, he could see Husk still holding the king at the open window, still with the knife at his throat. Padra had stationed groups of animals at points all around the tower and the island, but he himself had stayed with Arran and a few others before the Gathering Chamber windows. By the campfire light, their faces were warm and fierce.

Pulling his cloak around him, Padra massaged his painful shoulder and walked around the tower until he stood under Fir's turret. The small, bent figure stood framed in light in the arch of a window.

"Brother Fir!" called Padra, and saw the priest's head tilt toward him.

"Dearest Padra!" called Fir. It was too dark to see him clearly, but Padra heard his smile. "I have prayed for you. Dear son, stand firm."

"Do you have all you need?" called Padra. "Do they treat you well?"

"I have the company of four excellent moles," replied Fir. "They are here to make sure that I don't leap from windows, nor take up a sword against them. Four of them, Padra! With weapons! Two in here, and two at the door! They must think me a most formidable warrior; I'm thoroughly flattered. And I have bread and water, which is all . . . my goodness! There's a star! A riding star!"

"It can't be!" Padra turned to look as a spark of silver flew across the sky. "But you always tell us when we're going to have riding stars!"

"Hm," said Fir. "Well, this time I didn't, because I didn't know. Extraordinary!"

For good or for harm, thought Padra, thinking of Crispin and all that had happened since the last night of riding stars. *Good or harm?* He knelt on the cold rock.

"May I have your blessing, Brother Fir?" he asked. And however old Fir was, however weary, the paw he lifted in blessing was firm and did not tremble. He turned his face to the skies.

The night grew colder. Stars flocked, danced, stopped, and began again. The besiegers slept in snatches. Padra slipped into a rock pool to ease his injuries in salt water. Husk muttered to himself, to the king, to Aspen. All watched the stars. And Fir, standing at his window, looked beyond the riding stars and saw the first pale gold light tracing across the eastern sky. With a great leap of his heart and a surge of joy, he saw in the distance the faraway specks of Mistmantle's deliverance.

CHAPTER TWENTY-FIVE

URCHIN KNELT IN FEATHERS, STRETCHING FORWARD as he held tight to the strong, white neck of the swan. The rush of cold air through his fur chilled him, but his legs were warm, pressed against the swan's body. He gazed forward and upward past its head, into the sky, not daring to look down.

They were flying higher. The beat and beat and beat of the powerful white wings swished in the air as they rose.

"I'm flying!" Urchin told himself again, breathless, his eyes wide. "I'm really flying!" It was wonderful and impossible, but it was happening.

Crispin flew ahead of him, his head up, his hind paws anchored in the space between the wings. For Urchin, if there was one thing better than flying back to Mistmantle, it was flying back with Crispin—and Crispin was himself again.

He wondered at the strength and endurance of the birds. The swans had told him how noble they were, and how they were not birds of burden to carry lesser animals, but for once, only once, for Crispin's sake, they would do this. For hour upon hour they had flown, as the night sky clouded and the air seemed dense around them.

"It's the mist!" Crispin had cried. "We're going home!"

"Wonderful swans!" called Urchin. "Beautiful, wonderful swans!"

He didn't know if they could hear, and swans didn't care about the praises of a common tree-rat. But he had to say it. Mists curled around them. White wings rose and fell, rose and fell.

"Captain Crispin, sir!" called Urchin. "I can't see you!" Through mist and darkness, he heard Crispin laugh.

"Don't be anxious! I'm still here!"

Something silver rushed toward them, so that Urchin gasped and ducked.

"Crispin!" he called. "Did you see? A star!"

"The stars are riding for us, Urchin!" cried Crispin. And Urchin, who had thought nothing could be more wonderful than this, caught his breath. The stars that had danced on the night of his birth were sweeping through the sky to bring him home to Mistmantle, and he rode among them.

On Mistmantle, dawn was cold. Aspen had ordered the kindling of a fire in the hearth and stood beside it to warm herself, but Husk would not leave the king. He remained, fierce-eyed with terrifying delight. Gleaner gave the king drinks from the flask whether he asked for them or not. It was her way of helping Lady Aspen.

Cold air from the window, and the spring water Lugg had put in his flask, had helped to clear the king's head. His wits were his own again, and he understood only too well.

At last he knew he had been Husk's puppet. He had been drunk half the time and doped the rest, and in his weakness and grief he had let Husk get away with it. He no longer deserved to be king. But he *was* king, and it was up to him to save the island. He remembered the days when he had been young, sharp, and ready for action. He dozed and woke again; and each time he woke he was more fully himself.

Husk's dagger was at his throat, but his sword was still sheathed. If only he could free his left paw. If he concentrated and summoned all his old skill, he could whip that sword away and with a quick twist send the dagger flying from Husk's paw. Then he would be free, and Padra could storm the tower. He himself might not last against Husk and Aspen until Padra reached him, but he would take the chance.

Gradually, slowly, in the tiniest movements, he wriggled his left paw in the ropes. It might take until morning, but he could do it.

Aspen left the warmth of the fire to watch him. The king stopped trying to free his arm, and turned his head a little. Although the window was wide open, he could, from this angle, see a reflection in the glass. He watched and watched, seeing the stars ride across the sky while the night seemed to last forever, until at last Husk's eyelids drooped, and Lady Aspen yawned.

He slipped his paw up a little farther. Husk's eyes snapped open.

"Stand still!" he ordered.

"Husk," he said wearily, trying another way, "enough blood has been shed. Let me abdicate. The crown is yours. That's what you wanted, isn't it?"

"What, and leave you alive so they can all plot behind my back to make you king again?" snarled Husk. "And let that otter get away with it? I could have been king by now, and nobody would have drawn a single sword. And this island would be perfect. Perfect! They'd all obey me. We'd have weapons. We could conquer other islands. The beasts would only have to obey me and not think too much, that's all! It would be so easy! I will not be content until I have personally hacked that otter into pieces and put his head on a spike over the priest's tower. And I will. Do you see the riding stars? They are for me! The stars proclaim me king! Stop wriggling, you!"

The king looked down to see Padra near a campfire, watching the window. Far away, golden light streaked across the sky. It was nearly day, and his paw was free. He couldn't tell how clearly Padra could see him, but he looked directly down and hoped.

"Now," he mouthed silently. "Ready. Now."

Aspen had been falling asleep on her paws. With a jerk she woke, shook herself, and turned sharply to watch.

"The king!" she cried, and leaped forward as the king swept Husk's

257

sword from its sheath and spun the dagger from his paw. With a kick, she sent the king careering off balance and, with her dagger in her paw, fell on him with a force that flung them both to the floor. Picking himself up, Husk dashed forward to grapple for the sword, screaming something about the window.

It was too late. As Husk shouted, Aspen and the king were on the window ledge. Husk was still screaming as the two fell and crashed onto the rocks.

CHAPTER TWENTY-SIX

TAKE THE TOWER!" shouted Padra, and with a rush and a roar the ranks tore forward. Padra glanced about for the oldest and slowest.

"Look to the king," he ordered, "and to Lady Aspen."

As the troops streamed past to the tower, he bent over Aspen and the king. A sword lay on the rocks. The king's eyes were closed, but he moaned softly. Lady Aspen lay absolutely still, with a pool of blood darkening the rocks behind her head.

Padra put a paw to her throat. There was still a pulse. Both were wounded, and the sword and the dagger were both bloodied.

"Do your best for them both," he said shortly, and ran for the tower as Husk's terrified guards either flew for their lives or fell back to the Gathering Chamber. Padra's forces rushed in: squirrels scrambling through windows, moles pouring from tunnels, otters and hedgehogs surging through every gate. As Padra ran for the Gathering Chamber, Arran was leaping down a staircase.

"Release Fir!" he called.

"Done it!" she said. "He was off like a fish, I don't know where to."

Battle cries and the clash of swords came from the Gathering Chamber. Husk's supporters must be making a last fight of it. Padra found squirrels and hedgehogs, moles and otters battling with teeth, claws, and weapons. Husk had armed himself again, and with a sword in one paw and a dagger in the other, fought with all the passion and fury of his life. Padra raised his sword in both paws, and with all his might, gritting his teeth against the pain in his shoulder, rang it against the doorway.

"In the king's name!" he yelled.

The fighting stopped. All eyes turned to him. The animals stepped back, breathing hard, leaning on their swords, nursing their wounds.

He had thought of this moment, and prepared for it. His shoulder still ached and his hind paw stung. He wasn't as fast as Husk, but he was stronger and heavier.

"Enough blood has been shed," he said. "Husk: deceiver, murderer, traitor to your king and to Mistmantle, I challenge you to single combat in the names of the ones you have wronged. I come for King Brushen, Queen Spindle, and Prince Tumble. I come for Captain Crispin the Exile, and for Urchin of the Riding Stars. I come for the Isle of Mistmantle."

"And I come for Husk," growled Husk, crouching over his sword. "Captain Husk, Lord Husk, Husk the Triumphant, King Husk." His voice rose high and wild. "For the great King Husk, and for Queen Aspen!" He raised his sword in both paws.

Padra raised his own sword, and kissed the blade. He was suddenly aware of a hedgehog running past him, and recognized Needle as she dashed to the window.

"Look!" cried Needle with joy. "All of you! *LOOK!*"

All heads except Husk's turned to look. All stared, wide-eyed, hushed with wonder.

"It's a trick!" sneered Husk, but nobody listened. They were watching the sky as something emerged through the mist, something that flew high and steadily toward them. "Squirrels on swans!" whispered Needle in awe. "Captain Padra, sir, it's . . ."

"Yes," said Padra, and felt his heart would burst with joy. And Husk, too, heard the depths of his own heart.

Fear nothing until squirrels fly through the air.

Slowly, sickeningly, he felt his courage drain. He did not want to see what the rest of them saw, but he turned to the window, leaned out, and screamed at the archers.

"Fire! Wake up, you fools! *FIRE!*"

Urchin's ears were sharply pricked, and his eyes shone with joy. The tower was before them. But why were those animals huddled on the rocks, and why was nobody else about?

"Get down, Urchin!" yelled Crispin. "Arrows!"

Urchin ducked, pressed his head down against the swan's neck, and gripped tightly. The swan swerved, bobbed, and rose so steeply that it took all of Urchin's balance to stay on. He raised his head a little, just to anticipate the next flight of arrows.

"Urchin!" called Crispin. "We're putting the swans in danger! We'll have to jump. Ready?"

"Yes, captain!" called Urchin. Still holding on, he struggled to his hind paws. He saw Crispin spring, all paws extended, to the windows of the Gathering Chamber. Then the swan swerved and, for the third time in his life, Urchin fell from the sky.

He landed on soft sand beyond the Spring Gate, rolled, and drew his sword as he ran at the gate. Nobody was there to stop him, and he was dashing to the Gathering Chamber when a noise from below the ground made him stop.

It was the thin, quavering voice of a young animal in distress. A hedgehog, from the sound of it. It was too far away to hear the words, but the voice was angry and close to tears at the same time. There were other voices, too, unpleasant ones.

Irritation ran through Urchin. He should be with Crispin, flying into the Gathering Chamber in triumph. But somewhere nearby was a very young animal in distress, and almost certainly in danger. He knew what Crispin would want him to do.

Urchin didn't often use tunnels. Trying to remember what Padra had taught him about them, he found an entrance in a corner of the wall. The frightened hedgehog voice was closer, and so was cruel laughter and then, to his horror, the rasp of a sword being drawn. Urchin tore toward it.

The tunnel opened out so suddenly that Urchin wasn't ready for what he saw, and had to pull himself together. He was in some sort of guard room, where a platter lay on a small table, a lamp glowed on a wall, and two moles, who neither looked nor sounded like Mistmantle moles, had their backs to him. They were pointing their swords toward a hedgehog so small, so scruffy, and so brave in its terror that fury fired Urchin.

"I'll fight you . . ." the hedgehog was saying, though his voice was thin and his mouth trembled. "I'll fight you. One at a time. But you'll have to lend me a sword, or it's not fair."

Soundlessly, Urchin sprang onto the table and picked up the platter for a shield. If the hedgehog had seen him, it was wise enough to keep quiet. The entrance was free, so the moles would probably escape rather than fight.

"Captain Padra will be very cross," said the hedgehog, trying very hard not to cry.

"Aah! Poor ickle hedgehog!" said a mole.

"Aah!" said the other, and was turning away as Urchin sprang from the table. "Aaaarh!"

There was no need to fight. The moles had seen, not a young squirrel, but a raging armed warrior. The first fled, and the other followed as the flat of Urchin's sword skimmed across his flank. Urchin slipped the sword back into its sheath and knelt by the trembling hedgehog to stroke the soft spines. It snarled, but not very convincingly.

"I won't hurt you," said Urchin gently. "The moles have gone. My name's Urchin: I'm Captain Padra's page. Who are you?"

"I'm Hope," said the hedgehog. "I've heard about you. The funny-colored squirrel?"

"That's me," said Urchin, remembering the nearsighted hedgehog from the nursery.

"Thank you for chasing the moles away," said Hope. "I would have fought them, you know, sir."

"Yes, I know," said Urchin, and wondered what to do next. He really wanted to rush to wherever Crispin was, but he couldn't leave the hedgehog. It could hardly even see where it was going, and the moles might find it again.

He sighed quietly. It had been like this before he came to the tower. Since then he'd served two great captains, nearly been killed, crossed the sea in a storm, and flown through the mists on a swan. Now he was back to looking after infants.

"Come on, then," he said, and lifted the lamp from its bracket on the wall. "Where are you meant to be?"

"I think I can manage now, sir," said the hedgehog. "I can do tunnels."

"It's a good thing one of us can," muttered Urchin, who had just realized that he wasn't at all sure which way he'd come in. The hedgehog trundled along at his side as Urchin tried to remember Padra's map of the tunnels. He must be heading either back to the Spring Gate or forward to the Gathering Chamber. As his confidence returned, the hedgehog chattered to Urchin about how he'd had a lovely time at the Spring Festival except he didn't see his mummy, and she might be sad at missing him, so he thought he'd better go to the tower and find her, because he knew how to do tunnels.

"She works here," he explained. "She makes Threadings. She's very clever. And very, very beautiful." He told Urchin how he had got a little bit lost and a very little bit frightened, but he'd kept searching. It was a long time, and he'd got very hungry.

"I should have thought of that," said Urchin, and slipped the satchel from his shoulder. There was a bottle of water and some very squashed biscuits and berries. The squashed berries were impossible to eat without making a mess, especially in a dusty old tunnel, but the hedgehog enjoyed them and didn't notice the stains of juice on his chest and the stickiness that glued cobwebs to his spines. They hurried on, Urchin carrying the lamp, Hope walking on his hind legs with a biscuit in his paw, talking with his mouth full. The moles had found him and asked him a lot of questions, "and they were very rude about my mummy," he said indignantly. Then he dropped to all fours and sniffed.

"It's this way," he said. "There's a nasty smell and a nice one. Yes, this way."

"But it's downhill!" said Urchin.

"It'll go up again," said the hedgehog. "It gets nasty farther on, but I can smell candlelight. And a squirrel. A nice squirrel."

"It's narrow, too," said Urchin. He didn't know of any other way, and he couldn't leave Hope. But something about this tunnel made his fur bristle with cold. He didn't want to go on.

Husk didn't know how he came to be in the middle of the hall. He supposed he must have backed away as Crispin sprang down from the swan. *Squirrels flying through the air.* This should be his hour of triumph, and everything had turned against him.

Padra's joy shone in his face as Crispin balanced on the windowsill. And Padra knew that Crispin did not come with bitterness, or for revenge. It was simply time to finish what should never have started, and he was the one to do it.

"Padra, please send someone to find Urchin," said Crispin, but his eyes rested on Husk. Padra nodded to a few eager squirrels.

"And Padra," Crispin went on, "if you were about to settle this vermin, will you please stand back?"

"You have a higher right to it," said Padra, and took a pace backward. Needle, not wanting to be in the way, scurried away to a side door to watch.

Silence had settled on the hall. Miraculously, wonderfully, Crispin was here, in command, raising his sword, kissing the blade, his face steady and set against the wild-eyed Husk. Then with a scream of outrage, Husk lifted his sword and leaped at Crispin, who darted from beneath the blade and swung to face him, parrying the swinging blow. The creatures gasped.

Husk fought furiously, but skill and planning were deserting him. He turned his back to the window. No, no, he mustn't let Crispin force him to that open window. He swung around, his back to the door—but then Padra was behind him. . . .

There was a passageway from this room. A passageway, a flight of stairs, a tunnel reaching to draw him down to welcoming darkness. That darkness called him. The absorbing, breathable evil of the pit drew him. Nobody was near that door, except a young hedgehog.

He fought on, letting Crispin force him back to the place where he wanted to be. He could feel it behind him, the side door, the sharp turn through the shadowed gap in the wall. Nearly there, and as Crispin's sword plunged toward his heart, he slipped backward through the door, turned sharply, and was running wildly to the place where he belonged.

Needle whisked around the corner just in time to glimpse Husk's vanishing tail tip.

"That way, sir!" she called, and Crispin darted after him. Padra followed, twisting his way through the gap, with Needle at his heels. As they raced after Husk into darkness, they followed the sound of squirrel paws and wild laughter.

Husk ran through the tunnels as if he ran to destiny, faster, faster, leaping over stones: fierce, wild, and driven. The place of darkness would save him. He only had to lead them to it, open the door, and stand his ground. It was too narrow for them to come at him in a rush.

They would come one at a time, and he could pick them off one by one and fling them into the pit, alive if necessary. Crispin first, then Padra, then any animal that still dared challenge him. He could hear the paws that followed him. Let them follow. He gathered speed. He was nearly there when horror transfixed him.

It was the horror of light.

The door of the dungeon stood open. Light glowed from inside it, the dancing light of hundreds upon hundreds of candle flames, flickering as if they were laughing. Even the water and slime twisting down the walls were transformed into gleams of gold and silver. Husk put a shaking paw against the wall. Fear gathered around and inside him, all his fear, his nightmares, and the greatest fear of all, the terrible fear of all his life, the fear of helplessness, crippled him. His nerve failed. The sword fell from his paw.

He could not go back. Crispin and Padra were there. With both paws to the walls, he inched forward, creeping past the open door of the dungeon. Then he saw the unspeakable thing.

He closed his eyes, and looked again. Aspen was not there to wake him up, and the thing of nightmare was running toward him. But he knew he was awake. It was real. Prince Tumble was stumbling toward him, cobwebs hanging from his prickles, his eyes half closed as he sniffed out his murderer. The stain on his chest was deep and drying, just as he remembered it. Unstoppably, the prince came on. Light followed him.

Urchin followed Hope, staying close, holding up the lamp before him, taking shallow breaths and holding his courage together. He remembered this place with its terrible smell of death and fear, but Hope needed him, and as he went on, there was light ahead. He kept going. There in the dim tunnel ahead of him was Husk, and Urchin had never seen such terror.

Husk was backing away. His eyes were staring, his paws shaking, his coat bristling. "No!" whispered Husk. "No!"

"It's only me, sir," said the hedgehog.

"Stay away!" pleaded Husk. "Away, you!" He inched backward, staggering. No!"

From the dungeon, Urchin heard Brother Fir's voice. "Husk! Stop! Take care!"

Urchin dashed past Hope. Crispin and Padra were running in from the other direction.

There was no time to take it all in. He was aware of a grim place softened by candlelight; Brother Fir hobbling forward, stretching out his paws; a last cry—then somehow Husk disappeared, and the cry sounded farther and farther down and turned into something that was half a cry and half bitter laughter—then it stopped.

"Keep away from the edge," said Fir sharply. "All of you."

Urchin stepped back and put out a paw to stop the hedgehog from going any farther. Crispin and Padra were beside him. He saw and smelled a damp cellar, but its slimy walls were softened by the shining of candles, rows and rows of them, like jewels. There was a faint scent of beeswax. Deep sorrow lay in Brother Fir's dark eyes. Padra's warm paw was across Urchin's shoulders.

"What is this place?" asked Crispin.

"It is a place of ancient evil," said Fir gravely. "I myself have only just found it and attempted to cleanse it of its past. We should leave it for now."

"The king," said Padra. "What's the quickest way out?"

"Excuse me," whispered the hedgehog. "What happened?"

"Never mind," said Urchin. "Come with me, and we'll find your mum."

Brother Fir led them away. Padra gave Urchin's shoulders a reassuring squeeze.

"It's over now," he said. "Well done."

"I didn't run away this time," said Urchin.

Padra's paw tightened on his shoulder, and there was a catch in his voice. "I know, Urchin. You didn't run away."

CHAPTER TWENTY-SEVEN

SAYING LITTLE, THEY MADE THEIR WAY BACK through the tunnels to the rocks below the Gathering Chamber. Urchin gulped the fresh sea air gladly. Waddling and wobbling, Apple ran to him, and he left Hope in her care while he followed Fir and the captains across the rocks.

Arran had taken charge of the king. He lay with his head in her lap; his wounds had been dressed, but Arran shook her head. A few paces from them, Gleaner knelt in a crumpled mess of torn silk and bent tearfully over Aspen, lifting her head to hold a drink to her lips. A dented bracelet lay on the rocks.

Urchin glanced from Aspen to the king. Sooner or later, somebody would tell him what had happened, but both were so wounded and bruised that it was impossible to work it out. Padra and Crispin were kneeling before the king, so Urchin did the same, and the king turned his head a little.

"The page," he said. "Nice young chap." With sorrow in his eyes, he turned to Crispin, struggling to speak, and Urchin felt Padra's paw on his shoulder.

"We should leave," he said. "Let them be alone."

There was real warmth in the morning sun. While Padra issued orders about the prisoners, Urchin stood on the shore and drew in deep, long breaths of Mistmantle air. Two swans glided across the bay toward him, and he waded out to meet them.

"Thank you," he said.

Lord Arcneck inclined his head. "The tree-rat who sent his mole to our island," he said. "Is he dead, servant?"

"Yes, Lord Arcneck," said Urchin.

"We have generously decided," said the swan, "to release Crispin from our service. You may tell him so."

"Thank you, Lord Arcneck," said Urchin.

"And we will rest here tonight before returning to our realm," said Lord Arcneck. "Direct us to fresh water."

Urchin led them around the shore, left them in the care of an otter, and returned to Padra.

"Crispin's still with the king," said Padra. "We should see what's happened to Aspen."

But they knew before they reached her. Gleaner was crouched over her, sobbing desperately, with Lady Aspen's paw in hers. When

Padra knelt beside them, she leaned across like a mother defending her young.

"Leave her alone!" she snarled.

"We'll do no harm," said Padra gently. He put a paw to Aspen's throat, and shook his head.

Gleaner dried her eyes on the back of her paw. "I tried to save her," she gulped. "She knew I tried."

"Of course you did," said Padra.

"I ran down here and she was still alive," Gleaner said. "She was trying to say something about the queen. I helped her to nurse the queen; I know all about the medicines; so I knew which was the queen's special medicine. Lady Aspen was most particular about it. She used it only for the queen, and it was only her and me that gave it to her. She wouldn't let anybody else near it."

Padra met Urchin's eyes across the body, but his face gave nothing away.

"It was the best medicine on the whole island," said Gleaner, sniffing. "There wasn't much left. I took the last of it and mixed it like she taught me and ran down as fast as I could to give it to her. She tried to say something, but I don't think she knew what was going on. I got her to drink it. I don't think she wanted to, with it being so special and her being so noble, but I got it into her. I stayed with her all this time, but it's no good. My lady died!"

Apart from Gleaner's muffled sobbing, everything had become quiet. Urchin could hear the slow, painful rasp of the king's breathing.

Other animals stood anxiously at a distance. Some wept silently.

The king opened his eyes slowly, as if it took a great effort, and whispered to Fir. Urchin heard Crispin's name, and Brother Fir nodded as he placed a paw on the king's head.

"May the Heart claim you with joy and forgive you with love," he said gently. "May your heart fly freely to the Heart that gave you life."

Urchin wasn't sure exactly when the king died. He only became aware that the harsh breathing had stopped, and Arran was smoothing the king's face. Padra and Crispin removed their circlets. Urchin thought of the times when he had carried spring water to the Throne Room and the king had been so kind.

He realized that Padra had dropped to one knee. He had drawn his sword and was holding it by the blade across his clenched paw, with the hilt toward Crispin.

"Kneel to your king, Urchin," he prompted.

Urchin knelt, copying Padra, as he presented his sword. He tried not to look over his shoulder at such a solemn moment, but he heard the brush of fur as every animal knelt. Padra raised his head to look into Crispin's face, but he remained kneeling.

"Crispin of Mistmantle," he said, "I acknowledge you as rightful king and lord of this island and all its creatures. I ask that you rule with wisdom and love, and I place my sword, my captaincy, and myself at your service." There was a pause, then he added, "I confess to you that I have fought and shed the blood of Mistmantle creatures, and I ask Your Majesty's pardon."

Urchin raised his head and saw Crispin's eyes fixed on Padra's. It was as if Padra were prompting him, helping him to be the king.

"Mistmantle animals," said Crispin, "those who fought for King Brushen have done no wrong. You have no need of pardon. And I promise to be the best king your help and support can make me." And from all the animals came a great cheer for King Crispin, who seemed to Urchin to be the loneliest animal on Mistmantle.

Crispin knelt for Fir's blessing, and gave orders for the king's lying-in-state. "I need to know about that place," he said to Fir. "That terrible place, that dungeon where Husk fell."

"You certainly do need to know," said Fir sadly. "We'll go to Padra's chambers. Urchin, your captain has a wound that needs dressing. Come with us."

There was a spring breeze and a sense of freedom as they walked over the rocks to the Spring Gate. Urchin saw two hedgehogs scurrying toward them, and broke into a run.

"Hello, Hope!" he said. "You found your mum!"

Hope looked cleaner, neater, and a great deal happier now that he had found Thripple. He turned to gaze up at her with adoration as she curtsied awkwardly.

"I remember you, Thripple!" said Crispin. "When I was little you taught me to make boats out of birch bark! Your son has done us a great service."

"He was very brave," said Urchin.

Hope, at a nudge from his mother, trundled forward, took a deep breath, and said, "Thank you, Master Urchin, for fighting the moles away and looking after me, thank you, Master Urchin, sir."

"Moles?" said Padra.

"My beautiful mummy!" whispered Hope to Urchin.

"Very beautiful," Urchin whispered back.

"And may I take him home now, Your Majesty?" said Thripple.

"All the animals can go home," said Crispin. "And never mind the Threadings, Thripple. Enjoy being with him. Teach him to make bark boats."

Urchin watched the hedgehogs trundle away together. There would be no more culling, now that Crispin was king.

"I can't wait to hear about these moles, Master Urchin, sir." grinned Padra.

"I can't wait to scrap the work parties," said Crispin.

"Freedom!" Urchin whispered the word aloud. It was as if he could taste it. Apple bounded up to them, holding her hat on.

"Welcome back, Captain Crispin, Your Majesty, I should say, that'll take some getting used to, ooh, that was our Urchin flying on a swan, I never believed my eyes, and I hear our Urchin scared the daylights out of Captain Husk, and they're all having parties in the wood, do you want to come to a party, we'd forgotten what it was like to be free."

"So had I," said Padra. "Or I would have fought for it harder and sooner."

"Didn't I tell you it were better in them days?" said Apple. "Now,

I'll send a bottle of my best apple-and-mint to the tower for you."

She scampered away, and Fir hurried them to Padra's chambers. He sent for Arran and Needle, and Urchin soaked cloths in seawater to clean Padra's gashed leg.

"You must all know this," said Fir. "Needle and Urchin, you are young, but the young must hear this story, too. It is a story of Mistmantle, but it has never been spoken in the Gathering Chamber nor shown in the Threadings. It has been told in the greatest secrecy from king to king and from priest to priest.

"Long ago, before the moles built the Old Palace, there was an evil king in Mistmantle, a squirrel. He and his followers did not understand the Heart. They worshipped the darknesses in themselves. They honored all that destroys. They took joy in death, not in life. It was said that they had a dungeon under the rocks of the shore so dark and so hidden that no animal taken there could hope to see daylight again. Dead or alive, victims were thrown down a pit into darkness. The place became so evil that even the king feared it, and committed murder there as a sacrifice to it.

"But moles are determined creatures. Moles who survived being thrown into the pit made tunnels. Some made long, deep tunnels far under the sea. But others dug under the island and built a hiding place, where they formed an army. That place became the Old Palace, and from it that army defeated the squirrel king and established a peaceful kingdom. The dungeon was locked and sealed forever, not to be mentioned again. The tunnels to it were walled up, though it seems that over time the walls decayed, or some explorer broke through them."

"Husk was always trying to find the Old Palace," said Crispin. "He found that instead."

"And it drew him," said Fir. "Whatever pride, bitterness, resentment, greed, ambition—whatever was dangerous in Husk—it fed on the evil of that place. The pit claimed him."

"It was under the tower all this time," said Crispin. "And we didn't know."

"Hm," said Fir. "Exactly. It should never have been sealed. Its evil has festered all these years, waiting for someone like Husk. He nourished it, and it nourished him. When Urchin talked about what happened the night the queen died, I began to suspect that Husk had found the place, but even I did not know where it was. As soon as I found it, I set about cleansing it with light and prayer. It will still take days and nights of light and prayer until it is cleansed of its past. Every true and loving act on this island, every kindness, every simple goodness, will help. And now, Your Majesty, there's work to be done."

"And as I'm the only captain left, I suppose I'll have to do it," said Padra. "Your Majesty can't be a captain and the king at the same time, and I assume Granite's sacked."

"And you'll be next, if you keep calling me Your Majesty," said Crispin. "New captains, then."

Lugg and Arran were promptly made captains, and Mother Huggen and Moth were appointed to the Circle. Crispin and Padra toured the island, thanking their supporters, proclaiming the end of forced work parties and the culling law. The swans were thanked and offered the freedom of the island. The animals who had fought for Husk because they had been thoroughly deceived were pardoned. The rest, and the mercenaries, were to leave the island forever. There was some dispute about which were which.

"Gleaner's a pain," said Needle. "But whatever she did, she did it because she loved Aspen."

"And Tay?" said Crispin. "I think she really believed I was guilty. Keep her in prison. A pleasant, comfortable cell in the tower, but a prison."

Finally, Padra said he'd die if he didn't have a swim, and Urchin went with him to the sea. Padra lay on his back, easing his wrenched shoulder, while Urchin splashed about and jumped on and off boats as they heard each other's stories. He told Padra all about Whisper, while Padra muttered, "Verminous creeping mole," and then "Oh, poor Crispin!"

"He was going to leave the circlet on her burial cairn," said Urchin. "But I said it might be better to bring it with him. It's all he could keep of her. It was the closest he could come to bringing her back with him."

"Well done," said Padra.

"I wish she were here," said Urchin. "I wish we had her for our queen." He was quiet for a while, watching Hope and Thripple building a sand castle on the shore.

"Padra," he said—he felt awkward about it but he said it anyway—

"do you think, if my mother could see me, she'd be proud of me?"

"Of course she would!" said Padra, and flipped over. "And she probably can. I don't know how it is, but I should think she's still watching you somehow."

Maybe she is, thought Urchin. But Arran was swimming toward them, and he swam away to leave them alone.

"How many times should I thank you?" said Padra as Arran swam alongside him. "You must have saved my life three times at least, just in the fight with Granite." He pulled himself onto a boat, and she scrambled up beside him. "I'm impressed."

Her tufts of wet fur stood out at severe angles. He opened his mouth to speak, looked down, and tried again.

"You know," he said, "after all this, and if you've got nothing better to do, you might marry me." And she hit him, and he laughed, and they swam back to shore together.

"We'll need Crispin's permission," he said. "But perhaps we should give him time."

Urchin went to find Needle. She was setting out bottles and plates on the shore.

"They'll all be hungry by now," she said. With the help of some of Arran's staff, they spread out a meal of cold pies, cordials, and leftovers from the feast, and laid it out on the rocks. It was a fine evening, and soon Crispin, Padra, Fir, Huggen, Moth, Lugg, and Arran had gathered, with Needle and Urchin serving them, and everyone talking and reliving the day.

Crispin took off his circlet and laid it down on his folded cloak, as if it should have a place of honor. Then he turned suddenly to Padra.

"You know, if you and Arran want to get married, you have my permission," he said.

"How did you . . ." began Padra. "Well, yes, were were going to ask."

"Did she hit you?" asked Crispin.

"Not very hard," said Padra.

Urchin and Needle scrambled onto a rock. They ate honey cakes and looked out to sea.

"Do you remember," said Needle, "you said once that you thought you should have something important to do? Well, I think you've done it."

"I'm not sure," said Urchin. "I mean, yes, I know I've done *something*. But it doesn't feel finished. There's more that I have to do. And more that I have to be. I mean, it's not as if you can do one special thing, and that's it. It's what you go on *being* that matters. Come to think of it, I don't know what I am anymore."

"You're that funny-looking squirrel," said Needle. But Urchin hopped down from the rock and bowed to Crispin.

"Please, Cap—Your Majesty," he said, "I don't know what I am anymore. Whose page am I now?"

Padra and Crispin looked at each other.

"We'll have to think about this," said Crispin. "You should be more than a page by now, but it would be too much to promote you to the Circle. You deserve it, but a lot of responsibilities go with it, and you should enjoy being young and free for a bit longer. Complete your training with Padra, but I think 'Companion to the King' is what you are. Both of you—Needle as well."

Urchin gabbled his thanks, but then he didn't know where to look. And he didn't know how to thank Padra, either, for all he'd done, so he just sat quietly at Padra's paws for a while, and knew that Padra understood. Finally, when nobody needed him, he went down to the shore. He needed to be by himself, to take in all that had happened.

"'Companion to the King,'" he repeated to himself. "Urchin of the Riding Stars." He wondered where he had come from, and what his future would be. And from their place on the rocks, Padra, Crispin, and Fir looked down at the pale young figure on the shore; and they, too, wondered what he would become.